The stranger's hand shot out and fastened on Emma's arm.

His grip was like an iron band. If she struggled, she would have bruises. He brought his face close to hers, and his unbelievably beautiful eyes held her spellbound.

She felt it then, that spark between them. The man-to-woman, hunter-to-hunted, connection. The bond of recognition that dwelled in the depths of instinct. The truth seared across her mind in a dazzling flash.

It was impossible.

But it was Bruce. *Bruce.* In a different body, a different person, but she knew it was *the same man!*

She couldn't move. Her pulse raced, her lungs heaved. Before a single sound could escape her frozen lips, he swooped closer and brought his mouth next to her ear. "Play along," he breathed. "Play along, or we're both dead."

Dear Reader,

Welcome once again to a month of excitingly romantic reading from Silhouette Intimate Moments. We have all sorts of goodies for you, including the final installment of one miniseries and the first book of another. That final installment is *MacDougall's Darling,* the story of the last of The Men of Midnight, Emilie Richards's latest trilogy. The promised first installment is Alicia Scott's *At the Midnight Hour,* beginning her family-themed miniseries, The Guiness Gang. And don't forget *The Cowboy and the Cossack,* the second book of Merline Lovelace's Code Name: Danger miniseries.

There's another special treat this month, too: *The Bachelor Party,* by Paula Detmer Riggs. For those of you who have been following the Always a Bridesmaid! continuity series from line to line, here is the awaited Intimate Moments chapter. And next month, check out Silhouette Shadows!

Finish off the month with new books by Jo Leigh and Ingrid Weaver. And then come back next month and every month for more romance, Intimate Moments style.

Enjoy!

Yours,

Leslie Wainger
Senior Editor and Editorial Coordinator

Please address questions and book requests to:
Silhouette Reader Service
U.S.: 3010 Walden Ave., P.O. Box 1325, Buffalo, NY 14269
Canadian: P.O. Box 609, Fort Erie, Ont. L2A 5X3

TRUE LIES

INGRID WEAVER

Silhouette® INTIMATE™ MOMENTS®

Published by Silhouette Books

America's Publisher of Contemporary Romance

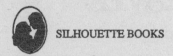 SILHOUETTE BOOKS

ISBN 0-373-07660-6

TRUE LIES

Copyright © 1995 by Ingrid Caris

Books by Ingrid Weaver

Silhouette Intimate Moments

True Blue #570
True Lies #660

INGRID WEAVER

admits to being a compulsive reader who loves a book that can make her cry. A former teacher, now a homemaker and mother, she delights in creating stories that reflect the wonder and adventure of falling in love. When she isn't writing or reading, she enjoys old "Star Trek" reruns, going on sweater-knitting binges, taking long walks with her husband and waking up early to canoe after camera-shy loons.

To Melanie, George and Karl—
three truly amazing people.

Chapter 1

Bruce Prentice hadn't used the tourist disguise in years, but it was one of his favorites. This time he wouldn't need to risk the inconvenience of a fake beard, since his own scruffy blond stubble had reached a length that buried his distinctive chin and jawline. The wads of gauze that he held against his gums effectively filled the lean hollows of his cheeks.

He flicked a quick, assessing glance at his reflection in the rearview mirror, then allowed himself a tight quirk of a smile as he noted the way the contacts turned his eyes a nondescript brown. Subtle props were the easiest to work with, like the padding that expanded his stomach four sizes and the baggy jacket that would allow him to curl his shoulders forward. The loose clothes had another advantage—they effectively concealed the gun that nestled in the custom-made holster at the small of his back.

He spotted the mailbox, a rusty red one that leaned on a post beside the ditch, half hidden by the swaying grass at the side of the road. He put down the clutch and let the van coast to a stop as he checked the name.

"Emma Cassidy," he read aloud, trying out the slightly nasal twang that he had decided to use. Bruce had learned that unsophisticated accents tended to put people at ease, making them more cooperative, and making the actual timbre of his voice less memorable. That was only one of the hundreds of tricks he had learned during the years he'd been working at the job.

The job. That's what he called it, when he took the time to think about it, even though it had long ago gone beyond the bounds of merely a way to make a living. He seldom concerned himself with money. He hadn't taken a vacation in four years. What he did became who he was, and who he was varied from day to day. A month ago he had been a homeless vagrant. A year ago he had been a priest. He was a tourist this time because it gave him a valid reason for nosing around these woods.

Through the open window floated an acrid trace of wood smoke, along with the sharp scent of the spruces that loomed over the road. Silence rolled back at him as the dark trees absorbed the last echoes of the engine. He pocketed his keys, giving himself a moment to observe his surroundings. Bruce was more accustomed to working the streets of Chicago, but Emma Cassidy had chosen to conduct her business at the end of a sparsely populated dirt road on the outskirts of Bethel Corners. The quaintly tiny Maine town was an unlikely setting, he thought, but there was no mistake. The trail he had been following for weeks had led him here.

He swiveled from his seat, then stooped over to walk to the back of the van and squatted down to unzip his camera bag. With quick, economical movements he snapped a telephoto lens in place, slipped the padded camera strap over his shoulder and opened the rear door. At the sudden squeak of metal, a squirrel chattered maniacally from the concealment of a bushy pine. Bruce stepped to the road, easing the door shut behind him.

The driveway that led into the woods was little more than a rutted track. In the damp depression beside a bas-

ketball-size boulder were the traces of wide, deep-treaded
tires. Automatically Bruce swung the camera up, focused,
and recorded the pattern. These tracks would be from the
blue four-wheel-drive pickup that had rattled past five
minutes ago. If she was going to town, she would be gone
for forty minutes, thirty minimum. If he was lucky, only
the squirrels would witness the brief reconnaissance foray
he'd planned. Still, with a caution learned from long experience, he maintained his stooped posture and shuffling
gait as he made his way through the shadows that dappled
the drive.

At the crest of a hill the trees abruptly gave way to an
open expanse of rock and low bushes. A small bungalow-
size log cabin perched on a rise that faced a sparkling blue
lake. To one side was a neatly stacked crib full of firewood and an open shed that was probably used as a garage, to the other side was a round cement well and a
fenced-in rectangle with rows of mounded dark earth and
trembling green sprouts. Bruce cataloged it all. Shelter,
fuel, water and food—she was practically self-sufficient
here. She could hole up for days, maybe weeks at a time.
A good place to hide, he decided, glancing behind him toward the road that was already lost to sight.

He angled his baseball cap to shade his eyes as he turned
in a slow circle. The cabin was isolated, not only by its location, but by the tight-lipped, mind-your-own-business
yankee character of the locals. A twinge of interest nibbled at his mind. Perhaps she was smarter than he had
thought.

Walking forward, he took several shots to record the
layout, then pointed the camera toward the shore of the
lake. As good as binoculars, the long lens gave him a clear
view of the gleaming white plane that bobbed gently at the
end of a wooden dock.

That's how she did it, of course. A float plane didn't
need to use runways. Or official border crossings. With
hundreds of miles of rugged bush between here and the St.
Lawrence, a skilled pilot could rendezvous in the black of

night, make a pickup, and bring the cargo back to this picturesquely peaceful lake with no witnesses except the moose and the muskrat.

Beneath the scruffy beard his jaw clenched. People in Cassidy's business were well paid for the risks they ran. Bruce had long ago stopped trying to figure out why they did it. There was no explaining human greed, no justifying the misery that resulted from even one midnight run. Getting rid of a link like this would only interrupt the flow, not stop it. But this was one way to get to the source. And before he was finished with Miss Emma Cassidy, he intended to make her useful, whether she wanted to cooperate or not.

The fine hairs at the back of his neck tingled. Although he couldn't identify any sound that had alerted him, suddenly Bruce knew that he was no longer alone. Careful to keep his movements casual, he swung the camera in a slow arc, scanning the dark forest, the rocky hillside, the cabin, the drive....

A lone woman stood on the crest of the hill, the sun at her back, her slim body braced against the breeze. Leather boots laced past her ankles, black denim clung to her long legs. The loose white shirt she wore fluttered, flattening briefly against compact but generous curves. Her face was shadowed by a broad-brimmed canvas hat, so he had only a quick impression of a delicate jaw and a dimpled chin before he clicked the shutter and lowered the camera.

"Hi, there," he called, using the voice he had chosen.

In response she moved forward. She walked with the easy stride of an athlete, each step a study in fluid grace. Without slowing down, she lifted her arms and unslung the weapon that she had been carrying on her back.

Despite the years of training and the countless times he had met the unexpected, Bruce couldn't help the tickle of surprise he felt as he realized what she held. It was a hunting bow. Its sleek curves gleamed in the sunlight, its long, narrow stabilizers bristled outward. The pulley-enhanced bowstring promised swift, silent penetration. There was something primitive about the way her fingers wrapped around the carved grip and casually clutched its deadly potential, something almost . . . sensual.

Bruce felt his pulse thud as blood coursed heavily through his gut. He couldn't remember the last time he had experienced this sudden thrill of anticipation before a job. She would be a worthy adversary, an entertaining prey.

"Was that your van at the foot of my driveway?" she asked. Her voice was low and steady, filled with an emotion that could have been anger.

The sun was still at her back. He couldn't see her eyes, so he kept his gaze on her hands, alert for any movement that might indicate her intentions. "You must be Miss Cassidy." He wiped his palm on his baggy multipocketed pants and stuck out his hand. "I'm Bruce Prendergast. I heard in town that I could find you out here."

She halted about six yards away, bracing her feet apart and pulling an arrow from the quiver at her waist with a controlled, insolent motion. "What do you want, Bruce Prendergast?"

He assessed the ease with which she handled her weapon. Chances were he wouldn't be able to get to his gun before she nocked the arrow, so the best course of action would be to play out his cover. It was too soon for a confrontation. That wasn't what he had planned.

Letting the hand he offered drop awkwardly to his side, he maintained his pose of amiable harmlessness. "I wanted to talk to you about hiring your plane."

Beneath the flowing white shirt her bow arm flexed. An oblong leather guard was strapped above the wrist, molding a suggestion of smooth muscle. "What would a reporter want with my plane?"

He cleared his throat, feigning a nervousness he didn't feel. Adrenaline was surging through his body. His muscles tingled with the urge to move, to act, to wrest control of the situation. He wouldn't be able to reach his gun, but if he dived to his left, away from the bow, and did a few quick rolls, he could probably take her down to the ground. She appeared to be around five foot six, more than half a foot shorter than his real height. He outweighed her by at least eighty pounds, so he wouldn't have any trouble subduing her if it came to physical contact. He'd keep the option in mind. "Reporter? I'm not a reporter, I'm an accountant. I'm just here to do some—"

"Then why the camera?"

"This?" He glanced down at the object in his hand as if he had forgotten he still held it. "Oh, heck. I always take tons of pictures when I'm on vacation. I've taken two rolls just since New Hampshire—it's beautiful country around here. I'm not much good at it, though. Taking pictures, I mean."

A gust of wind rippled her white shirt, pulling the open collar to one side. For the space of a heartbeat, sunlight slid over the upper curve of her breast before the supple fabric fell back into place. "This is private property, Mr. Prendergast."

He nodded quickly, then flapped a hand toward the plane behind him. "Sorry, I didn't mean to trespass. The fella at the gas station told me that you might be willing to fly me in to some of the lakes to the north of here, so I thought, why not?"

"Who sent you? What's the name of this fella you talked to?"

Within the concealment provided by his loose coat he slouched a little more. She had sounded suspicious, not only of what he had said, but of the way he had said it. Oh, yes. She would be a worthy adversary. "Hugh something. I don't know his last name. He sold me a bunch of fishing tackle from that shop he's got in the back." He crinkled his nose in a smile consistent with the inoffensive cowardice of his persona. "Uh, ma'am, that bow is making me nervous. Would you mind pointing it somewhere else?"

Her mouth twitched—was that a smirk? Instead of putting the weapon away, she began circling slowly to her left. "Do I really make you nervous, Bruce?"

She was doing it deliberately, he realized with a start. She thought she was frightening him, and she was playing her advantage to the maximum. The steady thud of his pulse was loud in his ears as the anticipation he felt heightened. He still couldn't see her eyes, so he couldn't be sure what she would do. The way she was moving would make it more difficult for him to take her—did she realize that? "Uh, ma'am?"

The fingers that held the shaft of the arrow were long and slender. Absently she ran her thumb over the trio of stubby feathers that were set into the blunt end. "Which lake were you interested in?"

"Uh, any lake as long as it has fish."

"You're a fisherman?"

He affected a nervous chuckle. "I'm not much good at that, either, but I've heard there's terrific fishing toward the Quebec border. While I was in the neighborhood, so to speak, I didn't want to miss the opportunity to try my luck." He attempted another smile. "Please, do you think you could put that bow away, now? If we're going to be doing business together—"

"That hasn't been established, yet." Her fingers moved over the arrow as she ran a fingertip along the smooth wooden shaft. It was a slow, unconsciously suggestive movement.

He watched her hand warily, moistening his lips with the tip of his tongue. "Hugh from the gas station said that you often fly parties of fishermen to some of the lakes that don't have road access," he said, adding a whine to his twang. "What's your usual rate?"

"I'm not a professional pilot. I've only got my recreational certificate, so all I can charge is the cost of the fuel. Accepting a fee is against the rules, and I wouldn't want to do anything illegal, now, would I?"

Her scruples had to be as phony as his potbelly, but he was willing to play her game. "Well, heck. That doesn't seem fair. How much does the fuel usually cost?"

Her mouth twitched again. Another smirk? "Depends where I buy it."

"Oh. I get it. No receipt, no income tax, right?"

She simply waited and fingered the arrow.

He made a show of fumbling in his pants pocket and withdrew a battered leather wallet. He knitted his brows in concentration as he thumbed through what he knew would appear to be a thick wad of bills. "I've only got another week before I have to be back in Chicago. How much would the fuel cost for one day?"

She remained silent, twirling the arrow in her fingers. For a long minute the only sounds were the whisper of the wind in the pines at the edge of the hill and the gentle, rhythmic lapping of waves against the lakeshore. Finally she exhaled on a gusty sigh and thrust the arrow back into the quiver. "Okay, Mr. Prendergast. You've got yourself a pilot."

"Great! Thanks. Are you free tomorrow?"

"I suppose so." She hesitated for another minute before she slung the bow onto her shoulder and used her thumb to tip up the concealing brim of her hat.

And for the first time, Bruce saw her face.

Dangerous, he thought. This woman is dangerous. Not because of the deadly weapon she carried so casually. No, he knew how to defend himself against physical threats. What he hadn't been prepared for was the impact of her gaze.

My God, he thought. *She's beautiful.*

Blue eyes as clear and deep and pure as a mountain lake sparkled up at him. He saw mischief, not malice. Vulnerability, not violence. Sunlight caressed cheeks that bore the pink kiss of the wind. Innocent freckles danced across the bridge of an impudent, upturned nose.

Everything he had carefully cataloged swept back on a wave of awareness. The long, slim legs, the athlete's stride, the hunter's nonchalant confidence and the aura of suppressed energy...the pale skin beneath the white shirt...the slender, competent fingers stroking the shaft of the arrow... the low, throaty voice, those lips that twitched with secret amusement ...

The simmering anticipation he had been feeling, that low-level excitement of the chase changed to something more basic, reached beyond the circumstances and beyond the job to touch the part of him that was simply, essentially male.

"Come to the house," she said. "We can go over my maps." Turning her back, she walked away.

Sweat trickled between his hunched shoulder blades as he clenched his hands into fists at his sides. Ruthlessly he willed this dangerous awareness to stop. He reined it in, breathing deeply through his nose until he thought he had regained control. But he had already taken three strides before he realized that he'd forgotten to use Prendergast's ambling shuffle. Instantly he dropped back into character, fumbling to draw a lens cap from the pocket on his thigh as he followed her toward the cabin.

She didn't look back. Evidently she had finally bought his story along with the amiable harmlessness of his persona.

But there was nothing harmless about this situation. He was shaken by his temporary lapse from the cool professionalism that had been second nature to him in the past. How could he forget, even for a second, who he was. And who she was. So what if she was beautiful, if she stirred something inside him that he had thought long dead? In the end it didn't make any difference. After all, he was here to do a job.

And part of his duties could include sending Emma Cassidy to prison.

Emma could feel his gaze on her, boring through the thin cotton of the shirt that was beginning to stick to her back. She clasped her hands in front of her, hoping he wouldn't see the tremors that shook them.

God, what a complete fool she had made of herself. He was nothing but some innocent accountant on vacation, and he had been scared practically witless by the sight of her hunting bow. She shouldn't have done it, but the moment she had seen that camera pointing in her direction, all the old memories had resurfaced and in her anger she hadn't been thinking straight.

Of course, he was nothing but a tourist. What else could he be up here? This was Maine, not New York. There was no longer any need to check through her curtains to see whether she could elude the reporters that had staked out the house. There were no flashbulbs to blind her as she moved freely about her property. No one knew her here. To her neighbors she was simply that lady with the plane. Besides, she was old news. It had been over three years since she'd changed her name and escaped from the fishbowl her life had become.

She glanced over her shoulder. Bruce Prendergast smiled with that endearing nose crinkle and juggled his camera in front of him while he fumbled with the lens cap. A twinge of remorse traveled through her. He hadn't done anything to deserve such a hostile welcome. He couldn't possibly know how she felt about reporters. She loathed them for what they had done to her and her family. She hated them almost as much as she hated cops.

Relax, she ordered herself as she pushed open the front door of the cabin and waited for Bruce to catch up. He stumbled on the slab of rock that served as a step, then tugged on the brim of his baseball cap and grinned sheepishly.

Poor soul, she thought as she led the way inside. He was no reporter. He was exactly what he appeared to be. Besides, so far Hugh hadn't sent her anyone who had caused her problems—the crusty old mechanic was a shrewd judge of character. How could she have felt threatened, even for a moment, by this awkward, soft, overweight tourist?

"Hey, nice place you have here," he said, pausing in the doorway to glance around the main room.

She took off her hat and hung it on the hook beside the door while she imagined how her home would appear to a stranger. It wouldn't tell him much about her. There were no photographs on display, no souvenirs of the trips she had once taken, no trace of the elegant furnishings that had graced the Long Island estate. Everything in this central, all-purpose room of her cabin was modest and functional, from the overstuffed blue corduroy sofa and armchair to the scratched, footstool-height coffee table. There was nothing here to steal, or to conceal, except what was locked inside the sturdy rolltop desk.

"You must be quite an avid reader." His shoes scuffed across the wood floor as he ambled toward the bookshelves that lined the far wall. With his hands in his pockets, his baggy jacket dragged on his rounded shoulders, emphasizing his stooped posture. "Wow. You've got everything from Stephen King to Jane Austen. I love to read whenever I can find the time."

"Oh? What interests you?"

"Anything, even the backs of cereal boxes." He turned in a slow circle, taking in the rest of the room. "But I have to admit that I'm partial to a good whodunit."

"Why don't you sit down?" she said, waving toward the oak table in front of the window. "I'll be right with you."

"Sure. Thanks again."

She waited until he had settled into one of the ladder-back chairs before she crossed to the opposite side of the room and fitted her bow into the rack over the fireplace.

"What kind of bow is that? Sure doesn't look like anything I've seen before. Were you hunting with it?"

"It's a compound bow, and no, I wasn't hunting today." She unstrapped the quiver from around her waist and placed it on the mantel. "I was planning on using the sand pit down the road to do some target practice. I passed your van on the way there, but when you didn't come back I thought I'd better investigate. Sometimes people get lost on these back roads."

His laugh sounded uncomfortable. "I'm sure glad you didn't decide to use me for a target. That thing looks deadly."

"Sorry. I thought you might be somebody else."

"I guess you have to be careful, being so isolated out here and all. Is there much of a criminal element in the Maine woods, Miss Cassidy?"

"Not that I know of." She moved to a low shelf and selected several rolled maps. "And you might as well call me Emma. No one's very formal around here."

"Okay. Emma."

"What kind of fish are you after, Bruce?"

He had smiled nervously often enough during the few minutes since they had met. This time, though, the smile that briefly crinkled the skin at the corners of his eyes seemed genuine. "When I go on a trip like this, I'm always hoping to catch the big ones."

For a moment she was distracted by the way the spark of amusement lent a trace of animation to his face. She had no more than a fleeting glimpse, though, before he lifted his hand to fidget with his baseball cap. She carried the maps to the table. "Everyone wants to catch the big ones."

"I was hoping you'd lead me to them."

"I'll see what I can do. Here, hold this corner for me," she instructed as she placed the first map in front of him and began to unroll it.

His knuckles bumped the edge of the table as he shifted to follow her instructions. His fingers were long and tanned and looked surprisingly strong for someone who pushed a pencil for a living. "I really appreciate this, Miss...uh, Emma. I'm glad you weren't already booked."

"Hugh does his best to steer customers my way, but I don't get all that much business." She leaned over to point out the black square near the bottom of the map. "This is my place. There are several good lakes to the northwest of here," she said, trailing her finger in a straight line.

"You can get pretty close to the border with that plane of yours. What's the range on it?"

"Far enough for what you'll need. If you don't have your own boat I can strap one of my canoes to a pontoon."

"That would be great. Can it handle the extra weight?"

"There's nothing to be nervous about, Bruce. I assure you, I'm a very good pilot."

"Am I that obvious?" He tipped his head away from her. The brim of his cap shielded his eyes, but the light from the window clearly etched the hint of a solid jaw beneath his dark blond beard. "Sorry. No offense meant."

"None taken." She pulled back, focusing more carefully on what was visible of his face. Despite the pudgy cheeks, he had a strong, masculine jaw, all right. It was a shame he wanted to hide it with that scraggy beard. The hair that poked out from the back band of the baseball cap was a few shades lighter, but just as unkempt. "How many people are with you?"

"Huh?"

"You've got a fishing buddy, don't you?"

"Uh, no. Just me. Like I said, it was a sort of spur of the moment decision." His pudgy cheeks creased into a hopeful smile. "That's okay, isn't it? I mean, you'll be acting as my guide for the day, won't you?"

"It'll cost you extra."

"Sure. Of course. What time would you want to leave?" he asked eagerly. His chair scraped loudly as he pushed himself to his feet. The map he had been holding rolled shut with a snap. For a moment he appeared to tower over her, but then he took a shuffling step away and bumped into the corner of the desk. Although the desktop was closed, there was a handful of unopened mail that was stacked on the top ledge. "Oh, heck. I'm sorry," he mumbled, squatting down to gather up the letters he'd knocked to the floor.

She watched his clumsy movements, restraining the urge to offer her help and risk insulting him. "Can you get here half an hour before sunrise?"

"Sure. Great." As he straightened up and replaced the mail, the strap of his camera slid from his shoulder. He juggled it awkwardly as he reached the door.

Poor soul, she thought again. He was so painfully nervous and clumsy. She had strong doubts whether he'd be able to catch anything at all. Well, she took advantage of any excuse to fly, and he would be paying for her fuel. He'd even be paying her to lounge around fishing all day, and she could use the time off. She held out her right hand as he stepped outside. "Until tomorrow, then."

He wiped his palm on his pants and reached for her hand. "I'm really looking forward to this, Emma."

"The weather should be..." Her words trailed off as his fingers closed gently around hers.

It was startling, that contact of flesh on flesh. Her skin tingled where he touched her, as if a connection were forming between them, as if some part of her was responding to... to what? What could she possibly be feeling for this awkward, painfully shy stranger? He wasn't remotely her type, if she even had a type. He was soft, and sloppy, and...

He straightened, and her gaze locked with his. It was difficult to do at first. The brown of his eyes seemed flat and elusive, as if she weren't really seeing him. Gradually she looked past the color to the long, thick lashes and the bold, straight eyebrows. She hadn't noticed them before. Until now he'd kept his head tilted so that the brim of his baseball cap had shielded him. Was it an illusion, or were his eyes really as compelling as they seemed? Were those actually hints of masculine strength and determination in the depths? Was the fragment of vulnerability she glimpsed real, or was it a reflection of her own?

The odd moment of connection lasted less than a heartbeat. He dropped her hand as awkwardly as he had taken it and shoved his fists into the deep pockets of his jacket. Stumbling backward, he tripped on the rock step again before he made it to the lawn. "Uh, I'll see you tomorrow morning."

She curled her fingers into her palm as she watched him move across the hill to the driveway. His shoulders slouched beneath the baggy coat, his scuffed running shoes stirred puffs of dust from the dry gravel. He was as clumsy and unappealing as he'd been before. Yet even after he had disappeared into the shadows of the pines, his presence seemed to linger.

A frown tightened her brow. She must have imagined it. Determination? Strength? Vulnerability? *Tingles?* She barely knew him. How could she possibly have felt anything at his touch?

Rubbing the lines from her forehead, she turned to go back into the cabin. Only the wind heard her whispered question. "What kind of man are you, Bruce Prendergast?"

Bruce lifted the last print from the rectangular tin and let it drip into the bathtub for a moment before he clipped it to the string with the others. He stepped back and hit the switch on the wall, flooding the tiny motel bathroom with light. Stark black-and-white photographs hung in an orderly line, marking the progress of his first day in Bethel Corners. The shots of the property by the lake would be useful if he needed to coordinate a team assault. Several shots he got of the white plane were detailed enough to make future identification easy. But it was the last print that he had developed that caught and held his attention.

Against the background of dark, towering evergreens, Emma's flowing white shirt and pale face made her look like a nymph that had just stepped out of the woods. The camera had captured the delicate features beneath the broad hat brim and Bruce found himself staring, entranced.

He had seen beautiful women before, had worked closely with a number of them. What was it about this one that made her so special? What had happened on her doorstep when they had parted? It had been nothing but a handshake, a polite, impersonal way to seal a business arrangement. It had held him rooted to the spot the instant her skin had touched his.

That was twice in one day. In the short time he had been with Emma, she had managed to get past his persona twice. What was the matter with him?

Maybe the strain of the continual undercover jobs was beginning to take its toll. Xavier Jones, his contact at the task force headquarters, had been trying to convince him for months now to take a vacation. Maybe Bruce Prentice wanted to be like Bruce Prendergast and have nothing to worry about other than lounging in a canoe all day with a fishing rod in his hand. If fatigue was responsible for those inexcusable slips he had made today, then perhaps after this operation was wrapped up he should think seriously about using some of that time off that he had coming to him.

He pushed his glasses up his nose and leaned closer to the photograph of Emma. He'd taken out his contacts and stripped down to his shorts as soon as he'd locked the door behind him for the night. She didn't know what color his eyes were, or what his true size and shape was, or what the contours of his face looked like. Yet she had flushed when he had held her hand. He'd seen her eyes widen, and felt the tremor in her fingers, and he'd known that she must have been experiencing at least a hint of the mindless pull that had raged through his body. It was crazy. It was unbelievable.

It was damned inconvenient and wouldn't happen again.

The background check that he'd initiated this morning was far from complete, and the preliminary findings were too sparse to either condemn or exonerate. He had learned that her cabin and the ten acres that surrounded it were mortgage-free and her property tax was always paid on time. Her plane was her own, her license was a recreational one, as she had said, complete with the extra provision to allow her to fly a float plane. He'd had no more than a brief glance at the pile of envelopes that he'd deliberately knocked off her desk, but it had been enough to note the return addresses. Her sole visible means of support were the occasional fishing charters she flew, so what business would she have with the managers of seven banks from here to Connecticut?

Handling the damp print carefully, Bruce unclipped it from the string and carried it to the bed in the other room. The springs creaked as he lithely settled himself cross-legged in the center of the mattress, propped his elbows on his knees, steepled his fingers and studied Emma's image.

Even in this cheap motel room, with the yellow glare from the overhead fixture and the stale traces of a previous occupant's cigarette smoke, Bruce merely had to look at her face and he felt as if he were back on that hillside with the pine-scented breeze. And even though the image in front of him was black and white, he could feel the impact of her clear blue gaze.

He leaned closer, pleased to see that his trusty old camera had captured the smattering of freckles and the delicate indentation in the center of her chin. No more than a few stray wisps of hair were visible against her cheeks. A hint of a smile softened his mouth as he remembered how the deep brown strands shone with auburn highlights, and how the locks she had tucked behind her ears had swung loose when she had leaned over the table to show him the map, and how that loose white blouse had gaped....

His smile dissolved before it could develop. He was a professional; he never let himself get personally involved when he was working on a case. But he couldn't remember experiencing such an overwhelming sense of connection with anyone before. His instinct, his gut and the odd tingling from his subconscious that had never led him wrong in the past all shouted at him that she couldn't be guilty. He would need to be more cautious than ever. The stakes in this game, and the penalty for an error, were too high to let his feelings color his judgment.

He moved his hand to the photograph, holding his fingertips a breath away from her lips. Innocent bystander, or clever criminal? "What kind of woman are you, Emma Cassidy?"

Chapter 2

The morning started too early, with the shrill of the telephone and another argument with Simon. Emma raked stiff fingers through her hair and hooked the phone with her other hand, pacing as far as the side window as she tried to hold on to her patience. "No, Simon. The last time I let you borrow it, you left the tanks empty."

"I said I was sorry. Please, Emma. Plee—eease?"

It was the same drawn out whine that he'd perfected during his childhood when he wanted to wheedle something out of his big sister. Despite her firm intentions, she felt herself soften. "You know how important the log is. Even if you didn't want to take the trouble to record it in the book, you could have at least left a note on the window. That's what I keep that grease pencil in the cockpit for."

"I won't forget again, I promise. Scout's honor. Hope to die. But I really, really need to get to that lake. The assay results on my last samples were encouraging. This might be the break I was looking for."

"Not today, Simon. I have a customer."

"Another fisherman?"

"Uh-huh."

"I don't understand why you persist in that penny-ante stuff. I know you started out flying those charters so the locals wouldn't wonder where your money was coming from, but you've been there three years, so your cover is solid enough. You don't have to continue the farce about needing the work."

"I like to fly. I like to fish. I consider it a vacation."

"Listen, Emma, I was counting on you. If I wait until tomorrow, another prospector might have already staked the claim."

"If it's that important, why don't you find another plane? There are plenty of pilots for hire in Bangor. Surely you've still got enough money left from last quarter's dividends to allow you—"

"I don't want anyone else to know where I'm going. Not until I've got this sewn up."

"I can understand that, but—"

"You're not going to change your mind, are you?" His voice had switched from wheedling to sulky. "I thought you wanted to help me. You said I could count on you."

"Not today, Simon."

There was a pause. "Tomorrow? I promise I'll top off the fuel and fill in the log like a good boy."

She had to fight against the urge to give him what he wanted. He was a twenty-three-year-old man, not the bewildered child that she'd protected and coddled ten years ago.

"Emma? You still there?"

She rubbed her face briskly. "I've got to go."

"Wait! This is really important."

His sporadic efforts at prospecting were really important. That's what he'd said about the candy factory, the hat store and the mail-order perfume business. She clenched her jaw, hating the weakness that had her on the verge of giving in to her brother. "Call me tonight after I get back. We can talk about it then."

"You're a peach, Emma. Thanks."

"Right," she said, but the dial tone was already humming in her ear. Sighing, she replaced the receiver and carried the phone back to the desk.

How could she simply turn off ten years of mothering? Simon was old enough to take charge of his own life and support himself—God knows, she had done all that and more when she had been younger than he was now—but she still felt responsible for him. Oh, he knew perfectly well how to pull her strings. For his own good, she had been trying to wean him away from her support to force him to grow up and stand on his own feet. Was she being too harsh? The nightmare of their youth had affected Simon far deeper than her, perhaps because she'd been too busy trying to hold the family together. She hadn't had the chance to indulge in helplessness or self-pity or dependence.

No, she wouldn't let herself criticize her brother. He had his faults, but basically he was a loving, warm person. Once he gained some self-confidence and learned to take responsibility for his actions, things would be different. Maybe his new interest in prospecting would put him on the right track. Perhaps she shouldn't have refused him outright. She might have worked out a way to help...

"Oh, just stop it," she muttered to herself. She strode to the corner that served as her kitchen and snatched the coffeepot off the stove. Pouring herself another cup, she tried to focus her energy on the day ahead.

Simon had been right about her not needing the money from these tourist fishing charters. But there was so much more to life than money. She loved to fly and she welcomed the excuse to spend a day fishing. Above all, she still got a kick out of the pocket change that she didn't declare on her tax return—after what she and her family had endured in the name of law and justice, she had little respect for rules.

A beam of light swept across the front of the bookshelves. Emma twisted around in time to see Bruce's van bump past the crest of the hill and pull to a jerky stop in front of her garage. Gears ground loudly in the predawn hush before the engine shuddered to silence.

He drove as awkwardly as he walked.

She hadn't forgotten the strange reaction that had followed his touch. How could she? Yesterday she had tried to convince herself that the momentary awareness had to have been a fluke. Or an hallucination. But there was no denying the flutter in her stomach as she heard the loud creak of the van's door.

A thud, followed by a metallic clatter heralded Bruce's arrival at her front step. She paused to fortify herself with a gulp of scalding coffee before she went to answer his timid knock.

"Hi," Bruce said, moving well back from the doorway. He ducked his head, glancing at the pile of gear at his feet. "I hope I'm not too early."

She scrutinized his slouched form. There was nothing in the least appealing about his appearance today. If anything, his baseball cap was grimier, his coat was baggier and his shoulders more rounded. She waited until he raised his eyes. Instead of glowing with intensity, his gaze slid harmlessly off hers as he ducked his head again to fumble with his camera.

Could the flash of masculine strength that had surprised her yesterday have been a figment of her imagination? She sipped another mouthful of her coffee. The awkward, sloppy man in front of her definitely wouldn't be the type to inspire a woman's attention. And yet...there was something about him. She could sense it now, as if touching him yesterday had triggered some weird undercurrent. She felt it, the way steel senses a magnet.

"Sorry about the mess here," he said, stooping over to retrieve the contents of his tackle box. "I, uh, tripped over the step somehow."

Emma studied the hard profile that was etched against the pearly dawn. His nose was long and narrow, with a subtle bump in the center. Like the jaw that she could barely glimpse beneath that awful beard, his nose looked boldly masculine. Even with the extra weight he carried, his features, what she could see of them, were well-defined. If it wasn't for his poor posture and the vacant, ingratiating expression he wore, he would look entirely different.

Curiosity stirred. And interest, simple feminine interest. Thoughtfully, she stole another glance at Bruce's profile before she picked up the lunch she had packed and led the way to the dock.

The plane roared across the lake, its pontoons throwing up twin tails of glittering spray. There was still plenty of flat water to spare when the nose tipped upward and they became airborne. Bruce was impressed. He had flown in a large variety of aircraft with pilots of widely varying competency, so he could tell immediately that he was in the hands of a natural. Emma continued the easy climb until they were well above the trees. Dipping one wing, she banked in a wide turn before leveling off and easing back on the throttle.

This was a single engine Cessna, nothing fancy, just a reliable little plane. Xavier had filled him in on the specifications and capabilities late last night, and the information supported his original suspicions. The plane was fully capable of the round trip from here to the St. Lawrence. Yes, the plane was capable of playing a vital role in the pipeline. But was the pilot?

She was dressed much the same as yesterday, with her well broken-in boots laced over her ankles and a pair of dark blue denims molding snugly to her legs. She'd thrown a red-and-black plaid jacket over her loose blouse and had crammed that wide-brimmed black hat over her luxurious hair, but the clothes didn't diminish her femininity. Or the renewed pull he'd felt the moment he'd seen her.

Although Bruce had resolved not to let his personal feelings become any more involved in this case, he hadn't been able to prevent that sudden stab of pleasure he'd experienced when his chief suspect had opened her door this morning. The mist had been curling off the lake like a silent embrace, the lonely dawn calls of a pair of loons had warbled in the distance. Silhouetted by the soft glow of the cabin light, Emma had appeared warm and too damn welcoming.

He'd stared at her photograph for hours last night, trying to discern the woman behind the beautiful face. But that was something the film couldn't show him. Even in the all-too-distracting flesh, she kept her thoughts hidden. When he'd deliberately dropped his fishing gear on her doorstep and had stood there looking like a pathetic klutz, he hadn't seen derision or ridicule or pity in her gaze. She'd been studying him, as if she were trying to see the man beneath the baggy clothes.

From the corner of his eye he watched her. She was a seat-of-the-pants flyer, using her instruments merely to confirm what she already knew through other cues, like the feel of the controls and the level of noise. The cool, clear day was ideal for flying. She handled the controls with a gentle touch, using subtle nudges of her hands and feet to make the steady flight seem effortless. Dark aviator sunglasses hid her eyes, but she made no effort to hide the expression of sheer enjoyment on her face. Obviously, she loved to fly.

And obviously, she would be skilled enough to pull off the dangerous night smuggling runs.

Resolutely, Bruce redirected his gaze to the panoramic view beneath the wing. He was on the verge of letting his feelings interfere with his professional detachment again. Yet he simply couldn't imagine Emma participating in something so abhorrent. Not with this plane, not with the way she loved to fly. Would someone with her exceptional competence willingly pervert their skill?

He hoped the answer was no.

"Are you okay so far?" she asked, raising her voice over the noise of the engine and the air rushing against the windshield.

"Sure," he answered. "Hey, it's beautiful way out here, isn't it? You really can't tell from the ground. I'm glad Hugh steered me your way."

She started a lazy turn, nudging the rudder with her foot to minimize the stomach-wrenching slide typical of less skillful pilots. "So am I." Sunlight flashed briefly from her sunglasses as she glanced toward him. "Everyone needs a vacation now and then, Bruce."

Her smile took him by surprise. It was sudden, and as brilliant as the rising sun that glowed above the forested hills. Her cheeks rounded, displaying an unexpected dimple at one corner of her mouth. Her entire face relaxed with uncomplicated pleasure and innocent joy.

Bruce clenched the fist he'd jammed into his pocket, reminding himself yet again to maintain his objectivity as well as his cover. Being alone for the day on an isolated lake would put him in an ideal position to learn more about Emma Cassidy. Even if there was a possibility that she wasn't guilty of being part of the smuggling ring, the trail *had* led to her, so she would have to know something about it. If he gained her trust, got closer to her, he could use her to lead him to the criminals.

Without warning, a memory surfaced from a case he had worked on the previous year. He had used someone then, too. In order to do his job, he had manipulated an innocent man into risking his life. He had accomplished what he had set out to do, but at what cost?

You used him. You and your disgusting masquerades, you don't care who gets hurt. All you see is your job, your rigid picture of right and wrong...

But he was a cop. It was his job to see nothing but right and wrong. This job was his life, it was all he had. After Lizzie's death, it had been all that had kept him going. He'd never experienced these kinds of doubts before.

God, maybe he really did need a vacation.

A light breeze had sprung up by the time they reached the lake Emma had pointed out on her map. She used the pattern of the ripples on the surface to gauge the direction and strength of the ground level wind, expertly bringing the plane to a near stall seconds before the pontoons kissed the water.

They spent the morning fishing for bass. She took Bruce to spots she had found on past trips, like the place near a pair of rocky islands where on a calm day you could actually look down and see the dark shapes of the fish moving below, but as she had already guessed, Bruce was hopeless as far as his angling skills were concerned. By the time the sun drew overhead, he had managed to land no more than two small fish, even though the brand new rod that Hugh had sold him had bent double with heavy strikes several times.

Emma lounged against a life jacket in the stern, her hat tipped over her face so that she could study Bruce unobtrusively. Not that there was much to see. Dark glasses covered his eyes, and he had a way of tipping his face so that the brim of that grimy baseball cap obscured what the beard didn't.

It almost appeared as if he were trying to hide. She knew all about hiding, but what made Bruce do so? Was it because of his weight? His clumsiness?

The canoe wobbled alarmingly as he juggled his rod to a different position. Another bass fought its way to freedom. "Oh, heck," he muttered.

Reaching into the padded lunch sack in front of her, Emma withdrew an apple and held it up. "Would you like to have something to eat?"

He propped his rod against the bow and twisted to face her, setting the canoe into motion once more. "Thanks, but I don't have much of an appetite today."

"Neither do the fish." She took a bite of the apple. "We might have better luck later in the day."

"You mean around sunset?"

"A few hours before sunset. I don't like to fly after dark."

"You don't? How come?"

"I'm not instrument rated. The Cessna doesn't have any of those state-of-the-art gadgets that would keep me from slamming into the side of Mount Katahdin."

He glanced toward the forest-cloaked hills on the horizon and moistened his lips nervously. "We're not near that, are we? If something delayed us and you needed to fly at dusk, we wouldn't really, uh, hit a mountain, would we?"

"I was exaggerating, Bruce. I'd be more likely to graze it than to slam into the side."

"Uh, that's reassuring."

"Don't worry," she said, her voice softening. Had he always been this timid a person? He must have had a terrible time during his childhood. "I chart my course before I fly, and I can calculate my position by dead reckoning or by simply looking out the window."

"Have you ever flown at night?"

She bit into her apple again and nodded. "Not much, and not for long. It's too risky."

"But theoretically, you could do it?"

"Sure. In an emergency, I suppose any pilot could, as long as the weather was clear."

"You seem to enjoy flying. How long have you been a pilot?"

"Since I was old enough to drive." Stretching her legs in front of her, she crossed her ankles on the gunnel and nibbled at her apple. She couldn't prevent the smile as she remembered the wonder of her first time at the controls of an aircraft. "My first lesson was in an old Piper Cub that must have been held together with chewing gum and baling wire. It was the scariest and most exhilarating experience of my life. And I knew then and there that I would do anything to get the chance to fly solo. The feeling of total freedom that you get when you're in the air is like nothing else. For that brief time you leave all your problems on the ground and escape into a world where nothing matters but the sound of the wind and the feel of the rudder pedals beneath your feet and the stick in your hands—" She broke off, realizing that Bruce was looking at her oddly. "Sorry. Don't ever ask a pilot about flying."

"Not that it's my business, but why haven't you gone for your professional license? You could make more money if you could charge a higher fee. If you advertised in some of the tourist magazines you could get a nice little business going here."

"The money's not important. And I've got other obligations."

"Oh. Sorry. I guess I'm always thinking like an accountant. I'd never dream of doing anything as risky as flying a plane," he murmured.

What could she say to that? In a way he reminded her of her brother, not that they resembled each other physically, but Bruce and Simon both seemed to suffer from a lack of self-confidence. She assessed the way Bruce sat, with his shoulders hunched awkwardly and his hands clasped loosely between his legs. His posture was the picture of dejection. She should be feeling sorry for him. But that was another way in which Bruce differed from Simon. As far as this timid accountant was concerned, her feelings weren't exactly sisterly.

She bit down hard on her apple. She had done this fishing routine with plenty of other men, but the seventeen foot aluminum canoe had never seemed so small before. Even with his face essentially concealed and the bulky red life jacket swelled around his body, she *still* felt that odd awareness of his presence. "How long have you been an accountant, Bruce?"

"I've been working at the same job since I finished college."

"Do you like your work?"

"Oh, yes." He hesitated. "It's all I do. I keep myself very busy with my job. Most of the time it's interesting and challenging, but lately I've been starting to wonder whether I'm letting myself become too personally involved."

"You're a workaholic, right?"

"That about *sums* it up." He laughed and self-consciously tugged at the brim of his cap. "Sorry. Accountant humor."

Emma was intrigued at the glimpse of wit. She felt as if a chink had opened in the bland facade he was projecting. "Did you bring your camera with you today?"

"Huh? Oh, yeah. It's in my pack."

"You know, just because you hired me and my plane to bring you fishing, doesn't mean you have to fish. There are some nice scenes to photograph around here, and in this sunlight the colors should be spectacular."

"Hey, that's a great idea!" he exclaimed, quickly leaning forward. Unfortunately, his hand caught the edge of the thermos of coffee that she'd brought, knocking it heavily against the side of the canoe. Glass crunched as the interior liner shattered with the impact. "Aw, heck."

His hand must have bumped it awfully hard to make it break like that, she thought. "It's okay, Bruce."

"I'm sorry. I'll replace it for you when I get back to town."

"Don't worry about it. It was old and liable to break anytime."

"No, it was my fault. I insist."

"You don't have to do that."

"Yes, I do." His voice deepened and held a trace of regret. "I'm sorry, Emma." He pulled his camera out of his pack and juggled the ruined thermos inside.

With the curtains drawn and the door securely bolted, Bruce stretched facedown on the carpet and started into another set of push-ups. His shoulders flexed rhythmically and his biceps swelled as the blood pounded through his veins, but twenty repetitions barely had him breathing hard. Clenching his jaw, he angled his legs apart, curled his left hand onto the small of his back, and did ten more using only his right arm. He followed with ten more using his left arm.

The waiting was frustrating. He had lifted a perfect set of prints from the broken thermos and had faxed them to Xavier hours ago. That should break through the dead end that they'd run up against with the background check. It seemed that there were no records of Emma Cassidy prior to three years ago when she had suddenly appeared out of nowhere and bought the cabin at the lake. It had taken him by surprise, and he didn't like that. After the day he had spent with her, he had been almost convinced of her innocence, so this new development had hit him hard. If she had nothing to hide, why had she gone to so much trouble to cover her tracks?

He rolled over, clasped his hands behind his head, and continued his workout with sit-ups. A sheen of sweat dampened his bare skin, glistening on the swells of lean muscle that ridged along his abdomen. Angry red stripes wrapped around his waist where he'd ripped off the adhesive tape that had held his false paunch in place. Emma didn't seem to care about the extra weight that Bruce Prendergast lugged around. Her manner toward him had actually softened as the day had worn on. By the time they had returned to her cabin, they had started a tentative friendship. It was exactly what he'd hoped would happen. Once he established a degree of trust, he would be able to use her. Use. There was that word again.

With a muttered curse, he let his head thump back against the carpet. She hadn't cared about his weight, and she had barely taken notice of the money he'd given her before he'd left. And when she had said goodbye and had wished him luck on the rest of his vacation, she'd sounded sincere. She'd even gently cautioned him against buying any more fishing gear from Hugh. Bruce had already seen how that wily old man who ran the Bethel Corners gas station overcharged the unwary tourist. Knowing the way these things worked, Bruce suspected that Hugh would be getting a tidy kickback for sending Emma some business.

At the first ring of the telephone, Bruce jackknifed to his feet and padded across the room to answer. As soon as he heard Xavier's gravelly voice, he tucked the receiver against his shoulder, grabbed his glasses and his notebook and sat down on the edge of the bed. "Okay, what have you got?"

"That's quite a fishing trip you're on up there."

"Did you get anything from those prints?"

"Oh, yeah. I found out who your Emma Cassidy is. Her full name is Emmaline Cassidy Duprey."

"Duprey." He paused a moment. "Doesn't ring a bell."

"Her father was Lewis Duprey. Old money, estate on Long Island, your typical high-flying corporate executive type until he served four years in prison for stock market fraud. Kept a low profile once he was released, died under suspicious circumstances three years ago."

Bruce underlined a word in his notebook. "Three years? That's when Emma bought the property here."

"Uh-huh. She was a real society princess until she shortened her name and dropped out of sight after the funeral. Still heads an investment group and has a place on the board of directors at a half dozen companies, but she's managed to shun publicity."

Bruce jotted down Xavier's revelations. A society princess? Dressed in an old plaid jacket, lounging in a canoe with her booted feet resting on the gunnel? Right now he would deal with the facts. He'd think about what it all meant later. "Was a fine imposed along with Duprey's prison sentence?"

"A hefty one. He declared bankruptcy, but he managed to shield a large chunk of the family fortune in trust funds for his children. His daughter stepped in to take over what was left of the finances while he was in prison. From what I could dig up, she was even more successful than Lewis. There were plenty of rumors that she was as crooked as the old man, but if she was doing anything illegal, she was smart enough not to get caught."

"She must have been just a kid."

"Eighteen when Lewis was convicted."

"How many other children?"

"There's one brother, Simon, five years younger. He was in and out of trouble as a juvenile."

"What about the mother?"

"In and out of substance abuse clinics until she over-dosed on sleeping pills several years ago."

Another image of Emma flashed through his mind. Smiling, carefree, with the endless sky reflected in her aviator sunglasses. She'd said she loved to fly. She'd said it made her feel free.

"Hey, you still there, Bruce?"

"Yeah. How did her father die?"

"Hunting accident."

"You mentioned suspicious circumstances."

"The inquest concluded alcohol was involved. There were no witnesses. I could find out more by tomorrow." The *snick-snick* tap of a computer keyboard sounded in the background. "I've got to hand it to you, Bruce. I thought you were on a wild-goose chase when you started this, but it looks as if you've stumbled onto something."

"Possibly."

"Possibly? Come on. Do you think it's only coincidence that someone with Emmaline Duprey's record pops up in the middle of an investigation like this? I'm going to arrange backup—"

"Hold off on that, okay?"

"Why?"

"It's a small town. Too many strangers will spook the locals. Give me a few more days to feel things out."

"We could contact the Bethel Corners sheriff."

"Hold off on that, too. If Emma's involved in this, she couldn't be doing it alone. We don't know how far the network reaches."

"*If* she's involved? I thought you were already convinced."

He lifted his glasses to rub his eyes, then swung his gaze to the glossy photograph that he'd propped against the lamp. Delicate chin, innocent freckles, sparkling eyes peering warily from beneath a wide hat brim. "I've already established a solid contact with her. I can work from there and see what else I can learn. Give me a few more days,'' he repeated.

"It's going to take that long to coordinate our operation with the coast guard and the Mounties. I think you're on the right track, though. Emmaline Duprey is smart. And she's one tough woman.''

"She'd have to be, if she took over the care of her brother and the family finances when she was a teenager.''

"Yeah, well she's no angel. Don't you want to know why her fingerprints were on record?''

Startled, Bruce realized he hadn't even asked. "Why?''

The noise of shuffling papers came through the line. "Shortly before she made herself disappear to that cabin in Maine, Emmaline Duprey was arrested.''

"I thought you said she didn't get caught like her father.''

"She had some high-priced legal help hushing things up and settling out of court, but this had nothing to do with fraud or white-collar stuff. She was arrested for assault.''

"Give me the details.''

"I can't. Like I said, someone hushed it up. I'll keep digging.'' There was a brief silence. "I don't need to tell you to be careful, do I?''

Bruce continued to study the stark black and white of Emma's image, his mind filling in what wasn't captured on the film. The athlete's stride, the deadly, purposeful way she held her hunting bow... the haunting beauty of her smile. She was full of contrasts. She was a puzzle he longed to solve, a woman he longed to know.

A muscle twitched in his cheek as the pencil he held snapped in two. "No, you don't have to remind me,'' he said quietly. "I've already decided the woman is dangerous.''

Chapter 3

The orange rays of sunset gilded the tops of the trees on the opposite shore of the lake. Emma stood alone at the end of the empty dock, watching the ripples slowly flatten to a dark mirror in the dying breeze. Simon had managed to talk her into lending him the plane, but he appeared to understand that this would be the last time. Her earlier firmness must have made an impression on him. He'd seemed sincere when he'd assured her that he would be logging his flying miles and topping off the fuel tanks before he brought the plane back in the morning. He'd sounded pleased and excited, full of the youthful enthusiasm that had always managed to make her smile. His prospecting must be working out well.

Tiredly, she ran her fingers through her hair. How long would she be keeping this up? She was not Simon's mother. Or his father. She had done her best, even when she hadn't been much more than a child herself. It wasn't fair that she'd had to bail him out of one scrape after another, or that she'd had to relinquish her own hopes and dreams in order to hold what was left of the family together. When was it going to be her turn? Perhaps happiness was too much to hope for, but didn't she deserve a tiny bit of peace?

Peace. That's what she had sought when she'd turned her back on the lifestyle she had been raised in. She'd never regretted her decision. With the modem hooked up to the computer on her desk, she had been able to run the family business from here just as well as she'd managed it from the glass-and-steel tower where she used to have her office. She didn't miss the parties or all that phony posturing, or the constant need to weigh the significance of every phrase and gesture. She was glad to be rid of the vicious gossip and the lies and the superficial relationships. She seldom dwelled on the loneliness that arose on calm evenings like this when there was no one to share a sunset with.

A loon called, its solitary cry like an echo of her state of mind. She thought about the odd friendship she had begun with the intriguing Bruce Prendergast. They'd had a pleasant afternoon yesterday. Once he'd given up the pretense of fishing, he'd relaxed and their conversation became easy and entertaining. He had a dry sense of humor, a quick wit, and an inquisitive mind. All in all, the shy, awkward man was a genuinely nice guy. And she was already becoming fond of him.

Fond? Fascinated better described her feelings about the man.

Cool, damp air swirled over the water as the sun sank below the horizon. Emma wrapped her arms around herself for warmth and looked over the empty lake. Bruce had called this morning to invite her to have dinner with him tonight. She had accepted readily. Why? It wasn't because she felt sorry for him, and it wasn't because of the pleasant conversation they'd had the day before. It was because she was becoming, well, attracted to him.

It was almost laughable, considering all the successful, perfectly groomed, suavely handsome men who had pursued her when she'd still been part of society. They'd had the slick moves and the slick lines, but none of them had sparked that sense of instant connection like the one that had whispered through her body when Bruce had first touched her.

He hadn't touched her since. After that first and only handshake, he'd seemed to have gone out of his way to make sure they didn't come into contact with each other again.

What did she think would happen if he did touch her? Did she hope he would suddenly transform into some kind of dream lover who could sweep her into his arms? Bruce, the klutzy accountant?

She shook her head. As intriguing as this was, nothing could come of it, anyway. She had seen what devotion to one man had done to her mother, and she had experienced the pain of rejection herself. Okay, she did find something inexplicably compelling about Bruce, but she had no intention of complicating her life by having a romantic fling with a passing stranger. Turning her back on the twilit lake, she climbed the hill to her truck.

Darkness had fallen completely by the time she reached town. She left her truck in the parking lot beside the hardware store and walked the half block to the Stardust Café. It was one of the two restaurants in Bethel Corners, the fancier one. The tables boasted white tablecloths and candles in green glass jars, and on weekends a trio of local musicians provided entertainment. This was Thursday, though, so the music came from the jukebox. Emma paused inside the door and waved when she spotted Bruce.

He beamed her that endearingly awkward smile and half rose from his chair. His elbow caught the edge of the table and he made a dive for his wobbling water glass before it could tip over.

This was the first time she had seen him without his hat, Emma realized as she walked past the handful of other diners. Because of that beat-up baseball cap he usually pulled down over his forehead, his hair had always been hidden. Now she saw that it was a beautiful, warm, sun-streaked blond, several shades lighter than his scruffy beard. Cut on the long side, it curled boyishly over the tops of his ears and skimmed his collar. In the subdued lighting of the Stardust Café, his hair looked . . . attractive.

Emma's step faltered. It wasn't only his hair. This was her first unobstructed view of his face. The scruffy beard still camouflaged his jaw, but not the high cheekbones or the strong bone structure. Was it the lighting, or was he really . . . handsome?

"Hi," he said. Her scrutiny of his features was interrupted as he leaned sideways to reach under the table and pull out a white plastic bag. "I got you another coffee thermos. Hugh didn't have anything exactly the same as the one I broke, but it's pretty close."

She took the bag and glanced inside. "Thanks. You didn't have to do this."

Smiling timidly, he sank back into his chair as she sat across from him. "I needed some excuse to invite you to dinner, didn't I? Oh, I don't mean that I'd need an excuse to have dinner with someone as pretty as you, I meant that you'd probably have plenty of other invitations and wouldn't want . . . I mean, thanks for coming."

He wore a white shirt and an incredibly ugly brown tie that was half-hidden by his baggy beige cardigan. It was as if he were deliberately trying to appear unattractive.

She focused on his face more carefully. The more she looked, the more she realized that above the beard his features were in fact strikingly masculine. He tilted his head and scratched his ear, once more drawing her attention with his awkwardness. Emma's gaze strayed back to his hair as a waitress brought their menus.

"The food here is really good, Emma," he said, patting his protruding stomach, almost as if he were trying to distract her. "I should know. Too bad I didn't get enough fish for a meal yesterday. The waitress said they could have fixed it up for me."

Beneath the table she wiped her palm on her skirt. His smile was shy and awkward, but his teeth were perfect, straight and white. His mouth was partly concealed by his beard, but from what she could see, his lips were beautifully formed. She wished she could see what he looked like without the beard. And she had the craziest urge to reach out and test the texture of his tempting hair and wrap one of his golden curls around her finger.

Pulling herself back to the conversation, Emma asked, "How did your photographs turn out? Did you get those rolls developed yet?"

"Yes, there are some fascinating images that I managed to capture. It's so nice around here. Is your family from Bethel Corners?"

"No, I was born in New York. I moved to the cabin about three years ago." She found herself staring at his eyes. He still didn't like to meet her gaze, but without his hat, he was unable to hide his bold eyebrows or long lashes. The color was all wrong, though. His plain brown eyes didn't seem to belong with the strong bone structure of the rest of his face.... Where had that thought come from? "I like the privacy out by the lake, and the freedom to do what I want," she continued.

"You mean like flying your plane?"

"Don't get me started on talking about flying again."

Bruce ducked his head as he opened the menu. Talking about flying was exactly what he wanted her to do. Or talking about anything, as long as it distracted him from her appearance.

The moment she had walked into the restaurant he'd known his objectivity was in trouble. Gone were the heavy boots and plaid jacket he had last seen her wear. Tonight she wore a pale green dress that fitted subtly to her generous breasts and nipped in snugly at her narrow waist. The delicate color brought out the auburn highlights in her hair and lent a tinge of aquamarine to the pure blue of her eyes.

His response to her beauty had been immediate and completely unprofessional. He had to remind himself that he was here in order to use her, that the cunningly simple dress he found so enticing was probably part of an expensive designer wardrobe paid for by the shady wealth of the Duprey family, or possibly by Emma's own criminal ventures.

Sure, he could tell his brain to be cautious, but he had no control over the chemistry that was going on elsewhere in his body. He shouldn't have stayed up half the night staring at her picture and thinking about what Xavier had told him. He should be concentrating on solving the puzzle of this case, not the puzzle of the woman.

"Okay, we won't talk about flying, and I won't talk about my job, since I'm supposed to be on vacation," he said when he decided he had command over his voice once more. "What about books?"

"That's something we have in common."

"Have you read Clive Cussler's new novel?"

"Do you mean the one where Dirk Pitt saves the world from total economic collapse and environmental disaster?"

"You'll have to be more specific. He did that in the last three books."

She laughed and leaned her chin on her hand. "I love those stories. It's great to immerse yourself in another reality that way."

Time to steer the conversation to something useful, Bruce decided. "I know what you mean. Books always kept me company. I was kind of lonely growing up, being an only child. Have you got any brothers or sisters?"

"One brother. Simon's five years younger than me."

"It must have been nice to have someone to play with when you were a kid."

"I was more of a mother figure than a playmate," she said, her expression turning serious. "When he was a teenager our parents weren't around, so the responsibility of raising him fell on me."

Bruce felt pleased that she hadn't lied about anything so far. He'd chosen the right persona to slip under her guard. He could see that she was relaxing, so he decided to probe a little further. "Do you see him often?"

"No, he was going to college when I moved to Bethel Corners. He visits from time to time, but he moves around quite a bit these days. At the moment he's prospecting for copper in the area northwest of here."

"Prospecting? Do people really do that anymore? Like with a burro and a pickax?"

"I think that particular style went out with the wild west, Bruce, but there are still plenty of exploration geologists and independent prospectors around. Buying and selling mining claims is a big business in Canada."

"I didn't know there was any mining in Maine."

"Oh, there's an old copper and zinc mine in Hancock County south of here, and plenty of activity across the border in Quebec. I know it's a long shot, but the north woods have always been popular with amateur rock hounds, so there's a chance Simon might find something."

"So your brother's a geologist?"

"Well, not really. He took some courses in that at college, along with plenty of other things. He's still trying to figure out what he wants to do, though. I hope this works out for him." She picked up the menu and ran her fingertips over the cover. "I'm glad you invited me to dinner tonight. If I'd stayed home alone, I probably would have done nothing but worry about Simon."

"You sound like a mother."

"I do, don't I?" She glanced up and smiled wryly. "Maybe I should be more worried about my plane than about my brother."

He was distracted by the way the dimple in her cheek appeared with her smile. For a moment he almost missed what she had said. "Your plane?"

"He talked me into loaning it to him again. This is the last time, though. I think I'm too much of a pushover. Maybe it's a good thing that I never had kids of my own or they'd run me ragged."

Bruce felt the distinctive clutch in his gut that meant something had fallen into place. The brother, the one who

had a record as a juvenile and "moved around quite a bit"
had access to Emma's plane. Could it be possible? "But
it's dark now. Does he fly at night?"

"No, he set up a camp where he's working. He stays
overnight quite often."

The clutch in his gut intensified, and with it came a sense
of satisfaction. His instinct about Emma might have been
right after all. If it was Simon Duprey who was making
those midnight flights, then there was a possibility that
Emma could be innocent, despite her background.

The waitress returned and asked them if they were ready
to order yet. Bruce knew that he would have had trouble
eating anything while he kept the gauze pads in his cheeks,
so he had taken the risk and left them out tonight. He was
glad he had, since for the first time in days he felt hungry.

There was a strong irony about their conversation
throughout their meal. Although Emma didn't go so far
as to reveal her true name or her family background, she
was completely honest about the facts that she did mention. So was Bruce. Like the subtle props he used with his
disguises, he kept the lies necessary for his cover to a minimum. Even in the disguise of the wimpy Bruce Prendergast, he was able to be honest when the topic turned to his
favorite books, his love of jazz, and his childhood in a
middle-class suburb of Chicago.

At some point he became vaguely aware that their conversation wasn't providing any useful information, but he
didn't care. How long had it been since he had enjoyed a
dinner with a beautiful, interesting woman? What harm
could it do if they had a lively discussion about the thera-
peutic properties of chocolate as they sampled each other's desserts? As the evening progressed the tentative
friendship they had established the day before deepened.

This was exactly what he had hoped for. Yes, it was all
going according to plan...except for the growing discomfort Bruce felt each time Emma smiled.

How could he be jealous of his own character? He was
in the middle of an investigation. It was complete idiocy to

wish he could drop his disguise so that when she looked at him she would see him as he really was. It would be sheer insanity to open up the rest of his past to her, to tell her about his tragic marriage and his obsession with his job and his crazy pangs of conscience over what he was doing here tonight.

He had to keep reminding himself that this wasn't merely Emma Cassidy, the reclusive beauty who happened to hunt with a bow and fly a plane. This was Emmaline Duprey, who had been charged with assault, and whose record was tainted with a cloud of suspicion. Even if there was a possibility of her innocence, it was still just a possibility. Despite his personal feelings, he had to consider her his suspect. Damn!

There was no more than a scattering of cars on the town's main street as he walked Emma to her truck. A shaded spotlight fixed high on the wall of the hardware store was the only illumination in the parking lot. The cool night breeze ruffled her skirt and she shivered a little, crossing her arms and rubbing the bare skin below her short sleeves.

It would have been natural to offer her his sweater, or to put his arm around her and draw her close to his side for warmth. But the sweater concealed his gun, and if she touched his body, she would know that he wasn't the soft weakling he portrayed. So instead of doing what came naturally, Bruce clenched his jaw and did his job.

Emma stopped when they reached the blue pickup and dug through her purse for her keys. "Thanks for dinner, Bruce. I had a great time."

"It was my pleasure, Emma." Hunching his shoulders, he kicked at a piece of loose gravel. "I know this is a lot to ask, seeing as you probably have plenty of other things to do, but I was hoping that I might be able to hire you and your plane once more before I have to leave. Even though I didn't have much luck fishing, yesterday was the high point of my entire vacation."

She paused, her keys dangling from her hand. "Oh. I'm not sure..."

"I'm sorry. I forgot about your brother. I guess he'll be using your plane for a few more days, right?"

"No, he's due back tomorrow morning. He'll probably get in around 9:00."

"He'll be staying with you for a while, won't he? I wouldn't want to butt in."

"Simon will be hauling his crates of samples to the assay office, as he always does. I'm not sure where it is, someplace near Bangor, I think." She flipped her keys into her palm and closed her hand over them, then looked up and smiled. "Why don't you call me tomorrow once I've had a chance to check out my plane? I'll let you know then."

"Thanks, Emma. That'll be great."

"And if my brother remembered to fill the tanks, I might not need to charge you for the fuel this time." She shifted her keys and the bag with the new thermos to her left hand. "I have to go."

"Thanks again for having dinner with me. Vacationing alone can get lonely sometimes."

"I know."

"Well, I'll call you tomorrow."

She was silent for a moment, as if debating something in her mind. Her smile faded as she studied his face. Slowly, almost deliberately, she extended her right hand. "Good night, Bruce."

He stared at the delicate hand she was offering. He should have anticipated this. How else would they have said good night? For a split second he considered not responding—since that handshake at her front door, he had been careful not to touch her. He couldn't risk letting his persona slip, especially now that he had a solid lead to pursue with respect to her brother. He could still avoid it. He could stumble over his feet, or knock the bottle he had given her to the ground, or produce any number of clumsy distractions to avoid physical contact with her.

Yet he did none of those things. Until now he'd suppressed his own needs and desires so that he could do his job. Was it so wrong to want this one moment for himself? The impulse was reckless, and possibly dangerous, but he couldn't seem to stop. Bruce Prendergast might have made her smile all evening, but it was Bruce Prentice who reached out and clasped her hand in his.

The shock traveled through Emma's skin and lodged somewhere in the center of her body. The tingle she had experienced that first time was back, and it was too strong to be an illusion. She felt his male energy surge against her, as if a switch had been thrown somewhere inside him and he no longer tried to shut off his masculine aura. She'd been watching for it all evening and had managed to catch glimpses, when he held his head a certain way, or when she surprised him into meeting her eyes, or when he was distracted and moved with a smooth, controlled grace instead of his usual clumsiness. He wasn't clumsy now. The way his thumb slid over her skin was turning her knees to jelly.

His soft blond hair glowed molten beneath the harsh light on the wall. Everything about him seemed to suddenly come into focus. The muscles of his face lost their slackness, lean hollows shadowed his cheeks. He was transforming, like a skilled actor dropping his role.

Her pulse thudded, her breathing grew shallow. My God, she thought. He's more than handsome, he's gorgeous. Why would he want to conceal that? The bland facade he had been projecting cracked wide open, and the expression in his eyes held her spellbound. He was looking at her, really looking this time. His gaze held a compelling swirl of emotions, from vulnerability to regret. He leaned closer, and she could clearly see the longing.

His grip on her hand tightened. His fingers were long and supple, his palm hard. She felt enveloped by his strength and overcome by a wave of awareness. She was close enough to feel the heat from his body, and smell the clean tang of his soap and the underlying scent of maleness that sent her heart tripping.

He raised his other hand to her face. As gently as the kiss of the breeze, he touched her cheek with his fingertips. "Ah, Emma," he murmured. His voice had changed, grown deeper. "You have no idea what you do to me."

His caress tingled over her sensitized skin, sending tendrils of pleasure all the way to her toes. Never had she felt a reaction this immediate. She didn't try to figure it out or justify it—there was no justifying the chemistry between two people. It was more than his looks, more than his friendly, engaging manner. This was what she had found so fascinating about him, this was the *something* that she'd known was there.

Warm breath tickled her skin as he leaned closer, his features blurring.

Closing her eyes, she pressed her cheek to his palm.

"Evenin' Miss Cassidy."

At the loud voice her eyes flew open. Nate Haskin, Bethel Corner's sheriff, was standing at the corner of the hardware store.

Bruce immediately released her hand and took a shuffling step back. Emma blinked, taking a moment to bring her breathing under control. The connection was broken, the instant of closeness cruelly shattered.

Sheriff Haskin moved nearer. "Everything all right?"

"Everything's fine," she said. Her voice shook, her whole body was trembling from the sudden withdrawal of Bruce's warmth.

"We haven't seen you in town lately, Miss Cassidy."

Defensively, she straightened her spine. This was a cop. She couldn't let him see any trace of her weakness. Glancing at Bruce, she saw that he had drawn into himself again, refusing to meet her eye.

"Have you seen that brother of yours lately, Miss Cassidy?" Haskin said.

"Not lately."

"Expecting to see him soon?"

"No," she said without hesitation.

"When you do, you tell him I want to talk to him, okay?"

"Certainly."

He gave her a glare, then dismissed them both by turning his back and walking away.

Swagger would be a kind way to describe Haskin's rolling gait. He reminded Emma of a school yard bully, with his close-set gray eyes and the fleshy lips that seemed to be set permanently into a sneer. Hugh had warned her about the sheriff when she had moved here, and so far she had kept out of his way. Of course, she didn't need any prompting to avoid a cop.

Bruce waited until the sheriff's loud footsteps had faded before he shoved his hands into the pockets of his loose cardigan and turned toward her. "Why did you lie to him?"

Where was the man who had just sent her pulse soaring with the touch of his hand? Could this really be the same person who had stroked her cheek so sweetly? He was frowning, his bold, straight brows drawn together with displeasure.

Emma crossed her arms over her chest and took a step closer to her truck. "It was a reflex action," she answered. "An acquired habit."

A flash of what looked like disappointment tightened his features for an instant. Then he sighed and rubbed his eyes. When he dropped his hand, his bland expression almost veiled his handsomeness once more.

Almost, but not quite.

He lowered his gaze. "I get the impression that you don't like that sheriff."

She didn't want to talk about this. She was shaken by the reaction his touch had once more managed to wring from her body, but now the mood had irretrievably shifted. She wrenched open the door of her pickup and climbed onto the driver's seat. "No, I don't," she said finally.

Bruce seemed to withdraw into himself even further, tilting his head so that his face was completely shadowed. "Why not?"

"I've always hated cops."

To Bruce, her parting comment was a slap of reality. Motionless, he watched the taillights from Emma's truck disappear into the night. Fool! He had been about to risk everything, and for what? Simply to hold a woman's hand, to have her smile?

No, it had been more than that. He didn't merely want to hold her hand and make her smile. He wanted to pull her against him, cover her mouth with his and make her moan.

What the hell was happening to him? He knew she was strong, and intelligent. Had he thought her to be honest? She could have been playing him along all evening. She came across all sensitive and innocent, but then she had lied to that sheriff without blinking an eye.

I've always hated cops.

And that's what he was. That's all he was, and all he lived for. He had felt the pull between them, and had heard her breathless sigh when he'd touched her cheek. He'd seen the warmth in her eyes.

What would he have seen if he'd revealed who he was?

What would she have said if she knew how he planned to use the information she had given him to call in reinforcements who would follow her baby brother and his cartons of rock samples tomorrow?

And just how did he think she would react when she found out he was probably going to send her last living relative to prison?

Whirling around, Bruce slapped his palm against the brick wall of the hardware store. He wished he'd never started to have those doubts about his job. Things were so much simpler when viewed through rigid ideals of right and wrong. The anticipation he had felt at the start of this case had changed to urgency. He wanted this to be over. As far as Emma Cassidy Duprey was concerned, his objectivity wasn't merely in trouble, it was shot to hell.

Chapter 4

Emma paced to the end of the empty dock and raised the binoculars for what had to be the eighth time in the last hour. She should have spent the morning working on the new prospectus for the fund her group was going to introduce next year, but she hadn't been able to concentrate. A dull ache throbbed behind her eyes from a sleepless night. Each time she had been about to doze off, she saw Bruce's face in her mind. Only it wasn't Bruce's face. And she heard his voice, but it was deeper and more resonant than she remembered. And he was touching her hand, and the heat that flooded her body had her twisting the sheets until morning.

She kept replaying their parting handshake over and over in her mind. The sense of connection she'd felt with him had been no illusion. Her eyes might have deceived her at first, seeing only what Bruce wanted her to see, letting him use his gestures and his expressions to distract her from his appearance, but her body had known from the moment he had touched her that he was someone... special.

Why did he want to disguise his good looks? Was it really due to his shyness? Was he unaware of his appeal? Or did it all come down to the eye of the beholder?

Frustrated, Emma dropped the binoculars, letting them dangle from the strap around her neck while she rubbed her eyes. Her thoughts were chasing around pointlessly, as they had last night. Bruce was an enigma, a mystery. Yet whatever he was, beneath his puzzling exterior there was a man who was on the verge of reaching past all her defensive barriers. She liked him, she found him attractive, and the lightest brush of his skin against hers made her tremble. Bruce. The klutz.

Only, he wasn't, was he? Not all the time.

What would have happened if Sheriff Haskin hadn't interrupted them? But he had. And he had asked about Simon. What was her brother into now?

"I don't need this," she muttered. "I really don't need this."

The white speck appeared on the northwestern horizon long before any noise from the engine could reach her. Emma checked her watch. Almost 10:30. Simon usually arrived by 9:00. He was always in a frenzy to unload his crates and get them to the assayer's. She lifted the binoculars back to her eyes and adjusted the focus, following the progress of the aircraft. It roared overhead as it made a circuit of the lake, dipping a wing in a sliding turn before it lined up for its descent. The pontoons bounced from the water twice before the airspeed reduced enough to eliminate the lift. Emma grimaced at the sloppy technique. Simon didn't share her natural love of flying. To him, a plane was simply a convenient mode of transportation.

The Cessna taxied toward the dock. Simon cut the engine and stepped out of the cockpit to toss her a line as the pontoon collided with the row of tires. Emma winced at the jolt that shuddered through her plane.

Simon leapt to the dock and gave her a grin. He had the easy charm of their father, with his clean-cut features and sparkling green eyes. His brown hair was brushed back stylishly, the auburn streaks lifting in the strong breeze. He was barely an inch taller than her own five foot six, so he was able to duck under the wing of the plane easily as he came toward her. "I'm glad you're here, Emma. I ran into a bad head wind. Be a sweetheart and help me unload my crates, would you?"

She fastened the last of the lines to the heavy rings in the dock boards. "Did you fill up the fuel tanks?"

"No time, I'm running late," he said, brushing past her at a jog. "I have to be at the assayer's in less than an hour."

"Simon!" She straightened up and called after him. "Simon, you promised."

He gunned the engine of the Wagoneer that he'd parked in her shed and backed it over the rocky hillside to the dock. He jerked it to a stop and jumped down to open the tailgate. "I'll do it next time, honest. But I was running late today, and I really have to get rid of this stuff."

Well, what had she expected? Did she think he would actually keep a promise to her? She set her jaw as she stepped onto a pontoon and began an inspection of the plane. Her palm glided along the smooth aluminum of the fuselage as she looked for signs of stress.

"Aw, quit worrying about that thing. It's only a lump of machinery." Simon ducked through the open door and pulled out a wooden crate. "I thought you were going to help me unload."

Only a lump of machinery? Hardly. This plane was like an extension of herself. She always cared for it with the attention a horse trainer gave a thoroughbred, or a biker gave his Harley. This was her freedom, her way of escaping from the world from the time she had realized that the world wasn't always a great place to be. "Simon, I'm not going to let you use this again."

Another bulky crate hit the dock with a thud. Simon pushed it aside and swung down another. "Look, I'm sorry, Emma, but I'm really trying hard to do well at this prospecting. I thought you wanted me to succeed."

He was trying to manipulate her again. God, why was it so difficult to take a stand against him? "Of course, I want you to succeed. I'm very proud of the way you're sticking with this venture, but you have to learn the importance of—" She caught her breath on a gasp. Bending down quickly, she looked at the ugly scar on the pontoon.

The metal had been dented for a span of more than a foot. Two rivets had been sheared off at the head, and a rust red scrape mark extended to the waterline. Anger tightened her hands into fists as she stepped carefully back onto the dock. "What the hell is that from?" she said, her voice dangerously low.

Simon glanced around, then quickly hefted a box and carried it to the back of the Wagoneer. "Oh, sorry about that, Emma. The water was a bit rough where I tied up, and the chain I was using sort of slipped."

"That's it," she stated. "That's the very last time."

He maneuvered the rest of his samples to his vehicle and came back to take her hands in his. "I'm sorry, sis," he said, his green eyes glowing with sincerity. "You're so terrific to put up with me. And I haven't even thanked you yet." He leaned forward, aiming a kiss for her cheek.

Glaring at him, she yanked her hands loose. "No, Simon. This plane is now off-limits to you. Permanently."

"Aw, you don't mean that. I'll fix that damage and—"

"No." She looked at the scrape mark again, outrage giving her the strength that she'd lacked before. "No more. I've given everything I could to you for ten years, but no more."

For the first time, his face lost its charming smile. He looked worried. "Emma, I apologized. I'll get it fixed. But I really need to use it again this week. I've made commitments."

She shook her head from side to side in a slow negative. "Make some other arrangements for your prospecting. I'm through letting you use me this way."

"You don't know what you're saying. I have to make one more run, that's all. Then I'll be finished."

"Run?"

"Emma." He grabbed her hands, squeezing painfully. "Listen to me. When I say I've made commitments, I mean real, serious commitments. This isn't just a job, this is life or death."

"How can looking for a copper mine be a matter of life or death?"

"I'm in debt, Emma," he said desperately. "Real, serious debt. I'm doing this to work it off, but if I stop now, they'll kill me."

"*What?*"

"I had a bad streak at cards. It was only supposed to be a friendly poker game, and I kept thinking my luck would turn. I didn't know what kind of people they were. Oh, Emma, you've got to help me. Let me do this last run and then I'll have paid it off."

A coldness crept over her, a familiar coldness replacing her anger. They'd been through this before, so many times. She thought he had changed. "You're not prospecting. You never were."

"I really do want you to be proud of me, Emma. I tried—"

"What are you into this time, Simon? What are you doing? Why do you keep calling it a run?"

"These people I owe money to, they need to bring their product into the country without attracting any attention, so I pick it up at night in the St. Lawrence and bring it—"

She grasped his arms and shook him. "Simon, what have you done?"

"I haven't touched the stuff. I just take it to their warehouse in these sample crates and—"

"*Simon!*"

He inhaled shakily, hanging his head. "It's cocaine, Emma."

As quickly as she had seized him, she released her grip and stepped backward. Revulsion slithered through her body. "My plane? You were using my plane, and my dock and my property to bring that . . . that filth into the country?'' Her stomach turned over. She battled the urge to be sick. "No. Oh, dear God, no."

"Just one more time, Emma. Then I'll quit. I promise."

She turned her head to look at the open tailgate of the Wagoneer, then ran forward and ripped the lid off the nearest crate. She didn't want to believe it. Digging desperately through the broken rocks on the surface, she kept going until her fingers touched something smooth. It was a rectangular package the length of her forearm, wrapped tightly in thick brown paper. She sank her nails into the end and tore it open. There was plastic under the paper. And white powder under the plastic.

"No," she repeated, as if saying it enough times would make what she was seeing untrue. He had lied to her all his life. Why couldn't he have lied about this, too? The trouble he'd gotten into as a kid, the vandalism, the joyriding, the petty theft, all that she'd been able to smooth over for him. But *this?* What could she do this time? With a sob, she wrestled the crate into her arms.

"Emma," Simon said, hurrying to her side. "What are you doing?"

Clenching her jaw, she carried the crate to the end of the dock.

"Oh, my God, no!" he cried, catching up to her just before she could heave the box into the lake. "No, don't destroy it. They'll kill me. Emma, please!"

She hadn't known she could feel such rage. It rose like a red mist in her brain. "Drugs! After our mother killed herself with drugs. After I ruined what was left of my reputation to give you another chance. After I moved here for some peace, you bring this to my very door!"

"Help me, Emma. Please. I don't know what to do, I don't know how to get out of this. Can't you see that I have to do what they say?" He struggled to pull the crate out of her grasp. "Please, Emma. I'm in too deep to stop now."

"You have to stop. You have to turn yourself in."

"Go the police? Trust them? If the mob doesn't kill me, prison will. Don't you remember what happened to our father? He was a broken man by the time he got out. He couldn't survive. Don't do the same thing to me."

At the painful memories his words evoked, her arms went slack. She released her grip on the crate.

Simon carried it away and stored it with the rest, then closed the tailgate and got in the driver's seat, slamming the door shut.

The noise made her whip around. She strode forward and clutched the driver's door at the open window. "No more, Simon. it stops now. You tell them that."

He inhaled shakily. Tears glistened in his eyes. "I'm so scared, Emma. And ashamed. Please, can you ever forgive me?"

She didn't answer. She couldn't. Emotions had thickened her throat.

"Emma. Please." He wiped his eyes with the backs of his knuckles, the same way he used to as a child. "I'm begging you. Don't send me to prison. I couldn't survive it. We're all that's left of the family, don't turn in your own brother."

What else could she do? Oh, Lord, what could she do?

This was her brother, the child she had coddled and sheltered. The people who owned those drugs would kill him if he didn't deliver. They would probably kill him if he sought help from the police. Or if they didn't, then prison would finish the job, just as it had with their father. She had to decide, to choose between her brother and the law.

The law. Since when had she felt any obligation to the law? But how could she make him stop this unthinkable thing he was doing without betraying him?

Simon's chin trembled. "I owe them a lot of money, Emma."

"And I've got a lot of money. I'll bail you out. As always. I'll pay your debt to get you out of this, but it stops now. You tell them to find someone else, because you're not doing this again, for any reason."

"But how—"

"It stops now," she repeated. "Call me after you tell them. I'll arrange to get them the money."

He reached through the open window and squeezed her hand. "I love you, sis."

Right now, she couldn't bear the thought of him touching her. She raised her palms and backed away. "Get off my property. Just get out of my sight before I change my mind."

Simon knew he had pushed her beyond her limit. He didn't say another word. He started his engine and drove over the hill.

She watched him disappear along with his obscene cargo, then stood with her fists clenched in frustration for long, agonizing minutes while she wished she could have thrown every one of those crates into the lake. She would pay Simon's debt, and get him out of this situation. But then she would make sure the police knew exactly where to find and destroy those drugs. Not for the sake of the law, but for the sake of the victims.

Numbly, she turned to walk back to her plane. Kneeling on the edge of the dock, she stretched out to touch the scraped pontoon. It was scarred, now. Tainted. It would never be the same. This lake and this cabin would never be the same, either. And she had thought she had achieved a measure of peace.

It was her fault. She was the one who had formed Simon into the man he was. Where had she gone wrong? What could she have done differently? Was she wrong to have let Simon go? Should she have made him face up to what he had done and take the consequences? Was her coddling responsible for the way he had turned out?

Water lapped against the dock. A gull screeched overhead and a squirrel launched into a raucous, chattering scold. The familiar noises seemed cruelly magnified, scraping across her raw nerves. She pulled her hand back from the plane and drew her knees to her chest, feeling the urge to scream.

"Emma?" The voice was soft and deep, moving over her like a gentle caress.

"Bruce?" She twisted around.

He was walking toward her, his familiar shuffling gait making scraping noises on the dock, his shoulders hunched inside his baggy coat. He tilted his head and the shadow from his cap brim slid over his sunglasses to shade his features. "Is something wrong?"

Something wrong? Hysterical laughter threatened to burst from the lump in her throat. She shook her head quickly. Why was he here? She felt brittle enough to shatter. On top of everything Simon had dumped on her, she couldn't handle the puzzle this man presented.

He stopped when he stood beside her. "I'm sorry for dropping in like this, but there was no answer when I called and..." He paused. "You're crying."

She dragged the back of her hand across her eyes and turned away from him.

"Emma? What's the matter?"

Shaking her head again, she wrapped her arms around her legs and pressed her face to her knees. No one had ever seen her cry, no matter what. "This isn't a good time, Bruce," she managed. "I'll..." She swallowed hard. "I'll call you later."

Instead of leaving, he squatted down beside her. "Aw, heck. I'm sorry. Is there anything I can do to help? Not that I'm much good at fixing things. I always seem to barge in on people when they'd rather be alone and— Heck, what happened to your plane?"

A fresh spurt of tears gushed against the denim that covered her knees. "It's scraped."

The boards of the dock vibrated as he sat down heavily. "No wonder you're upset. You love that plane, don't you? I could tell by the way you look when you fly it. It can be repaired, can't it?"

She could fix it, but it would never be the same.

"Emma? Can I get you a glass of water or something?"

A sob hiccuped past her lips. She tried to stop it, but it was out before she had a chance. His kindness was threatening to be the final blow to her self-control.

A stud from the open front of his coat scraped along the dock as he moved closer. His warmth flowed out to her even before he lifted his hand to her back. It was no more than a whisper of contact. "Do you want to tell me about what happened?"

It was tempting, that offer to share. She couldn't, though. For too long she'd had no one but herself to rely on. She had been the one to find solutions.

He shifted his legs, twisting so that he could slip his arm around her. His touch was tentative, his long fingers resting gently on her shoulder.

She didn't uncurl from the defensive ball she'd wrapped herself in. Instead, she tightened her grasp on her legs, keeping her eyes pressed stubbornly to her knees. She was so stiff the muscles in her back were cramping. Oh, to let go and trust someone for once in her life. She'd never been able to in the past. Not her parents, not the man who had said that he loved her. She couldn't even trust her own brother anymore.

"I know it isn't any of my business, but you might feel better if you talked about it."

"I can't," she whispered.

He was silent for a while. "Is it your brother? Was he the one who damaged your plane?"

She didn't answer.

"I think he passed me on the road. He was driving pretty fast. Did you two have an argument?"

An argument? If only it were that simple.

At her continued silence, he sighed. "Okay. You don't have to answer anything if you don't want to. But if you want to cry, go ahead. I promise I won't look."

That did it. Helpless to stop them now, Emma felt the tears scald her cheeks. With a muffled groan, she turned to press her face against Bruce's neck.

"Shh. It's okay, Emma." He rubbed her back in soothing circles. "It'll be all right."

No, it wouldn't be all right, but surrounded by Bruce's gentle strength like this, she could pretend for a while, couldn't she? She rubbed her cheek against the coarse fabric of his jacket. His beard tickled her forehead and she nuzzled closer, her nose touching the skin of his throat.

God, he smelled good. It was the same as the night before, that clean tang of soap overlying the unique scent of masculinity. She inhaled shakily, her tears trickling into his collar.

He raised his hand to her head, tangling his fingers in her hair. "Emma?"

She didn't want to move. Instead of answering, she brushed her lips over his neck.

"Emma, you're upset. You don't know what you're doing."

No, he was wrong. She knew exactly what she was doing. She kissed him again, sliding her mouth downward to the place where the pulse beat at the base of his throat. His taste was as unique as his scent. And she wanted to taste more, because she didn't want to cry.

His fingers tightened, tipping her head back. "I can't do this to you," he said hoarsely.

It was Bruce's voice, but not his voice. Opening her eyes, she looked up at him. Where was the man who had made her laugh, who had shared his chocolate cheesecake, who had worn that ugly tie? Where was the stranger who had made her quiver with the mere brush of his hand on her cheek? Which one was he now? She frowned at his dark glasses and baseball cap, suddenly impatient. Lifting her hand quickly, she grasped the brim of his cap and flipped it off.

He jerked. His hair gleamed in the sunlight. The beautiful, pale-streaked locks stirred softly in the breeze from the lake. A loose curl flopped over his forehead. "What are you doing?"

Recklessly, she grabbed his glasses and dropped them to the dock behind him. They struck the boards with a clatter that echoed through her head. Now the only shadows on his face were the subtle contours of his lean cheeks. Through vision still blurred by her tears, she saw his chameleon features harden into chiseled handsomeness.

Like a leaf caught helplessly in a high wind, her need for comfort flipped over to another side of need altogether. Her emotions were too raw to control. Fingers trembling, she traced his face, learning the taut texture of his skin and the bristling coarseness of his beard. Her thumb touched the edge of his mouth. She felt him shudder.

"Emma," he whispered. "No."

"Kiss me, Bruce."

His eyes glowed with an intensity that made her lungs heave. He moved with the swiftness of a coiled spring that had suddenly been released as he rose to his knees beside her and fastened his hands on her shoulders.

"Kiss m—"

There was no need for her to ask a second time. His mouth covered hers with a solid sureness that stole her breath.

This was what she needed, she thought as she tipped her head back and felt the firmness of his lips. Later she would worry about the sheer madness of this moment, but right now she wanted to lose herself in this simple, basic contact of flesh on flesh. What he looked like, where they were, and what she would have to do tomorrow could be forgotten as long as he was giving her this kiss.

Sweet, Bruce thought as he closed his eyes and tasted her lips. Not the cloying sweetness of sugared candy, but the rich flavor of a full-bodied wine. And just as dangerously intoxicating.

What was he doing? What the *hell* was he doing? Prendergast might have sat beside her and offered his comfort, but that persona never would have folded her in a tender embrace. And he sure wouldn't be kissing her. Kissing her wasn't going to get him any of the answers he wanted. It wouldn't help him wrap up this case any sooner. It was insane.

But Prendergast's hat and sunglasses lay discarded on the rough wood of the dock. She had yanked them off and thrown them away, turning the tables on him, probing his secrets with the lethal swiftness that he had hoped to use on her own.

Her fingers fluttered over his cheek and slid upward to thrust into his hair, and a soft sound of satisfaction rose from her throat.

Bruce parted his lips and took the sound into his mouth. He was glad that she'd knocked off his hat and that she found pleasure in touching his hair. He was glad that he hadn't bothered to pad his cheeks with gauze today and that she liked what her fingers had traced. The cop in him should be worried about losing the props of his disguise, but the man in him rejoiced. Increasing the pressure of the kiss, he cradled her face in his palms.

She returned everything he gave her. When his tongue traced the seam of her lips, she opened them readily. Unable to stop himself, he plunged into her warmth and his senses reeled. Had he thought she tasted like wine? She was nectar, a pungent, heady mixture of sensuality and strength.

If her mouth tasted like this, what would the rest of her be like? What would it feel like to graze his lips down her throat and part the loose blouse that molded her curves? How would her breasts weigh in his palms, and how would they look if he bared them to the sunlight and the gentle breeze?

The primitiveness of his response startled him. His hands tightened on her cheeks as his entire body trembled with tension. He wanted her. In broad daylight, on these rough wooden boards, beside the plane that had probably been filled with cocaine an hour ago.

Cocaine smuggled into the country by her brother.

Or maybe even by her.

Sanity belatedly filtered through the desire that dulled his brain. She had lied to the sheriff last night. She was Emmaline Duprey, she had been arrested for assault. He was supposed to establish a useful friendship with the woman, not seduce her. And he wasn't even sure which one of them was being seduced.

Her fingers slid through his hair and curled around the back of his neck.

He lifted a hand to catch her wrist before she could learn the broadness of his shoulders.

She nipped at his lower lip and moved her free hand to his arm.

Letting go of her face, he grabbed her other wrist before she could feel the hard muscle beneath his loose sleeve.

Close. He couldn't believe how close he had just come. Ruthlessly he attempted to rein in the desire that shook him. Emma pulled against his grip on her wrists, but he held her firmly, bringing her hands between them. He tried to ease his mouth from hers.

With a whimper, she followed him as he withdrew. She shifted to her knees and leaned toward him, refusing to let him end the kiss.

He didn't waste energy on cataloging all the "if only's." There was no changing the cruel and ironic reality of their situation by wishful thinking. Somehow he found the strength to wrench his mouth free.

They were both struggling for air as much as for control. The sound of their ragged breathing was as loud as the pulse that hammered in his ears. He leaned his forehead against hers and lowered her hands to her lap.

She didn't move away, and she didn't try to lean closer. She stayed where she was, her entire body quaking with reaction. "Oh, my God," she said, her voice breaking.

"I'm sorry, Emma." He stroked the backs of her hands with his thumbs. "I'm sorry, I took unfair advantage of the situation."

Her forehead rolled against his as she shook her head. "Don't be sorry, Bruce."

"I acted unforgivably. You were upset, and I—"

"I asked you to kiss me. Please, don't be sorry."

It wasn't the kiss that he regretted. It was who they were, and all the reasons why they had to stop. Clenching his jaw, he released her hands and swiveled away from her. He stretched his arm to pick up his sunglasses, then pushed himself awkwardly to his feet. His hat was nowhere in sight.

"It blew into the lake," she said.

"What?"

"Your baseball cap." She sat back on her heels and rubbed a hand over her face.

He fitted his sunglasses over the bump on his nose and raked his fingers through his hair distractedly, trying to salvage what was left of his Prendergast persona. He dipped his head, slouched his shoulders and shuffled to the end of the dock. A dark crescent bobbed on the ripples twenty feet from the back of the plane. His hat was sinking beneath the water.

"It was Simon who put the scratch on the pontoon," she said. "And we did have a terrible argument before he left."

The freely volunteered information hit him like a blow to the gut. She hadn't wanted to tell him before. But now that he'd held her, and kissed her, she was willing to take him into her confidence. Rather than being the disaster he'd feared, his slip out of character might work to his advantage. He'd be able to use her.

He should have been pleased.

Instead, he felt as if the splendor of their spontaneous embrace had just been irrevocably sullied.

And for the first time in his life, Bruce wished that he wasn't a cop.

Chapter 5

"My full name is Emmaline Cassidy Duprey." Emma propped her elbows on the edge of the table and sighed shakily before dropping her chin into her hands. She had thought this would be difficult, but it wasn't. It felt wonderful to be able to share this with someone. No, not just someone, with Bruce.

He sat at the opposite end of the small table where they'd looked at her maps three days ago—was it only three days ago? He leaned his forehead on his hand in a way that partly shielded his face, but he could no longer hide himself from her. She had kissed him. She had tasted the man, not the outward appearance, and she had felt something precious begin to grow.

"I head an investment group and occasionally act as a management consultant, but I changed my name three years ago and moved here to escape what I decided was an intolerable situation," she continued. "I still have an embarrassing amount of wealth, so I apologize for taking your money for that fishing trip the other day."

"You don't have to tell me this," he said quietly. "We all have good reasons for the masquerades we choose to employ."

The sunlight sparkled through the window, casting a pattern of bars on the table between them. She knew she didn't have to tell him anything, but she wanted to. It was the same instinctive urge to reach out to him that she'd felt when she'd sat on the dock and let her tears fall on the skin of his throat. So she told him about her childhood, how alone she'd felt when her father had been sent to prison, and how she had found herself responsible for raising her brother. Throughout it all, he sat motionless and listened without saying a word.

"The damage Simon did to my plane hurts more than it should," she said. "I brought that Cessna with me when I moved here, outfitted it with pontoons and amended my pilot's license. It's my own form of escape therapy, I suppose, just like those books that take up two walls of this cabin."

"My apartment in Chicago's the same way," Bruce said. "Only my bookshelves overflowed onto the floor a few years ago."

"I think we have a lot in common."

He hesitated. "I didn't mean to interrupt. Go on. You were telling me about what happened today."

She turned her face toward the window and looked over the lake. "I've always tried to smooth things over for my brother. It's second nature to me to pull him out of one scrape after another. But this time he's mixed up in something deadly serious, and I'm not sure if either of us can handle it."

"What's the problem?"

"He's been lying to me. Not that the fact that he lied is such a big surprise—he's been pulling my strings for years. But now he's in serious trouble with some very nasty people."

"Is he into something illegal?"

She flinched. "I don't have much respect for legalities, Bruce. It's like my basic loathing for the police."

He was silent for a moment. "I remember. You said you hated cops."

"My family was destroyed by the police and our justice system. I know what my father did was wrong, but he paid for his mistake. He gave the money back, he served his time in prison, but that wasn't enough. The law had to take it all. His self-respect, his reputation and his future were ruined the moment he was convicted. The press considered it open season on the entire Duprey family. My mother couldn't live with the scandal. She retreated into her own private cocoon, getting more and more dependent on the tranquilizers the doctors prescribed. I tried to help her. I pushed her into one rehab program after another, but she chose to escape permanently." Emma broke off and swallowed hard before she went on. "She didn't even leave a note. Her suicide killed my father, but it took him two more years to die. He became an alcoholic the day he left prison."

"I'm sorry, Emma."

"Simon and I are all that's left."

"But if your brother is in trouble, maybe it would be best to go to the police."

"No. I can't. That's out of the question."

"Maybe you should reconsider." Bruce pushed himself up from the table, awkwardly knocking his chair backward. He grabbed it before it could topple over and moved to her side. With a hesitant, tentative motion, he placed his hand on her shoulder. "I'd like to help you, Emma."

She reached up and covered his hand with hers. "You have. You held me while I cried. Did you know that I'm twenty-eight years old, and no one has ever done that before?"

His grip tightened. He exhaled harshly, his breath stirring her hair. "I have no business taking advantage of you this way."

"You're not doing anything that I don't want you to do." Still holding his hand, she rose from her chair and turned to face him.

He ducked his head, raising his free hand to scratch his beard. "Maybe I could help you with your brother. I've done work for all kinds of people. I remember the name of one man who had some sort of job in the justice department, a guy by the name of Jones. If Simon is mixed up in something illegal and he wants out, you could call this guy and say you were a friend of mine. I bet he would help you."

"You're a truly kind man, Bruce," she murmured.

"No, I'm not."

She was startled by the vehemence of his denial. Stepping closer, she angled her head so that she could look into his face. "Yes, you are. You're also very handsome."

"Emma, I don't want to take advant—"

"Oh, stop it." She shook off his grip and raised her hands to frame his face. "You are. I saw it from the start. You have a handsome nose, and a broad forehead and strong, thick eyebrows and beautiful, long eyelashes and your beard can't completely cover those sexy hollows beneath your cheekbones."

"Sexy?" he said, his voice unsteady. "Me? Heck, how can you say that? I know what I look like."

She slid her fingers into his hair, feeling the soft curls caress her skin. "How can you want to cover this gorgeous hair with a hat?"

He caught her wrists and brought her hands between them. "Emma, don't. Please. I don't want you to hate me."

"Hate you?" She looked into his eyes. His plain brown gaze was sparkling with vulnerability. "Whatever hang-up you have about your appearance, I don't hate you, Bruce. I think, given enough time, I might even grow to—"

"Don't say any more!"

She stared at him, hurt beginning to replace the warmth she had been feeling. "What's wrong?"

"This thing that's happening between us is impossible. It shouldn't have started. It can't go anywhere. So please, don't say anything you're going to regret later."

Her arms dropped to her sides and she took a step away from him. Of course, he was right, but that didn't stop her from wanting to kiss him again. "I'm making a fool of myself," she said finally.

He swore suddenly and viciously in language that she never would have suspected the gentle accountant would know. In a heartbeat he closed the distance she had put between them and caught her chin in his hand. He looked at her for a long minute while a muscle twitched in his cheek. "I think the situation is making fools out of both of us," he said cryptically.

"Bruce, I—"

He moved his forefinger over her lips. "I'm leaving Bethel Corners this afternoon."

She had only known him for three days. The disappointment she was feeling shouldn't be this deep. "I thought you wanted me to take you up one last time."

"What I want has very little to do with this. You have a way of making me forget about my job, but I won't let myself. I have to go back to work."

"You said you had a few more days."

"My vacation is over. I really have no choice, I have to leave. As much as I want to stay here and get to know you better, I can't." He traced the outline of her mouth as if committing it to memory. "I can't. My job has to come first, Emma. It's all I have in my life."

She was struck by the stark loneliness of his statement. "Why is that, Bruce?"

"What?"

"Your job is your life. Why? What happened to you that made you want to hide yourself like this?"

Indecision flickered across his face and for an instant he seemed about to answer. Instead, he slipped his hand around to her nape and held her head steady while he touched his lips to hers in a quick, light kiss. He drew back, his eyes filled with regret.

"Bruce?"

"I want you to promise that you'll call my friend to help you with your brother."

"I don't know."

He kissed her again, his mouth pressing harder until her lips parted. His tongue slid inside, a short, breathtaking plunge that lasted less than a second. Then he was nibbling at her lower lip in tiny, teasing tastes. "Say you will, Emma. Give the law another chance."

She closed her eyes and homed in on the pleasure he gave her, tilting her head so their mouths could mesh more closely. With a simple kiss he was doing things to her that she'd never felt before. She yearned for him. The tingling awareness that he'd inspired with no more than a touch had been merely an overture to this. The kiss after her tears had been an emotional reaction. This was so much more. It stirred long-forgotten dreams of having someone who would be there to hold her the next time she cried.

She raised her arms to his shoulders, but he caught her wrists and roughly broke off the kiss.

"I have to go." His voice was deep, and as unsteady as his breathing.

"Are you coming back?"

The silence stretched out while he drew into himself. His expression became shuttered, his features slackened, and the slouch of his shoulders seemed to intensify. She had seen him do it many times before, so she shouldn't have been annoyed. Yet she was. And she was confused, and frustrated.

He released her and took a stumbling step away. "No. I'm sorry, Emma. It would be best for both of us if we didn't see each other again."

She fought against the urge to reach out to him. She knew he was right. He was just passing through, wasn't he? Last night, as she had stood on her dock and listened to the lonely cry of the loon, she had known that what-

ever feelings she might have for Bruce could have no future. But the solitude she felt was worse now that she'd had
someone to share it with for a brief time.

Bruce glanced around the room, then picked up a pen
from on top of her desk and wrote something out on the
back of an empty envelope. "This is the number of the
man I told you about," he said, placing the envelope beside her phone. "Call him, okay?"

"I'll think about it."

"Say you'll do it, Emma."

"I won't lie to you, Bruce. I'll think about it, that's all."

He fidgeted with the pen, turning it over and over in his
fingers. "Is there some other reason you don't want to go
to the police, something besides the suffering your family
went through when your father was arrested?"

"I won't betray my brother. It's my fault he's in this
trouble to begin with."

His fingers tightened over the pen. "What?"

"It's my fault. I was the one who encouraged him. I
thought I was helping, but I should have known it would
backfire."

"What do you mean? Are you saying that you're involved in Simon's problems, too?"

Should she open up to him again? Share her conflicting
feelings about her brother, the guilt and the responsibility? Bruce was leaving. The comfort she'd found with him
was only temporary. She shook her head. "I think I've said
enough. It's not that I don't appreciate the kindness you've
shown me—"

The pen dropped to the floor. Bruce swore sharply and
stooped to pick it up, then slammed it on the ledge of the
desk. He pulled his sunglasses from a pocket of his jacket
and scuffed his way to the door. "I have to leave."

"Yes. You told me."

He fumbled with the doorknob for a moment. "Take
care of yourself, Emma."

She felt her lower lip quiver. Ruthlessly she pressed her nails into her palms. She didn't offer her hand. Touching him again would only make this worse.

Bruce opened the door and stepped outside without looking back. It was the most difficult thing he could remember having to do, but somehow he managed to keep his shoulders hunched and his head down as he crossed the hill to his van. His body strained against the awkward shuffle. He longed to run, but he wasn't sure he knew where he would go. He wanted answers, but he didn't know if he had the courage to ask the questions.

It had been a risk to give her Xavier's number, but it was a calculated one. If she was innocent, it gave her an option. If she was guilty, it hadn't blown his cover. If. If. He still didn't know, he still couldn't be sure. Yet Bruce knew that if he had stayed in that cabin one more minute, he would have blown not only his cover but his investigation. So he buried his feelings in his duty, ground the van's abused gears and drove jerkily down the bumpy driveway until he was sure he was out of sight.

He pulled to a stop on the far side of Emma's mailbox, his knuckles white where he clutched the wheel. A stocky man behind a surveyor's tripod waved. Bruce watched critically as the man motioned to his partner to stay put while he crossed the ditch toward the van. Xavier had arranged the increased surveillance with his usual efficiency, but the road crew pose was hardly original.

"You've gained some weight, Prentice."

Bruce scowled. "Any word yet, O'Hara?"

"I just heard from Epstein. Duprey's passed the turnoff to Millinocket and is still heading south on I-95." The phony surveyor tugged at his fluorescent vest, centering the large X over his chest. "We're packing it in here. One of the neighbors has already been by to ask what we're doing."

"What did you tell him?"

"Same as always. I said the county sends us out to measure things without telling us why, and that I'm just a working guy doing his job. He bought it."

"Don't get too cute."

O'Hara frowned. "I know what I'm doing, Prentice. What about you? Any luck with the sister?"

"I don't know."

At the barely suppressed violence in Bruce's tone, O'Hara jerked back. "What's eating you, Prentice?"

"Nothing."

"If you've got a problem here, better tell Xavier before—"

"I'll handle it," he snapped.

"Take it easy. We're making progress."

"Not fast enough," Bruce muttered, jamming the van into gear. He felt like punching something. Instead, he gunned the engine and channeled his frustration into seeing how fast he could navigate over the winding dirt road to Bethel Corners. He barely slowed down as he passed through town, almost hoping that Sheriff Haskin would pull him over. He needed a fight, an outlet, anything to keep him from turning around and going back to Emma.

But that was impossible. There was no longer even a whiff of objectivity attached to his relationship with her. What he had said before he'd left her had been the stark truth. With him, his job had to come first, it was all he had in his life. And if he went back to Emma again, it wouldn't be as a cop.

Bruce automatically locked the door and drew the curtains when he reached the motel. He didn't pause to check in with Xavier. There was something he needed to do first. He walked directly to the bathroom, braced his hands against the edge of the sink, and stared straight into the mirror.

Emma had called him handsome. She'd run her fingers through his hair and over his beard, and she'd looked at him as a woman looks at a man she wants.

Swearing under his breath, he leaned over and touched a finger to each eyeball in turn. His face twisted with revulsion as he stared at the brown contact lenses that wobbled on his fingertips. He raised his gaze to the man in the mirror, focusing on the vibrant color that shone from beneath his dark brows. The blue of his irises ranged from deep indigo around the rim to pale cerulean near the center. Surrounded by his long, dark brown lashes, the effect of the color was startling and memorable, one of the reasons why he usually tried to mask it.

Would Emma still want him if his eyes no longer looked like mud?

He shrugged off the baggy coat and flung it through the bathroom doorway. The loose shirt followed. With a vicious tug, he ripped the tape from his ribs and pulled the padding from his stomach. He watched his reflection straighten. Muscles stretched and rippled beneath firm skin as he rolled his shoulders. Would she have wanted him if her hand had discovered the breadth of his shoulders, or if her fingers had felt the rock hard swells of his biceps? He flexed his arm, watching the play of controlled power, then ran his hand over the crisp mat of hair on his chest to the washboard hardness of his abdomen. It was nothing but male vanity to wish that he had chosen a different persona, and that Emma could have known there wasn't an ounce of fat on his body.

Moving quickly now, he lifted the scissors from the counter and began to cut away the beard it had taken months to grow. Curling, dark blond clumps fell into the sink. When he had cut away as much as he could, he lathered his face and picked up the razor. Smooth, taut skin gleamed in a swath down his cheek. He shifted his jaw and puffed out the hollow she had called sexy, methodically scraping away his camouflage. When he had finished, he gave his face the same scrutiny he had been giving his body.

What would she think if she could see him now? Would she like the way the hollows emphasized his high cheekbones? What about the square jaw and the long, stubborn chin? Would she still call him handsome?

He seldom considered his looks, except when he thought of new ways to alter them. For a short-term cover, assuming a different expression would often do the trick—he was as skillful as any actor when it came to controlling the muscles of his face. His expression now, though, was as vulnerably naked as his freshly shaved cheeks.

I've always hated cops.

I don't hate you, Bruce.

But she would.

He threw the razor into the sink and strode to the other room, kicking his jacket aside as he passed. There was no going back. Prendergast had just disappeared forever. He could have used the new closeness to pressure Emma into revealing more about Simon, and her unwitting cooperation could have been a big advantage for the investigation, but Bruce could no longer stomach the deception. The woman who had broken down and cried against his neck didn't deserve any more lies.

But he couldn't tell her the truth. He knew how protective she was toward her brother, and if she knew that the police were already closing in, she might do something stupid and desperate. He had given her Xavier's number, but he didn't hold out much hope that she'd call it.

And there was still the possibility that she might be involved in the smuggling, no matter how much his heart wanted to believe in her innocence. The cop in him had known it from the start. Nothing she had told him had proven anything, one way or the other. Simply because she seemed to display genuine concern for her brother didn't mean that she wasn't doing something illegal herself. And plenty of criminals had a hard luck story they could tell about their childhood.

As it had at least a hundred times in the past few days, his gaze went to the photograph of Emma. He stared at the black-and-white image, this time seeing her as she had been that morning, curled into a ball, her cheeks streaked with tears and the lashes around her blue, blue eyes glistening in wet clumps.

No one had ever held her while she had cried. The admission had humbled him, and had sent a confusing blast of emotions through him. Guilt. Sympathy. Admiration. He'd heard her side of the story today, had learned of the suffering and pain that lay behind the naked facts Xavier had given him. He hadn't pushed her, but she had opened herself up to him as readily and honestly as she'd kissed him. While he'd been plotting on how to proceed with his case, how to use her, she had willingly invited him past her barriers.

She'd done it again. Since the moment he had first seen her unsling that hunting bow from her back, she had managed to surprise him. He had never met a woman so challenging before, or one who stirred his interest to this extent. Since the death of his wife, he had shut himself off from feeling anything other than his simple devotion to his duty. It was easier that way, less painful, less risky.

His hands tightened into fists at his sides. Emma had wanted him to stay with her. He'd seen the need written clearly on her face, and tasted it on her lips. No, not him. Prendergast. The overweight, clumsy, harmless tourist.

But he'd just killed off his alter ego as surely as he'd killed any chance of an honest relationship with Emma. He couldn't reveal himself to her as he really was. He couldn't jeopardize the investigation any further. And most of all, he couldn't bear to think about the hurt and the anger — and the hate — that he would see on her face if she ever learned of his betrayal.

But it wasn't a betrayal. He was just doing his job. Why should he feel guilty about that?

It was a hell of a situation, but there was only one way out. He would never be able to see Emma again.

Ten minutes later, he broke the news to Xavier.

"You can't do that!" Xavier shouted into the phone. "I want you right where you are. You've got an inside track with the Duprey woman."

"Too late. Prendergast left town permanently."

"Dammit, Bruce. That tip you gave us about Simon Duprey paid off big time. We followed him to a warehouse in Bangor. I just found out that it belongs to Carter McQuaig. The feds have had their eye on him for years, but haven't found anything more than innuendo and rumor. They're falling all over themselves to help, now that it looks as if we'll be able to tie McQuaig to narcotics."

"I figured the kid wasn't prospecting. Only his sister would have been gullible enough to swallow that story."

"There you go with the sister again. It was a good cover story. She probably helped him cook it up. Or if she didn't, then she got him involved. You should be cozying up to her and pumping her for more information—"

"That's not an option," he said harshly. "I want to bring this operation to a close as fast as possible."

"We all want that."

"I gave her your phone number."

In the sudden silence Xavier's indrawn breath sounded like a hiss. "You did what?"

"Considering her background, I couldn't reveal anything about our investigation, but I had to cover the possibility that she might be innocent so I gave her your number. You're a guy named Jones in the justice department that Prendergast did some work for. If Emma decides to turn to the police, you'll help her."

"Hell, Bruce, that wasn't part of the plan."

"The plan changed."

"This isn't like you."

"No, it isn't. I'm having some strong doubts about the things that I've been doing for the sake of my job—"

"You're a good cop. Don't start having some midlife crisis thing on me, now." His voice lowered to a tone of forced calmness. "Stay with me on this. You've got plenty of time off coming to you. When the case is wrapped up, you get yourself to somewhere tropical and laze around on a beach for a few weeks. How does that sound?"

"I'm not about to walk off the job, if that's what you're worried about. I told you, I want this wrapped up fast. That's why I've decided to go in from the other end. Get me everything you've got on Carter McQuaig."

There was another silence. "What are you planning?"

"When I started this investigation, I was after the head of the chain, not just the links. It's time to dig deeper." He rubbed his smooth chin, his eyes glittering with icy hardness. "Do we still have that black Corvette we impounded last February?"

"Yes, we do. Why?"

"Find out if McQuaig has any connection to the drug ring that I infiltrated in Chicago."

"No! Absolutely not. You're not going in that deep again."

"My cover wasn't breached. I'll use the same connections and get myself an invitation to—"

"Bruce, it's too dangerous. To go in that deep, we have to spend time setting it up. You don't know what you'll run into if you get close to McQuaig, or who else might be close to him. It's too risky."

He clenched his jaw. Too risky? Not when compared to the consequences of spending any more time around Emma Cassidy. "Depends how you look at it, Xavier."

The sun had set half an hour earlier. Shadows loomed in every corner of the cabin. With the darkness had come a creeping chill, but Emma didn't get up to start a fire. She was curled into a corner of the couch, her cheek on her updrawn knees. Although it was difficult to see more than a pale rectangular outline, she kept her gaze on the envelope that rested on the coffee table. The number that Bruce had scrawled in his bold, strong handwriting was no longer visible, but that didn't matter. She had no intention of using it.

She had tried to call Simon at least twenty times since Bruce had left. There had been no reply, nothing, not even a busy signal. She was worried. She was almost worried enough to pick up that envelope and carry it to the phone and put her trust in a cop. Almost. But not until her brother was out of this. Maybe Bruce was naive enough to think that his friend could get Simon a deal, but Emma wouldn't risk seeing another member of her family in prison.

"Simon," she whispered, "where are you?"

Had he told those people that he was quitting? Had he told them that she would pay his debt? She hadn't even thought to ask how much he owed. Likely she would need to liquidate some of her stock in order to cover it, but that didn't pose an insurmountable problem. She was good at making money. But she wasn't much good with people, was she? Dry-eyed, she turned her face toward the window and looked at the first faint stars that glowed above the horizon. Another sunset had come and gone, and she had dealt with it alone. She would deal with Simon's problem alone, too. She shouldn't have let herself get close to Bruce that way. She should have known better. Turner hadn't stuck around when the going got rough, either.

The sudden shrill of the telephone made her jump. She sprang from the couch, her heart tripping painfully. Before the second ring had finished she was across the room and lunging for the receiver.

"Emma?" The trembling voice belonged to her brother. "Emma, is that you?"

She pressed a hand over her chest and took a deep breath. "Simon. Thank God. Tell me what happened."

There was a fumbling noise before a new voice came on the line. "Miss Cassidy? Or perhaps I should say, Miss Duprey?"

"Who is this? Where's my brother?"

"I'm an associate of your brother's, Miss Duprey. We've been having a long conversation and I'm very distressed to learn that you don't approve of our business." The voice echoed slightly, as if the man were speaking from a tomb. "Simon tells me that you advised him to quit working for us. We can't permit that. It would leave us in an awkward situation."

She had to maintain a tight control over her mind, or she would be reduced to a pile of nerves. "Did he also tell you that I'm willing to pay you the money my brother owes?"

"But the money isn't the issue right now. It's the work, you see. We need people we can count on, and now we can't count on your brother anymore. Do you understand the problem? Wait, I'll let Simon explain it to you."

There was a muffled thud, and a sudden cry of pain. Emma steeled herself not to imagine what was happening at the other end of the phone line. If she did, she wouldn't be able to function.

"Emma? Are you there?"

"Simon, are you all right?"

"No. They're going to kill me. You never should have told me to quit. You can't quit something like this." His voice broke on a sob.

She felt sick. Even this was her fault. "Simon, hang on. I'll find a way to help—"

"Miss Duprey." It was the other voice again. "You can't think about contacting the police, or we will kill your brother." He said it with a cold, casual indifference, as if he were announcing they'd have bacon for breakfast.

Emma didn't doubt him for a moment. If she had even remotely considered going to the police before, that option was now eliminated. "I told you I'll pay you what he owes," she said quickly. "I'll pay more. How much do you want?"

"We don't want your money. We want you."

"What do you mean?"

"Simon tells me that he's been using your plane, and that your piloting skills are much superior to his. As far as we're concerned, the solution is simple. You will take over your brother's job while we keep him here as our guest."

Chapter 6

It was amazing how many different emotions could get tangled up with love. Emma knew she loved her brother, but right now she felt fear, worry, despair...and anger. She had seen the mixture before, when she had been at a shopping mall and a mother had found her lost child. The woman had cried with relief and hugged the wayward boy, then had held him by his shoulders and had shaken him like a rag doll, screaming at him not to wander off like that again, then had hugged him once more. The cycle repeated, over and over, as the pendulum of emotion swung. Love...and anger at the vulnerability of love.

If Simon was suddenly restored to her now, she wasn't sure whether she would hug him or shake him.

She eased her pickup into the shadows at the side of the warehouse, turned off the engine and slipped her keys into her purse. A bulb in a metal cage glowed weakly beside the sign on the wall. CM Imports. Business Hours 8:00 a.m. to 5:00 p.m. No Parking in Front of Door. Emma tipped her wrist toward the dim light and checked her watch. Almost 10:00. They would be coming for her soon.

The man who had phoned yesterday had been very specific when he had told her the time and the place. This was a test. They were telling her to jump, and they wanted her to answer "how high." Although she had never dealt with this particular strata of criminals before, she recognized intimidation when she saw it. She'd bargained with sharks and with slime in the business world, and that's how she had to handle this situation.

Her sober rust-colored suit with its padded shoulders and severe tailoring projected an impression of strength, her hair was carefully gelled into a sedate, backswept style, and her makeup was understated and elegant. She couldn't let them see her weakness. She couldn't let them know how her hands had shaken so badly that she'd taken five minutes to button her suit and three separate attempts to apply her lipstick.

She had to look at this as a business deal. They wanted something from her, she wanted something from them. It should have been simple, but her fear for her brother was clouding her thinking. It was there beneath the veneer of outward calmness like a raging current beneath an ice-covered stream.

Simon had cried on the phone. And they'd hit him.

A spasm shook her body. She tried to call up the strength that had gotten her this far. They wanted her to make one very important run and then they would let her brother go, they said. Every fiber of her rebelled at the thought of following their orders, but she had to play along with them until she could get Simon out. And once her brother was safe...

That was the point where her plans whirred to a stop. Hug him, or shake him?

The minute hand of her watch inched toward the hour. Emma sucked in deep, controlled breaths to pump oxygen to her screaming nerves, then reached for the door handle and stepped out of the truck.

Headlights blinked on from the darkness, exposing her where she stood. She forced herself not to flinch or to squint against the brightness. Crossing her arms over her chest, she took up a pose of patient waiting.

A car door opened. Crisp footsteps echoed across the pavement toward her until a slim man stepped into the headlights beam. He was completely bald. In the stark lighting, his face had the tight angles of a skull. "You're punctual, Miss Duprey. Good. Come with me."

It was the voice from the phone, the man who had struck her brother and made him cry out with pain. She wanted to lunge at him and claw out his eyes. "Where is Simon?"

"He isn't here." He walked toward the warehouse, evidently assuming she would follow.

"I won't go anywhere until I know that he's all right."

He turned, and his skull-like features tightened with impatience. "Let's get something straight here, Miss Duprey. You're in no position to give anyone orders. If I feel like it, I might let you speak with your brother when our business is completed for the evening, but until then, you do as I say."

She straightened her shoulders and followed him to the small door that was set into the wall beside the sign.

The interior was cavernous, the lone row of lights overhead barely denting the gloom. Emma's high heels gritted across a cement floor as the bald man led her through alternating pools of light and shadow toward a glassed-in office at the far end of the building. In the stark illumination from the fluorescent ceiling fixtures on the other side of the glass she could see a gray-haired man in a navy blue pin-striped suit. He sat behind a steel desk that held numerous papers, a coffee cup, a telephone and a gun. She focused on the gun, her throat closing with fear. She didn't have to know the make or model of it to understand its deadliness.

Oh, God. She couldn't handle this. She wanted to scream, turn around and run away, pretend this was all a bad dream and that Simon would be coming back with her plane in a minute and she would never scold him for his sloppy flying again and....

A firm hand on the small ̄of her back propelled her through the doorway into the office.

The man behind the desk looked up and Emma felt something inside her recoil. Everything about him, from the thin, almost nonexistent lips to the cold gray eyes, projected the merciless intensity of an executioner. Oh, Simon, what have you done?

It took only twenty-three minutes for them to explain exactly what Simon had done. The gray-haired man, whose name was McQuaig, detailed the flight path, the rendezvous point and the loading procedure. As the details mounted, so did Emma's horror. The chances Simon had taken were insane. She couldn't do this. She wouldn't.

Despite the tight control she kept on her feelings, something must have shown on her face. McQuaig paused, glanced at the other man, and snapped his fingers, pointing toward the telephone. "Let her talk to him, Harvey," he said tonelessly.

The bald man with the face like a skull was named Harvey? She thought the name was ludicrously ordinary, like Jimmy Stewart's giant rabbit. And on the heels of that thought came the realization that she was close to losing control. She dug her nails into her palms, her pulse counting off the seconds, while Harvey the skull man dialed and spoke a few terse words into the phone. He held the receiver out to her. "This isn't because you asked," he said. "It's because we chose to. Remember that."

She wiped her palm on her skirt and took the receiver. "Hello? Simon?" Nothing but silence greeted her. She felt her heart clench and looked at McQuaig. He stared back at her with flat indifference.

Suddenly, her brother's voice, weak but recognizable, drifted through the receiver. "Emma?"

Her breath whooshed out. "Simon! Are you all right?"

There was a long pause. Then he spoke quickly, his words running together as if he were worried about getting them all out. "Do what they say, Emma, please, please, I'm scared, they'll kill me if you don't."

"Simon, where—"

"That's enough," McQuaig said, pressing his finger down on the disconnect. The line went dead. "Don't try anything cute. Just do the job your brother was supposed to do, and we'll all come out of this satisfied."

From outside the warehouse came the sound of screeching tires and the throaty noise of a powerful engine. Both men glanced at each other as if already dismissing her presence. McQuaig gestured toward the emptiness on the other side of the glass wall of the office. "He's early. Bring him inside while I finish up with the pilot."

The pilot, she thought numbly. The word that had once connoted freedom now sounded dirty. Emma moved away from the phone on the desk, trying to hang on to the threads of her unraveling composure. Through the glass wall she watched Harvey walk across the cavernous gloom to the outer door.

The new arrival stepped into the first pool of light, suddenly materializing from the shadows. Emma felt her heart thump hard. Even with the width of the warehouse between them, this man looked more dangerous than either of the others. He was tall, maybe an inch or two over six feet. He moved with the sleek, fluid ease of a big cat as he peeled off his black leather jacket and held his arms extended outward at his sides. Harvey said something that elicited a negligent shrug, then passed his hands over the man's body in a swift but thorough check for weapons. Evidently nothing was found, and the man was waved forward.

He walked with a riveting combination of arrogance and grace. It was more subtle than a strut, the way his legs stretched confidently and his hips rolled just enough to suggest a casual sensuality. For a moment he faded into the shadows, then reappeared in the next pool of light, and Emma felt her palms sweat.

He hadn't put the jacket back on. He hooked it with two fingers, letting it hang over his shoulder—his bare shoulder. The olive drab undershirt he wore exposed almost as much skin as it concealed, and that skin was stretched taut over solid muscle. She tried to look away, hoping to ignore the involuntary clutch of...something that responded to his blatant masculinity. But she couldn't. He came closer, and she was able to see more details. He didn't have the sterile shape of a bodybuilder but rather the firm, rangy physique of a man who used his body hard.

"You can use the same crates as your brother."

She jerked, her gaze snapping back to the man behind the desk. "What?"

"Cover the merchandise with rocks, just like he did. But as long as you keep your mouth shut, you won't be stopped." He picked up his gun and sucked in his stomach in order to tuck the weapon into his waistband. "You'll have until 10:00 the morning after the pickup to deliver the merchandise to the location we tell you. Your brother will be waiting there. We remove one of his fingers for each minute you're late."

Dots danced in front of her eyes. Breathing in deeply, she grabbed on to the corner of a battered filing cabinet to steady herself. "I'll be there."

"Good."

The solid footsteps that were echoing from the concrete grew nearer. Clenching her jaw, she delved for a reserve of strength in order to straighten her spine. This was a business deal, she told herself. She couldn't let them see her weakness. "Fine. Then we have a deal, Mr. McQuaig. Just let me know the date and time."

"We'll be in touch." He glanced at the doorway. "Mr. Primeau?"

A deep, resonant voice replied. "Yeah. You McQuaig?"

"Yes. Please, come in."

Emma felt the man's presence the moment he stepped into the office. She kept her gaze on the floor until he moved into her field of vision. He wore black leather cowboy boots, not the dusty, beat-up kind but the highly polished, expensively tooled kind. Black, skintight denim hugged the muscular contours of his calves and thighs and clung indecently to his slim hips. The olive drab undershirt molded against washboard firmness. Emma tightened her fingers on the edge of the filing cabinet to keep from trembling.

"I've heard good things about you from our mutual acquaintance in Chicago," McQuaig was saying. "What brings you out here to the coast?"

"Business." He shifted to drop his jacket over the back of a chair and crossed his arms over his chest. "I heard you're reliable. My last source retired prematurely, and I'm looking for someone who can supply my customers on a regular basis. You interested?"

Something stirred at the back of Emma's mind as she listened to the voice. It was rich and deep-chested. She knew she would have remembered if she had heard it before, but still it seemed familiar. She looked at the man's powerful arms, then raised her gaze as far as his chin. It was a long, stubborn chin set in a square jaw. His skin gleamed with the tightness of a fresh shave, but he wore his hair on the long side. It was dark blond, slicked straight back from his face and caught into a short ponytail at the back of his head. A thin gold chain with a cross on the end of it dangled from his right earlobe.

On some men the ponytail and the earring might look effeminate. They had the opposite effect with this Primeau. Everything about him, from the sensual walk to the arrogant stance to the aura of leashed power in his lean muscles, exuded raw masculinity.

"As a matter of fact, a regular supply is what I guarantee," McQuaig said. "My network is second to none."

"That's what I heard."

"My latest shipment has already been distributed, but I should have several kilos by the end of the week. Harvey," he said, gesturing toward Emma. "Get her out of here."

That was one order that Emma was eager to comply with. She was unraveling. On top of the panic over the threats to Simon, and the horror of what she had to do, this gut-level reaction to the man called Primeau was making her sick with revulsion. She knew what he was. He was a drug dealer. He was the next link in the obscene chain, the one that would distribute the white death to its ultimate victims.

Until now, she had focused on his walk, his clothes and his body. As she was straightening up to leave, she raised her gaze to his face.

He was staring at her, and his eyes were...beautiful. The color was a brilliant blue, unlike anything she had seen in her life. Surrounded by long, thick lashes, his gaze was fascinating, like an unexpected glimpse of clear sky. His eyebrows were bold and straight, angled downward in a frown. His nose was long and narrow, with a subtle bump in the center...

She blinked. No, it was impossible. *Impossible.*

His cheekbones were high, with hollows carved beneath them that would be partly hidden by a beard...

Her breathing stopped, simply suspended on a gasp. This was crazy. She must have snapped from the tension, but this drug dealer bore an uncanny resemblance to...

No. It couldn't be.

Rapidly her gaze traveled over him again. There wasn't an ounce of fat on that tautly muscular body. There was nothing shy about his arrogant stance, nothing plain or awkward about the boots or the tight clothes or the earring that dangled defiantly down the side of his neck.

His firm, well-formed lips spread into a smile with no warmth. "Hi, there, sweet thing."

She stared at his lips. She knew their shape, and their texture. But this didn't make sense. She had never seen this drug-dealing scum in her life. Had she?

"Harvey, I told you to get her out of here."

"What's your hurry?" The man who called himself Primeau moved between Emma and the office door. "A woman like this does wonders for the decor in here, McQuaig. She yours?''

Disgust, along with anger, tightened Emma's stomach, adding to the insane suspicions whirling in her head. She tried to step around him, but he shifted smoothly, blocking her path.

McQuaig laughed, a low grating sound like an unused hinge. ''Primeau, meet Emma Duprey. She's our pilot.''

''Her? A woman?''

''She'll be bringing in the next shipment.''

''So she's working for you?''

''We have a mutual agreement, don't we, Miss Duprey?'' McQuaig drawled.

She nodded numbly, not taking her gaze from the man who stood in front of her. Were those hints of sun-streaked gold in his tightly slicked hair?

''Hey, she can fly my friendly skies anytime.''

The crude comment sickened her. She must be mistaken. The kind, gentle accountant would never—

Before she could move, Primeau's hand shot out and fastened on her upper arm. His grip was like an iron band. If she struggled, she would have bruises. He brought his face close to hers, his unbelievably beautiful eyes holding her spellbound.

She felt it then, that spark between them. The man-to-woman, hunter-to-hunted connection. The bond of recognition that dwelled in the depths of instinct. The truth seared across her mind in a dazzling flash.

It was impossible.

But it was Bruce. *Bruce.* In a different body, a different person, but she knew it was the *same man!*

Before a single sound could escape her frozen lips, he swooped closer and brought his mouth next to her ear. ''Play along,'' he breathed, ''or we're both dead.''

She couldn't move. Her pulse raced, her lungs heaved. She felt a swirling disorientation threaten to sap the last of the dwindling strength that kept her knees from dissolving.

He pulled back and stared straight into her eyes, the message in his gaze as clear as a shout. His mouth moved into a cold smile and he released her arm to rub the crest of his knuckles across her cheek.

The contact was a hollow parody of the tender caresses Bruce had given her in the past. Bruce. How? *Why?* Confusion fogged her brain. She could barely deal with her anxiety over her brother and her fear over what she had to do for these criminals. She couldn't deal with these questions that had no answers.

Bruce—yes, Bruce—grasped her wrist and tugged her forward, bringing her hard against the front of his body.

The impact of his solid, muscular form knocked her speechless. She squirmed, but that only intensified the contact of their bodies. No. *No!* This couldn't be happening. How could the nightmare be getting even worse? It was as if reality had shifted, like one of those children's pictures that changed if it was viewed from a different angle. She felt sick, and she felt instant heat spark along her skin from the proximity of this man, and that made her feel even sicker.

"What price are you asking for your merchandise, McQuaig?" Bruce asked.

McQuaig laughed his rusty hinge noise again. "Which kind, Primeau? The shipment at the end of the week, or what you're holding now?"

He answered with a chuckle that was deep and ugly. "I'm referring to business. What I'm holding is pure pleasure." He named a price for several kilos of cocaine that made those dots dance before Emma's eyes again. McQuaig haggled briefly and demanded a down payment. Bruce demanded to test a sample before he took delivery. A bargain was struck in less than a minute.

Emma felt as if she were going to throw up.

Bruce let go of her wrist and fastened a powerful forearm around the small of her back. He reached past her to pick up his jacket, then twisted quickly and propelled her toward the office door. "Looks like I'll have some time to kill around here, sweet thing." His fingers dug warningly into her ribs. "What do you say we go somewhere for a drink?"

She stumbled alongside him, her heels skidding on the gritty cement floor. She clutched at his hand, trying to pry it loose, but it was like trying to pry granite.

"You don't mind if I borrow your pilot for a few hours, do you, McQuaig?" he called over his shoulder.

"If you're thinking of striking a private deal with her, forget it," McQuaig replied. "We only use people we can rely on. Isn't that right, Miss Duprey? You wouldn't think of doing anything to change our arrangement, would you?"

Simon had cried on the phone. They would kill him if she didn't deliver. She shook her head. "Of course not."

"Then what you do on your own time doesn't concern me," McQuaig said. "Keep in touch, Primeau. Harvey will see you out."

Bruce held her firmly to his side as they walked through the pools of light, his body strung tight with tension. Emma felt it the same way she felt his simmering anger. Why was he here? What was he doing? She looked up at him as they reached the outer door. Who was he? *What* was he? A mad hiccup rumbled from the place where she was suppressing all her roiling emotions. This was *Bruce*. A blue-eyed, sexy-like-a-snake Bruce.

The night air was cool and damp as they stepped outside. A gleaming black car was parked beside her blue pickup. Of course, she thought, feeling another hiccup bubble to her throat. This Bruce wouldn't drive a beat-up old van, he would drive a Corvette. Did he trade in his vehicles like he traded in his clothes? And his body?

Bruce steered her toward the car. "This is for Harvey's benefit," he whispered, his mouth close to her ear. His grip on her loosened for a moment. Before she could pull away, he rubbed his hand up and down her arm. "I saw a place a few blocks from here, sweet thing," he said aloud in a voice that would be sure to carry to the man who still stood in the open warehouse doorway. "You can follow me in your truck."

She wanted to scream. *Bruce, you're not like this. You're gentle, and kind and tender. We shared our desserts. We talked about books. You held me while I cried, remember? You're a man I could grow to...*

His hand dropped to her hip, his fingers caressing the curve of her buttock.

The gesture was a travesty. Emma felt something shrivel inside her. The peace of her cabin by the isolated lake had already been shattered, her simple joy in her skills as a pilot was being corrupted. Why shouldn't the warmth of what she had shared with the shy accountant be destroyed, too? "Don't touch me."

His mouth stretched into a predatory smile as he tightened his grasp and pulled her closer. "It's not only Harvey," he said between his teeth. "There are eight men stationed around the warehouse. Get in your truck and follow me."

She had to tip back her head to look at the stranger who held her. He was tall. And strong. He couldn't be her Bruce. But he was.

With a low curse he moved his hand to her back and steered her to the passenger side of his car. "Okay, we'll do this the hard way," he muttered, opening the door and pushing her inside. Before she could recover enough to react, he had rounded the hood and jumped into the driver's side. The engine came to life with a powerful growl.

"No," she gasped, reaching for the door handle. "I'm not going anywhere with you."

He clicked the power locks and put the car into gear. The tires squealed on the pavement and she was thrown back against the seat. Bruce didn't even glance at her. In the sliding bars of light from the scattered streetlights they passed, his profile looked as if it were carved from stone.

Emma braced her hands against the dashboard, feeling her grip on reality slip another notch toward hysteria. This was no rusty old van he was driving. The black car could go almost as fast as her plane. And he knew perfectly well how to handle it. That clumsy performance with the grinding gears and jerky starts that he'd put on when he'd driven up her driveway had been as phony as his shambling walk. Why? If he was a drug dealer, why had he masqueraded as a klutzy tourist?

Wide-eyed, she looked at the large, strong hands that gripped the wheel. Her gaze traveled up his arms, halting briefly at the firm biceps before going on to the broad shoulders and coming to rest on his profile once more. He was the same man. The nose was the same, so was the forehead and the cheeks and the masculine jaw she had glimpsed through the beard. But he wasn't trying to hide his attractiveness. No, he was flaunting it. Her pulse raced, her thoughts spun like the tires that squealed across the darkened streets.

Bruce drove in silence. In a matter of minutes they had left the run-down area of the warehouse and were cruising toward a neon-lit strip of bars and old brick hotels. Without warning he abruptly turned the car into an alley and skidded to a stop.

"Okay, this will have to do," he said. He twisted toward her. In the dim light from the dashboard his features took on a harsh, threatening cast. "First of all, let me say as one professional to another that your act is one of the best I've ever seen."

No, she thought as she listened to the cruel tones. This wasn't Bruce's voice. Bruce was gentle, and sweet and understanding.

"You've managed to surprise me all along, but this tops everything," he continued. "I was wrong about you. I can see that now."

She shook her head, trying to regain some control over her wits. "Who are you?"

"You can forget the innocent act, Emma. I saw you with McQuaig. I heard you make your deal with him. You freely admitted that you were his pilot before you recognized me."

"But I'm not—"

"Enough lies. It's too late. From now on I'm going to do my job, and the hell with the way my body happens to react around you." He reached across the cramped space between them and grasped her chin in his hand. "I'm through trusting you. I almost blew this whole operation because of you, and that's not going to happen again. From now on, I'm not letting you out of my sight."

She jerked away from his touch. "What are you talking about?"

He draped one arm over the steering wheel and braced the other on the back of her seat. "Don't you think I saw the exact moment when you made me? I'm not going to give you the chance to tell your pals who I am. Until this is all over, I'll be sticking to you like glue, sweet thing."

He must be crazy, Emma thought. He wasn't making any sense. This entire situation didn't make any sense. Why? her mind screamed. Why, why, why? It became a litany, the question repeated so many times it began to lose its meaning. Why would a drug dealer assume another identity like that? Why would he need to? Why did he stop her from revealing what she knew about him to Harvey and McQuaig? And why had he told her to play along or they'd both be dead? Emma remembered the concern he had shown the day before, and how he had tried to convince her to go to the police.

Why would a drug dealer want her to go to the police?

The police?

The truth was too glaring, too huge to take in all at once. Emma felt her reeling thoughts converge into the only possible answer.

No. Oh, good God, *no!* Not Bruce.

But there was no other explanation. He had lied. He had masqueraded as a clumsy tourist to put her off guard. He had manipulated his way into her confidence, had faked a friendship, had even kissed her. And she had blindly opened up to him and given him information about herself and her brother....

She focused on the incredibly handsome face that was so close to hers. And in that moment, she felt the tender feelings that had once begun to grow wither and die.

"You're a cop," she said finally, woodenly.

"That's right."

If he had reached out and slapped her, it wouldn't have hurt worse. "Prendergast or Primeau?"

"It's Prentice, Bruce Prentice."

"It's cop. That's who you are. You're a damn cop." She pressed back against the door. Tears burned behind her eyes, but whether they were tears of anger, or disappointment or hurt, she didn't want to know. The one thing that she was certain of was that she wasn't going to let them fall. She wouldn't let him see her cry. Not again.

"A damn good cop, until I met you."

"A lying, sneaking, dirty—"

"Whatever you think of my job, it's a hell of a lot cleaner than yours."

"I'm not—"

"Oh, no. I'm not falling for the lies anymore, Emma. That was a good act you put on for me. I almost bought it, too. I almost believed you were innocent. I tried to ignore your background, and the way you lied to the sheriff. I even admired your skill with that airplane, the Cessna you're using to smuggle cocaine into the country. It's a neat little operation you've got going up at that private lake. How long have you been flying for them?"

She clenched her jaw, trying to keep her chin from trembling.

"And what's the story with your brother? Was he following in his big sister's footsteps? Did you suddenly have conscience pangs about what you got him into?"

At the mention of Simon, a new anxiety knifed through her mind. Bruce was a cop. What would happen if Mc-Quaig found out? They might think that she had led Bruce to them. They had already told her that they would kill Simon if she went to the police. But even if they didn't find out, what would happen to Simon if Bruce stopped her from doing that run? His interference could cost Simon his life.

Emma could feel the anger radiating from his tense body. He wouldn't believe her if she told him she was innocent. And to explain her innocence, she would have to admit Simon's guilt. She couldn't do that. The police had brought nothing but misery to her and her family throughout her life, and this cop was no exception. How could she even consider telling him the truth? He had lied to her from the very beginning. He had lied to her when he'd told her his name, and when he'd made her laugh and when he'd held her face between his palms and kissed her. The closeness had all been a lie. The feelings she'd had for him had been based on illusion.

"I asked you a question, Emma."

She gazed into the startling blue eyes that held no warmth or mercy and studied the man that she had thought she'd known. She remembered her father, and her mother and her own lost dreams. And just as she had when she was eighteen and her world had crashed around her, she straightened her spine against the pain and stared back into the face of the law defiantly. "Go to hell, Bruce."

Chapter 7

Bruce hung up the telephone and watched Emma warily. She stood by the front window of the cabin, her shoulders rigid beneath the wrinkled linen of her rust-colored suit. Her arms were crossed over her chest, her legs braced slightly apart, her chin tilted up combatively.

She had been standing there looking out at the darkness of the silent lake since they had arrived here almost an hour ago. Although she hadn't resisted when he had taken her back to the warehouse and instructed her to drive home, he had followed her cautiously, alert for any surprises. She'd had a few colorful words to say when he'd stored his Corvette in her shed and removed the distributor cap from her pickup, but she hadn't tried to stop him. Still, he wasn't fool enough to take her compliance for capitulation. He didn't want to underestimate her or misjudge her again.

He gave Emma's back a final glance before he squatted down and unplugged the telephone cord from the receptacle in the wall.

She pivoted to face him. "What are you doing?"

"What does it look like?" he snapped. He picked up the phone, wrapped the cord around it, and walked to the desk where he disconnected the modem and stacked it on top of the phone.

He'd done a thorough check of the layout of the place. The cabin might look rustic, but it wasn't primitive—the rolltop of this large desk had concealed a computer setup that could have belonged in a high-rise office. Besides the multipurpose main room, there was a bathroom with a deep, oversize tub and lush hanging ferns, a small spare room with colorful, woven wall hangings and a single bed, and Emma's bedroom, which was dominated by a big four-poster with a comfortable-looking mattress.

He headed toward her bedroom now. Forcing himself to ignore the traces of the woman who inhabited it, the discarded tube of lipstick on the long dresser, the pair of jeans that lay in front of the open closet, he crossed the floor to the phone that rested on the bedside table. He unplugged it like the other, then straightened up and turned around.

"I told you I wouldn't contact McQuaig," Emma said. She stood in the doorway, her face carefully expressionless. "I have my own reasons for not wanting anyone to know I was conned by a cop. This isn't necessary."

"I'll decide what's necessary and what isn't."

"Why don't you just gag and handcuff me and get it over with, Mr. Policeman."

"I think removing the telephones will be sufficient for the moment, but I'll keep your suggestion in mind, Miss Duprey."

She clenched her fists and spun around, muttering something under her breath.

Bruce followed her back to the main room and stuffed the phones into the large bag that he'd brought in from his car. Cutting off the communications was only temporary—he'd need to reconnect at least one of the phones in the morning so that McQuaig could contact her about this week's run.

His hand shook as he zipped the bag closed, and he paused to take a calming breath. His anger wasn't yet under control. It had been building since the moment he'd walked across that warehouse floor and had seen Emma through the office window. With her hair styled sedately and her feminine body subdued by that severely tailored power suit, she had looked every inch the cool professional. And that's exactly what she was, a professional businesswoman making a deal.

Xavier had been right about her all along. It had been nothing but mindless chemistry that had drawn Bruce to this woman, and like a fool he had been blinded by it. He'd mistaken his hormones for his conscience, and he had allowed dangerous doubts to disorder his thinking. From this point on, things were going to get back on track. No more confusing himself with his personas. No more questions about the morality of his job or the right and wrong of his duty. He wasn't going to let his professional detachment slip again.

He stored his bag under the rolltop desk and walked over to throw the bolt on the front door. "I think we'd better get a few things straight."

"Am I under arrest?"

"Not at the moment."

"Then I'd like you to leave."

"I'm not leaving until I'm finished with you."

"What's that supposed to mean?"

He moved to one of the overstuffed chairs and perched on the arm. "Sit down," he ordered, pointing to the couch.

She glared at him defiantly, then raised her hand and wiggled her middle finger.

"Emma, you can make this as difficult as you want. It's up to you. Don't you want to know my plans?"

"Oh, yes, please, Mr. Police—"

"Dammit, you keep that up and I'll gag you after all."

She didn't sit on the couch. She pulled one of the ladder-back chairs from the table by the window and set it in the middle of the floor. With the poise of a princess presiding over a garden party, she sat down, pinched her slim skirt and crossed her legs demurely. Clasping her hands together on her lap, she looked at him expectantly.

God help him, he didn't want to cover her mouth with a gag, he wanted to cover it with his lips. Even now that he knew the worst about her, he still found some uncontrollable part of him responding to the challenge she presented. Ruthlessly he forced himself to concentrate on the plan he had just hammered out with Xavier. "I know you're using your plane to transport cocaine for McQuaig's group, Emma. You're not going to waste our time by denying it, are you?"

She lifted a palm regally, motioning for him to continue.

"When I started this investigation, I was after the people at the top. I still am."

"The big ones," she said. "I remember you telling me that when I asked you what kind of fish you were after. What was that, a little cop humor?"

"I can make things easier for you if you cooperate. I want nothing to interfere with the next shipment that comes in. When McQuaig gives you the time and place, I want you to make the pickup and the delivery just the way you always do."

Her eyes narrowed. "What?"

"You heard me."

"Why?"

"I already told you. I'm after the people at the top."

"And you want me to lead you to them."

"Put simply, yes."

"You know where the warehouse is. You've met McQuaig and Harvey. Why don't you arrest them?"

"I need proof that will stand up in court."

"Ah, yes. The law and our wonderful justice system." She shifted, recrossing her legs with a whisper of nylon. "You want to catch them with the goods. That's why you demanded to test the merchandise. That's why you took on this latest masquerade. Let's see, what was it you said? We all have good reasons for the masquerades we choose to employ? Another very fitting comment, now that I know who you are.''

''Whatever your reasons are for running those drugs, whether it's the money or the thrill or some inner need to defy authority, I'm going to shut you down. But not before I make use of what you're doing. When you get the call from McQuaig, you're going to do exactly what he tells you.''

''Believe me, I wouldn't have let you stop me.''

''I won't stop you, I'll be right beside you.''

She waited, letting a tense silence spin out between them. ''So you get what you want, but what about me?''

''Xavier authorized me to offer you a deal. A lighter sentence if you cooperate.''

Another silence stretched out. Her knuckles whitened as she tightened her clasped hands. ''That's not acceptable. I want full immunity and time to collect the payoff McQuaig promised. You give me one hour after I deliver the cocaine before you move in.''

''That's out of the question.''

''Without me, you've got nothing. Take it or leave it.''

''Why? What are they offering you?''

''That's my business.''

''I'll have to think about it.''

''There's more. You leave my brother out of this. He hasn't done anything. You were right before. I got him involved in the drug smuggling and then had second thoughts. Immunity for me, an hour to collect my payoff and no charges against Simon. Those are the conditions that will guarantee my cooperation.''

''Why should I give you an hour before we make our move? That would be suicidal. With that much warning everyone in the entire ring would have enough time to—''

''I wouldn't warn anyone. I have no loyalty to those people. This is a business deal to me, nothing more. If the whole mob ended up in prison I wouldn't mind. I'd well come it. As long as you're using me to get what you want, I might as well use you. My only concern is my brother and myself." She rose to her feet, her fingers twining restlessly in the first outward show of nerves she had so far allowed. "Forget the hour. The second you see Simon and me leave the drop-off point, you can move in."

"Why would your brother be at the drop-off?"

"He's staying with them temporarily, and I want to be sure there won't be any retaliation against him when your people move in."

"So as long as you and your brother go free, you'll give us what we need to nail everyone else?"

"Yes. I'll fly you to the pickup, I'll lead you to the drop-off, everything you want, as long as you don't move in until you see Simon and me walk out."

It was all he could hope for, if he could believe her. "Give me a minute to think about it."

Emma turned away and dragged her chair back to the table, braced her hands against the edge and gazed blankly at the polished wood. Her body was shaking from the emotions she struggled to suppress. This was a deal, just like the one she'd been forced into with the criminals. She had to think. And she couldn't do that while she was looking at Bruce. There was no warmth in his spellbindingly beautiful blue eyes, no compassion in his hard, uncompromisingly masculine face. The lips that had once molded to hers were carved into a stony slash. He hadn't needed to rip her phones out of the wall to demonstrate his lack of trust. It was written in every line of his body.

She raised her head and looked past the reflection on the window to the blackness outside, forcing herself to assess the situation. Things might not be as bad as she had feared. She was still going to make the smuggling run that would free her brother. She hadn't had a plan of her own for what to do afterward, but if the cops moved in and arrested the entire drug ring, her problem would be solved. She didn't care what Bruce thought of her, as long as she got what she wanted.

Tell him the truth.

Gritting her teeth, she ignored the weakness she felt. For Simon's sake, she couldn't explain her situation. Her ingrained, instinctive protectiveness toward her brother wouldn't let her risk the possibility of prison for him simply to clear her name. She'd been through this before, and it had worked out all right. She was in a good position to negotiate. This deal would get her brother out of danger as well as keep him out of prison. She wouldn't settle for anything less than full immunity for herself, so it didn't matter what Bruce thought of her. He was a cop, part of the unfeeling system that had destroyed her family. Why should she care what he thought?

At the sound of movement behind her, she shifted her focus to the reflection in the window. It still jarred her perception of reality each time she saw Bruce move that lithe, powerful body. In the soft light from the lamp behind the couch she could see the subtle play of shifting muscles in his arms and shoulders as he lounged against the back of the chair. She had no control over the quick tightening of her stomach as she looked at him. With those black jeans clinging to his slim hips and that skimpy undershirt leaving half his torso bare, he was simply magnificent, a sleek male animal in his prime.

Her anger rekindled. He had lied to her and used her and made her like him. She'd been a fool, a lonely, trusting fool.

"I'll take your deal," he said, staring straight into her eyes through his reflection. "You give me your employers, and I'll let you and your brother walk."

She pushed away from the table and turned to face him. "Fine. I'll hold you to it."

"I guess this just goes to prove the old saying."

"What saying?"

"The one about no honor among thieves," he said, contempt plain in his deep voice.

"Honor?" she repeated, taking a step toward him. "You, of all people, dare to mention honor?" The iron control she had kept on her feelings throughout this endless evening was crumbling. Business deals were one thing, but what he had done to her as Prendergast wasn't business, it was personal. "Tell me something, Mr. Honorable Policeman. Do you get paid overtime for having to kiss your suspects?"

"Of course not."

"What about listening while they unload their family problems? Did you get yesterday afternoon's conversation on tape? I hope so, especially that part where I tried to convince you that you were actually handsome. You might get a bonus for that if you played it around the station house."

Bruce thought he heard a trace of pain beneath her angry words, but he wouldn't let himself be affected by it. This woman had made a fool of him too many times. He crossed his arms tightly and leaned toward her. "I don't get extra pay, and I don't get bonuses. And if I recall correctly, you were the one who wanted to take our relationship beyond friendship, not me."

"Friendship? You have a twisted definition of the word. You were using me from the start. Very skillful, weren't you? Play on my sympathy with that clumsy tourist routine, manufacture just enough phony sensitivity to make me lower my guard, pretend to be sweet and shy and interested in my feelings. Is that what they're teaching at the police academy these days? You must have been at the top of your disguise class." She strode forward and reached out to flick his dangling earring with her index finger. "How did you do it, Bruce? How did you manage to hide all this macho stuff under Prendergast's baggy coat?"

"Padding. And contact lenses."

She bent to bring her face level with his. "Today your eyes are blue. Very spectacular, much more interesting than the mud brown you wore before. Is it real this time?"

"Yes. The color is real."

"My compliments. Are these muscles real?" She poked her finger against his bare shoulder. "Oh, my, they certainly are. And I had thought that you were too self-conscious about your extra weight to dress in fitted clothes.''

Her touch, her proximity, even her unraveling temper was sparking a response despite his tight control. "That's enough, Emma.''

Deliberately she ran the back of her knuckles across his cheek. He recognized the gesture. It was the same one he had used in the warehouse office. "Getting rid of the beard was a definite improvement,'' she continued, her tone furious. She was no longer concealing her rage. It crackled around her like an electric haze. "And combing your hair back into that punk ponytail was an inspired idea. Did you have to practice the swagger and the sneer? The walk was very effective. You moved like a jungle cat.''

"Stop it, Emma,'' he warned. He slipped from the chair arm and rose quickly to his feet.

"No, you had your fun. Now it's my turn." She propped her hands on her hips and tipped her head to do a long, slow appraisal of his body. "You're what, six-one, six-two? You must have had a sore back from all that slouching you were doing under your baggy coat. Now I understand why you wouldn't let me touch you. That would have blown your cover completely, wouldn't it? Poor Prendergast. No wonder he vacations alone.''

He could sense the approaching danger. He knew what would happen if either of them let their temper explode. He tried once more to turn things back to a safer tack. "It's late. You'd better get some rest.''

"You want to know something funny? I was actually starting to like Prendergast, even though he hid his features under that damn baseball cap and the stupid, bland expression. When he kissed me, I thought he cared. His appearance didn't matter." She clenched her jaw and raked him with a gaze that could have scorched steel. "But he doesn't even exist. And as far as this strutting hunk-of-the-month I see in front of me goes, I sure as hell don't like him.''

He had wondered what she would think if she saw him as he really was. He had stood half-naked in front of the bathroom mirror in the motel and wished that she could have known he wasn't the overweight klutz he seemed. Now she did know. And now he saw the hate in her eyes. He fought against the regret that stabbed him by letting his own anger rise. "While we're on the subject of humor, how about this one? I made good use of the connection Prendergast had established with you. I could have kept pushing and really taken advantage of you, but I pulled out and became Primeau. Because of you, I almost ruined the entire investigation. It's just as well that you don't like me, because at this point I don't like you very much, either."

She blinked, but her gaze remained steady. "Good. I'm glad you don't like me. I've seen how you treat your friends. And Primeau's caveman approach to women makes Prendergast seem like Don Juan, sweet thing."

Recklessly he grasped her arms and pulled her closer. "Do you prefer weak men? Do you want a man you can feel sorry for, someone who doesn't challenge you or have needs of his own?"

"I don't want anyone," she said breathlessly. "Especially you."

"You liked Prendergast. That was me, Emma. My lips that kissed you, my tongue that tasted your sweetness."

"No. It was a lie. Everything you did was a lie."

"Not everything." He slid his arms around her back and drew her against his body. His brain shouted a warning, but a different, more primitive imperative directed his actions. "This is me." He splayed his fingers over her bottom, pressed her closer, and tilted his hips. "And this is me. I'm a cop, but I'm also a man."

She trembled. "I hate you."

"I know."

She brought her hands between them and pushed at his chest. "You used me."

"I know that, too. And I'm not finished with you." He lifted her higher and felt her fingers dig into his shoulders. "This thing between us has nothing to do with my job. I've wanted you since I first saw you striding across the hill toward me. It's sex, Emma. That's all. I don't have to like you to want you."

"You disgust me."

"And you're a liar." Tightening his hold, he crushed her to his chest. Through the barrier of her linen suit he could feel the firm, warm curves of her breasts. Each ragged breath she took forced her nearer, and he knew her trembling wasn't only from anger.

"I told you I'd cooperate. You don't need to put on this performance of macho passion. Or are you hoping to earn some kind of commendation for deeds above and beyond the call of duty?"

"Did you like the way Prendergast kissed you, Emma?"

"No."

"Liar. You didn't want to stop. You liked the way our mouths fit together, didn't you? And you tried to touch me. Well, go ahead and touch me. Find out exactly what I was hiding under the baggy clothes."

She let go of his shoulders and arched backward, but he wouldn't release his hold. Sudden, savage heat raged from the place where their lower bodies molded together and her lips parted on a wordless gasp.

"You asked whether I had a sore back from having to disguise myself," he said, his voice growing hoarse. "My back wasn't the only thing that ached by the end of the day."

Roiling, conflicting emotions glittered in the depths of her blue eyes. "You were only playing a role, you were only pretending."

He wished to God that's all he'd been doing, but she had gotten to him. It had been five years since anyone had done that, and of all people, it had to be Emma. He braced his legs apart and leaned over her, bringing his face to hers. "It's a hell of a situation, isn't it? I want you, and from what I can feel, you want me. But we're on opposite sides.

We're adversaries. We both detest what the other stands for."

Her hair swung behind her as she locked her hands around his neck for balance. "You're right about the detesting part."

"And about the wanting."

Her body quivered. She didn't need to answer aloud.

With a fierceness that would have appalled him if he'd been thinking straight, Bruce brought his mouth down on hers. The kiss was swift and hard and possessive, nothing like the tender connection they'd shared before. He kept his eyes open, watching the fury that blurred her gaze, knowing his own control was on the verge of snapping.

And then she surprised him. Again. As she had always managed to. Her grip on his neck tightened, her nails pressed sharply into his skin and she retaliated with a response as fierce as his. She took without giving, using her lips and her teeth to wring every ounce of sensation from the place where their bodies joined. It was a kiss filled with carnality but no feeling, heat but no warmth.

He pulled back, focusing on the tense, delicate features that had haunted him for a week, feeling his heart pound and his lungs scream for air. What had he hoped to prove by that kiss? He already knew he wanted her. He already knew he couldn't have her.

"You bastard," she whispered. She slipped from his loosened embrace and wiped the back of her hand across her mouth. Curling her fingers into a fist, she drew back her arm.

He saw the blow coming. For a split second he considered letting her strike him—it was what he deserved. Yet instinct took over and he dodged easily.

She backed away. "Get out."

"No."

"I don't want you touching me, I don't want you anywhere near me. Get out of my house. Get off my property."

"Not yet."

"We have our deal. I'm not going to tell Harvey or McQuaig anything about you, so there's no reason for you to stay."

Bruce used every last reserve of inner strength to shore up his crumbling self-control. The job, he reminded himself. It was the job that was his priority here, not the woman. "The reason I have to stay is simple, Emma. I don't trust you. I made a mistake once with you, and I can't afford to make another. Until this case is wrapped up, we're stuck with each other. That's why I'm staying."

"Trust is another word that sounds strange coming from you. How do I know that you'll give me what I asked for if I cooperate?"

"If you don't cooperate, I'll haul you in right now for conspiracy and take my chances that your friends will find someone else to bring in a shipment for Primeau."

The angry flush drained from her cheeks. "No."

"Then it seems as if you don't have a choice."

"So you've made me an offer I can't refuse."

Echoes of the conscience pangs that had led him into this predicament surfaced in Bruce's mind, but he tamped them down firmly. Emma wasn't innocent. She had willingly admitted her part in this ring. Besides, it wasn't his conscience that was bothering him, it was his rampaging libido. He rubbed a hand roughly over his face. "I was out of line a minute ago. It won't happen again."

"Damn right."

"I'll sleep out here on the couch."

"Don't bother trying to lock me into my room, Mr. Policeman. The bedroom door has a bolt on the inside, and I fully intend to use it."

An apology was there, trying to get out, but he refused to speak it aloud. He wasn't sorry that he'd held her and kissed her. He'd reveled in every second of their angry embrace. He was sorry that they'd stopped, and he was sorry he couldn't sweep her back into his arms and carry her to that big four-poster with the comfortable-looking mattress and feel the prick of her nails on his skin and the sting of her teeth on his lips and her potent, heady taste on his tongue. He was sorry he couldn't rip off her civilized clothes and feast on her ripe, feminine curves and let the passion of their bodies whirl them to a place where who and what they were didn't matter and...

Bruce cursed low and long under his breath and turned away. "Bolt the damn door, Emma. And do it quick."

Chapter 8

A flock of gulls wheeled along the edge of the mirror-calm lake, piercing the air with their strident cries. Although not a single cloud shadowed the brilliance of the sky, the morning held the breathless, sultry expectancy of an impending storm. According to the latest forecast, the warm front that had passed through the day before had brought a stable high pressure zone, and no rain was predicted until the end of the week, so Emma knew that the storm she sensed gathering had nothing to do with the weather.

The vinegary scent of epoxy drifted from the can that rested on the edge of the dock. Emma shifted her position on the pontoon and stretched to reach it.

"What are you doing down there?"

At the deep voice she jerked. Grabbing on to a strut for balance, she twisted to glance over her shoulder. Bruce was wearing Prendergast's sneakers, but his silent walk could have been pure Primeau. The voice was somewhere in between, though. Maybe it was his real one, if she could trust anything about him to be real.

"I want to seal the holes where the rivets were sheared off," she replied. "Pass me that can."

He squatted down to hand it to her, then straightened up and studied the Cessna. "Is there anything else you need to do to ready the plane?"

Her nose wrinkled at the smell as she dabbed the epoxy into the holes beside the long rusty scrape mark. She had filled up the fuel tanks the day after Harvey had phoned, the day after her peaceful solitude had been twisted into something brutal and ugly. Her stomach rolled, and it wasn't from the noxious glue. "I need to load the wooden crates that are in the shed."

"Those would be the boxes for the rock samples that your brother's phony prospecting trips produced. I suppose the cover story was your idea, right?"

"Instead of standing around goading me, why don't you carry them down here yourself, Mr. Policeman?"

"Don't goad me, either. I've had about enough of your sarcasm, Emma."

She splayed her hand on the pontoon and looked up, making no effort to hide her scrutiny as her gaze traveled over his tall form. Tight jeans molded his powerful legs. A plaid flannel shirt hung loosely around his hips but the rolled-up sleeves revealed firm, muscular forearms and the open collar showed a hint of the springy hair that covered his chest. The dangling earring was gone, along with the ponytail. His blond curls lay in finger-combed disarray. "Okay, what should I call you? Who have you decided to be today?"

The vibrant blue of his eyes glittered with ice. "Bruce," he stated.

"Okay, Bruce. Yes, it was all my idea, is that what you wanted to hear? The prospecting was a convenient ruse. Simon wasn't participating in the actual smuggling when he damaged my plane. He's still just a kid, he couldn't handle what I got him into."

"Some kid. His juvenile rap sheet includes everything from vandalism to car theft."

"You know?"

"Of course, I know. Until now you've managed to keep one step ahead of the law, though, despite the rumors about your shady business practices. Except for that assault charge three years ago. What happened?"

"Nothing. It was settled out of court."

"Why do you do it, Emma? Your affection for your brother seems genuine, so why get him involved in your criminal ventures? Is larceny in the Duprey genes?"

"Is this your idea of not goading me?"

"I'm just trying to get some things straight in my mind, sort out the truth from the smoke screen," he said steadily. "How many kilos of cocaine do you bring in on one run?"

"It varies," she improvised. "Why?"

"I'll be going along with you. It would simplify matters if no one else knew I was on the plane, so we need to rig something up at the back of the cabin, maybe a tarp I can conceal myself under. Will there be space?"

She did a quick mental calculation of the number of crates Simon had unloaded the last time. "Yes, I think so. We could leave out the camping gear."

"What camping gear?"

"Simon stayed overnight . . ." She went silent as she realized the depths of her brother's deception. He had camped overnight to mislead her, so she would swallow his story. God, she was gullible. "It doesn't concern you."

"Don't make any changes to your routine that might arouse suspicion."

"They won't be suspicious. They figure I'm going to do exactly what they say. I have no intention of tipping them off to your presence, because I want the deal they agreed to as much as I want yours."

"It's a dangerous game, playing both sides against the middle, Emma."

"The way I see it, Bruce, there isn't much difference between the sides. You and McQuaig are each using me to get what you want. Neither of you gives a damn about anyone caught in the middle.''

A muscle in his cheek twitched. "I'll give you a hand with those sample crates." Without looking at her again, he turned around and headed up the hill to the shed.

She watched him go. She couldn't help it. He didn't use an awkward shuffle or an arrogant swagger. The long, easy strides he took were those of a man who was confident of his strength and his purpose. Of course, she already knew his purpose. But cop or not, he still fascinated her. And drew her. She might have been able to lock her door against him last night, but she couldn't lock away her own desires so easily. How many more sleepless nights would he cause her?

You liked the way our mouths fit together. You wanted to touch me.

Oh, he'd been right about that. She'd wanted to touch him, to taste his kiss once more, to feel his taut muscles beneath her palms... to hear the sound of her fist striking his jaw.

But as he'd said, it wasn't necessary to like someone in order to want them. She liked who he used to be, but that had been just another lie, hadn't it? Biting her lip, she swung herself back to the dock and tossed the piece of wood she'd been using into the epoxy can. There were too many lies. She had to focus on her brother. He was the reason she was doing this. The situation was tangled enough already without adding this physical thing that was happening with Bruce. Or whoever he was.

From the direction of the driveway came the sound of a car engine. Emma stood up and turned toward the noise just as Bruce emerged from the shed with a pair of wooden crates held under each arm. Seconds later a blue-and-white police car nosed over the crest of the hill. The driver's door opened and a familiar, uniformed man emerged.

"Haskin," Emma said, her hands clenching by her sides. Of all the times for the Bethel Corners sheriff to choose to snoop around. Her breath caught. Had Bruce called him? Had he changed his mind about their deal? Did he mean to turn her in now?

Bruce barely gave the sheriff a glance. Adopting Primeau's smooth strut, he carried the empty crates to the dock. "Keep calm and act normal," he told her quietly as he stacked the boxes near the back of the plane. In front of her eyes his face settled into the insolent sneer of the character she had met the evening before.

"I thought he was on your side." She watched Haskin approach from the other direction. "Don't you trust your own team?"

"He's not a player." His shirttails bunched around his wrists as he shoved his hands into the pockets of his jeans and took up an ankles crossed, hips forward pose. Even without the costume props, he effectively projected the belligerent toughness of his Primeau character. Under other circumstances, Emma might have admired his skill. As it was, though, she didn't have room for anything but the tension that hummed through her nerves.

Haskin's close-set beady eyes were hidden behind reflective sunglasses. A small, dark brown blotch that was probably spilled coffee stained the shirt front that stretched across his ample stomach. He hitched up the belt that held his holster and came to a halt a foot away from the dock. "Hello, Miss Cassidy."

Emma forced herself to nod. "Sheriff."

He looked toward the stacked crates and studied Bruce for a moment before he turned to face her. "Fixing on taking a trip in your plane?"

"If the weather cooperates."

"Who's he?"

"A friend."

Bruce stirred into motion, easing his hands from his pockets as he moved to Emma's side. He looped an arm negligently around her shoulders. "Is there a problem here, sweet thing?"

The absurdity of the roles they were playing threatened to choke her. "Everything's fine, honey" she said between her teeth. At the warning squeeze of his fingers, she looked back to Haskin. "What brings you out here, Sheriff?"

"I was wondering when you last saw your brother, Miss Cassidy. I'm still waiting to talk to him."

"I have no idea where he is," she answered, for once truthfully. "Why?"

Instead of replying, Haskin pursed his fleshy lips and glanced toward the hill. Through the open doors of the shed the black Corvette was clearly visible. "Did you get a new car?"

"The 'Vette belongs to me," Bruce said, his tone holding a note of challenge.

The sheriff rested his hand on the holster at his hip. "That's some fancy car. Those aren't Maine plates."

"No, they're not."

"Yeah, that's some fancy car." Haskin climbed back up the hill, swerving toward the shed to take a closer look at the Corvette before he returned to his blue-and-white cruiser.

"What was that all about?" Bruce asked as the sheriff disappeared around the bend of the driveway.

"You've seen it before. He likes to hassle me about Simon."

"Why? Does he suspect what you two are doing?"

"I doubt it. Simon had a run-in with the sheriff over a speeding ticket when I first moved here, but my brother hasn't done anything since then."

"Yeah, your baby brother with the rap sheet's a real angel, all right."

Emma twisted to face him, and her sharp retort died unsaid. He was so close. He still had his arm around her shoulders, and the physical connection was all too easy and natural. Almost...enjoyable. Instantly, she stepped away. "Why did you become Primeau just now?"

"I told you. Haskin's not a player."

"You really don't trust anyone, do you? Not me, not even another uniform. Must be a lonely life, Bruce."

"Lonely?" He looked pointedly at her solitary cabin. "It seems to me that you've done a good job of making sure your own life turned out that way."

"If it hadn't been for the way the police persecuted my father, my life would have been—"

"Give it a rest, okay?"

"What?"

"Forget it," he muttered. Pivoting away from her, he began loading the empty crates into the plane.

To her disgust, she couldn't help watching him this time, either.

Shadows deepened in the corners of the main room. The air wafted with traces of the acrid, back-of-the-mouth sting of wood smoke from the fire Emma had lit at dusk, a fire that was more for comfort than for warmth. She sat on a cushion in front of the hearth, her chin on her updrawn knees, her arms wrapped around her legs, and gazed unseeingly at the randomly flickering pattern of flames. What if McQuaig wanted her to make a run tonight? Then again, it might be tomorrow, or the next day. All he'd said was that a shipment would be in before the end of the week. There was nothing to do but wait for his call, and the inactivity was grinding on her nerves.

"Are you sure you plugged the phone back in properly?" she asked.

"Yes, Emma. It's working fine."

She turned her head to look at Bruce. He was lounging comfortably in the middle of her couch, his long legs stretched out in front of him and his feet propped on the coffee table. He didn't even glance up from the thick book he was reading. It was hers, the most recent collection of short stories from Stephen King, and he had been quietly immersed in it for the past hour.

His calmness was another thing that was grinding on her nerves. "Did you check it?" she persisted.

He tipped his head and looked at her over the rims of his glasses. He wore glasses for reading. They made him look oddly boyish and appealing and...human. That bothered her. She didn't want to think of him as anything other than a cop.

"Yes, I checked it," he replied. "Why are you so anxious? Do you think McQuaig might call off your deal?"

She couldn't even consider that possibility. "I just want to get this over with. I don't like waiting."

"A large percentage of my job involves waiting of some kind or another. You get used to it."

"Is that when you do your reading? When you're on a stakeout? Or was that stuff about your fondness for books just another of your lies?"

He shut the book with a snap and set it on the cushion beside him. "Except for my occupation and my reason for seeing you, most of the things that Prendergast said were true. But I don't usually get the chance to read while I'm on a case."

"Then how do you handle the waiting?"

"I think, or I exercise, or I talk if I happen to be working with someone I get along with." He raised his arms over his head and stretched until his shoulders cracked audibly, then took off his glasses and set them down on the coffee table. He went over to his bag, removed a small pouch, and carried it back to the couch. "In this case, I think I'll clean my gun."

"You have a gun?"

He held her gaze while he reached behind him and slipped his hand beneath the loose tail of his flannel shirt. Half a second later he was holding a gleaming black handgun. "Of course."

She narrowed her eyes at the way he was deliberately displaying it for her. "What's this? An attempt to scare me? A typical police ploy to intimidate me into behaving?"

"Now, why would I need to do that?" He sat down and opened the pouch to take out a cloth and a small plastic bottle.

Frowning, she pushed herself to her feet. A log popped and fell over in the fireplace and she raised her gaze to the hunting bow over the mantel. "I don't know, Bruce," she said as she reached out and wrapped her fingers around the carved wooden grip. "Why would you?"

"What are you doing?"

She lifted the bow from the rack and balanced it on her palm a moment before she tipped it forward and checked the pulley action. Satisfied with the easy rotation, she extended her left arm to elevate it into a firing position. Keeping her body straight, she turned by using only her feet until she could sight on an imaginary target where the far wall joined the sloping ceiling. Smoothly she drew back the bowstring to the point when the kiss button nudged her lip.

"What the hell are you doing?"

"Since you're cleaning your weapon, I'll clean mine. Not that I'm trying to intimidate you or anything."

"I don't believe this."

"Don't worry." She eased the string down slowly so the empty snap wouldn't stress the bow, then glanced at Bruce. "It isn't loaded."

A glimmer of something that could have been admiration shone briefly in his gaze. Grinding his teeth, he tossed the cleaning cloth onto the coffee table. "Damn, you did it again."

"Did what?"

"Never mind." He shook his head and rubbed a palm over his face. "Just how good are you with that thing?"

"I always hit what I'm aiming at. What about you? Are you any good with that pistol?"

"I hit what I'm aiming at." He leaned forward in order to tuck the gun beneath his shirt, then relaxed against the cushions and draped his arms along the couch back on either side of him. "When did you learn to use a bow?"

She picked up a dish towel from the corner that served as a kitchen and walked across the room to join him. "I was on the archery team at the private school I went to. It was the only thing about that stuffy place that was worth-while.'' Sitting on the armchair, she propped the bow between her feet and began to polish it with the towel. "They didn't supply any compound bows, though. An arrow from this one could have gone through the gymnasium wall.''

"You had to quit school when your father was arrested, didn't you?''

"It sounds as if whatever background check you did was thorough. Did you know all this before I told you who I was?''

He waited a beat before he answered. "Yes."

"I should have guessed. I could have saved my breath."

"You talked mostly about your family, not about yourself.''

"Well? What else do you know?''

"You didn't finish college. Instead, you took over what was left of your father's business and were extremely successful, despite the cloud of suspicion concerning your ethics.''

"As soon as anyone's successful, there will always be people wanting to believe they had to cheat.''

"Undoubtedly. You had an active social life, and were frequently featured in the society pages because of your family's notoriety.''

"I was an easy target. Photographed well, too.''

His mouth tightened and he glanced quickly toward his bag. "I'm sure you did. A lot of people probably found your looks fascinating. Why did your fiancé break your engagement?''

"What?''

"You were engaged once. Turner Addison was his name, wasn't it?''

She dropped the towel and braced her hands on her knees, surprised that the bare facts could so easily bring back the memories. She had been so young, still clinging to her idealistic dreams of a fairy-tale wedding, still trust-

ing a man who had claimed to love her. "Chalk up another one to your blind justice system."

"What do you mean?"

"Turner's family couldn't stomach the scandal when my
father was convicted. He broke off the engagement in order to find a more socially acceptable mate."

"Sounds like a real prince, all right. You're probably
better off without him. Any man who couldn't stick by you
through the bad times likely wouldn't be strong enough to
handle you, anyway."

"Handle me? Of all the stupid macho attitudes—"

"You're a strong woman. It's obvious that you would
be best suited to a strong man. Maybe someone who didn't
intimidate easily."

"I don't want any man."

"That's obvious, too, considering the way you've hidden yourself away out here."

"I can see why you preferred cleaning your gun to having a conversation if this is an example of how you talk,
although I suppose that's about all I could expect from a
cop."

"Your conversation seems limited to finding new ways
to blame all your problems on the justice system."

"It caused all my problems. The moment the law got
involved, my life fell apart like a wall of dominoes."

"Is that why you run drugs? Is it vengeance? Wasn't it
enough to run away to this cabin and play bird with that
Cessna? Do you have some kind of inner need to defy authority?"

Stiffly she stood and carried the bow back to the rack
over the fireplace. "What about you?" She turned
around, bracing her elbows against the mantel. "You
weren't lying when you said your job is all you have in your
life. What made you that way, Bruce? Did you ever have
a life outside your disguises, or were you born a cop?"

He caught her gaze. Firelight flickered in his startling
blue eyes and augmented the harsh angles of his face. "I

think we'd better change the subject before we get into another argument.''

"Maybe you'd better take out your gun."

"Maybe I should. Because I remember quite vividly how our last argument turned out, and you wouldn't want to push me into forgetting I'm a cop again, would you?''

The relaxed pose he had maintained was a sham, she realized suddenly. He was strung almost as tightly as her bow.

His gaze hardened. "Or maybe you have a notion to pick up where we left off last night."

"Why don't you take your gun and stick it—"

The shrill ring of the lone telephone cut across her words. She jerked, and her elbows slid painfully over the edge of the stone mantel.

Bruce was on his feet in an instant. He snatched up his glasses, crossed to her desk to pick up a pen and a pad of paper, and pointed to the phone. "Answer it," he ordered.

Emma wiped her palms on her thighs, her hands trembling. Another ring echoed through the silent cabin.

He snapped his glasses open with a flick of his wrist and propped them on his nose. "Go on."

Somehow she made it across the floor and picked up the receiver without dropping it. "Yes?"

"Miss Duprey?" It was Harvey's voice.

"Yes."

"We need your services tonight."

Bruce moved beside her and motioned for her to tip the receiver so that he could hear. She nodded and held the phone slightly away from her ear. "What are the coordinates of the pickup?" she said, struggling to keep her voice level.

Paper rustled at the other end of the phone line. Harvey read out a string of numbers. Bruce transcribed them onto the pad he held. "The ship will be there at 1:00 a.m.," Harvey continued. "It will wait for thirty minutes, no more. When you reach it, signal by switching your landing lights on and off twice. They will spotlight the area you are to land in.''

Emma had already heard these details from McQuaig in the warehouse, but she still wasn't inured to the risk involved. "I'll do my best."

There was a pause. "I thought we had a deal, Miss Duprey."

The threat in the softly spoken words was clear. She thought she heard an echo of Simon's sobs. "Yes. Of course."

Another pause, this one more ominous. "And you will be on schedule with your delivery to us, won't you?"

Bruce scribbled something on the paper. Emma read his question aloud. "Where do you want it delivered this time?"

"The warehouse will do."

She brushed aside Bruce's paper and spoke urgently. "And when I make the delivery—"

"We'll keep our end of the deal. Use the crates like before. And don't be late."

The connection was broken. Emma stood numbly unmoving until Bruce eased the buzzing receiver from her fingers and hung up the phone. He waited an instant before he dialed a number and quickly repeated the coordinates he'd written on the paper.

It was in motion, she thought. The criminals would get their drugs, she would get her brother and the cops would shut down the smuggling ring once Bruce was led to the people at the top. She could do this, she told herself as she took deep breaths to calm her pulse. By this time tomorrow the nightmare would be over.

The flight was a nightmare, like plunging blindfolded through a maze. Bruce sat in the cockpit beside Emma and marveled at her stony composure. There was no smile that revealed the dimple in her cheek, no joy on her face as she navigated the Cessna between the hills that were little more than deeper shadows in the blackness. She was the epitome of controlled efficiency, using her sparse instruments, her charts and her pocket calculator to keep them on course. At least the weather was still good. The quarter moon reflected weakly from the scattered lakes they passed, yet other than those ghostly swaths of paleness, the land beneath was an unbroken carpet of darkness.

"Where are we now?" Bruce asked, raising his voice over the noise of the wind and the churning engine.

"Quebec," she answered tersely.

He hadn't been aware of when they had passed over the border, which was no surprise. Out here the line between the two countries was nothing but a clear-cut strip through the trees. "How long until we reach the St. Lawrence?"

She paused to check her instruments and clicked a few numbers into her calculator. "Eight minutes. I'll head northeast along the shore until I reach the pickup spot."

The location Harvey had given was among the scattered islands on the south shore of the river. It was a well thought out place, the islands serving as concealment as well as windbreaks. It would be risky to land the float plane unless the water surface was relatively calm. A gust of wind buffeted the nose of the Cessna and Bruce watched as Emma made an automatic adjustment to keep them on course. If anyone could do it, she could.

What an amazing woman. It was too bad that... No, he wouldn't let his thoughts take that direction. He was here to do a job. They both were.

Bruce took a small flashlight from his pocket and twisted around to shine it at the back of the plane. Every square foot of space appeared to be packed solid, but there was a cramped gap behind the camping gear and the empty crates that would provide adequate concealment for him while the drugs were being loaded. It was a dangerous situation, but he'd been in worse. Emma would be staying in the plane, so he would be able to hear if she tried to alert anyone to his presence. He didn't think she would, though. The deal she had insisted on was a good one for her, and she was too smart to risk screwing it up. She was more anxious than he was to make the final delivery.

He clicked off the flashlight and turned to study Emma's profile. The dim glow of the instruments revealed no more than a suggestion of her delicate, fascinating features, but Bruce had committed them to memory days ago.

"I'll try to baby it," she said as she dropped a wing to begin a long, slow turn. "But I don't know how choppy the river will be. Stay strapped in until we're down."

"Your concern is touching."

"I don't want to have to explain one slightly dented cop to the people who fill up those crates."

"You know that if anything happens to me, our deal is off."

"It's going to be cramped for you back there under the tarp. It would have been simpler if you had let me do this alone."

"And you know why that's not possible."

"Still don't trust me, Bruce?"

"About as much as you trust me, Emma."

A pale slash on the horizon stretched into a ribbon, then a sheet. In minutes they were heading northeast over the unrolling expanse of the St. Lawrence. The noise of the engine lowered as Emma dropped her airspeed and reduced her dangerously low altitude even further. Islands appeared beneath them, long dark humps sailing past on the dull glitter of the restless water. They were miles away from the regular shipping channel, so when Bruce spotted the lights from the freighter, he knew it was the ship they were looking for.

Emma circled, flashing her landing lights two times.

There was no response.

Bruce leaned toward the side window. "What's wrong?"

"I don't know. We're on time. We're at the right coordinates. They should have responded."

"Try again."

The engine roared as she banked into a steep turn and made another pass over the ship. This time a powerful floodlight burst across the port side, illuminating a surprisingly flat strip of water. The oblong island that lay off the far side of the ship had effectively blocked the swells and the waves from the wide part of the river.

"Doesn't look too bad," Bruce said. "Do you think you can put us down all right?"

"I'll do it." Emma clenched her jaw and circled one final time to line up for the landing. The lower she got, the more waves she could see on the water. They glittered on the edges of the floodlit path like moving runway lights. Even if the surface turned out to be calm enough to attempt a landing, she couldn't see whether there were any obstacles. There could be a waterlogged piece of debris in her path that could catch a pontoon and flip her over. Or the wind patterns could change without warning. Or the poor lighting could cause her to misjudge her altitude and hit the river too fast.

She called on all of her experience and ignored her instruments, using her instincts and the sense of rapport she had with the Cessna to feel her way down. The airspeed dropped. Ripples on the water's surface raced past in a blur of silver. The pontoons skimmed, then sliced, then settled firmly on the river as the plane lost its lift. Their forward motion slowed. Miraculously, they were down.

"I've had bumpier rides on dry tarmac at O'Hare," Bruce said as he unbuckled his seat belt. "Very impressive, Emma."

She exhaled sharply, blowing a strand of loose hair from her forehead. "Thanks."

He grunted, as if regretting the compliment. "Keep the nose pointed away from the ship for a minute." Nimbly he twisted out of his seat and worked his way toward the back of the plane.

Emma looked out the side window. A small launch was speeding across the water from the ship. "Better hurry," she said. "They're not wasting any time." She cut the engines and reached into the storage slot beside her seat to unsnap a large flashlight from its magnetic holder. She swung the beam around the cabin but there was no longer any trace of her passenger.

Something metallic clanked against the pontoon. Emma got to her feet and stooped over to open the door. Damp, cool air and a glaring light struck her full in the face. She lifted her hand to shade her eyes and could see the outline of the launch that had pulled alongside. The two men on board were little more than vague shapes against the spotlight that was clamped to the side.

"You Duprey?" The voice was rough, with a trace of an accent that elongated the vowels.

Emma nodded and braced herself as the wash from the boat's wake rocked the plane.

The other man leaned over to hold them in place with a boat hook. Metal scraped again. "This is the plane, all right. Give her the stuff and let's get out of here."

"Keep us steady." The first man picked up a square, paper-wrapped package and swung a leg over the side. He balanced on the pontoon and looked around the interior of the plane thoroughly before he handed the package to Emma.

McQuaig had told her what to expect, so she tried to keep the revulsion out of her expression as she fitted the package into one of the empty crates. She pushed it toward the back of the plane and returned to the doorway. The loading continued in silence. When half the crates were filled, the boat hook was withdrawn and the launch drifted away.

"Is that all?" Emma asked across the widening gap of water.

"You've got what McQuaig told us to give you," the man with the rough voice replied. He clicked off the light on the side and spoke to his companion. "Let's go." The boat's motor chugged to life, throwing a frothing wake against the plane.

Emma fastened the latch on the door and took a deep breath. It had all gone so quickly, so easily. She could hardly believe it was almost over. She felt her way into the pilot's seat, strapped herself in, and started the engine. "I've got one minute before the ship turns off that flood-light," she called. "I'm taking off now, whether you're in your seat or not."

Bruce was already behind her. He squeezed her shoulder, then slipped into his seat and clicked his belt shut.

The illuminated path stretched in front of her, the surface of the water stirring menacingly. She couldn't think about the risks. She had made it down, she would make it back up. She nosed the plane into position and opened the throttle, dropping the flaps to shorten her takeoff run. She had to compensate for the sharper angle by increasing her power, and the Cessna responded beautifully, climbing sharply into the vast blackness, soaring away from the launch and the dark bulk of the freighter as if it were as anxious to be away from this place as she was. When she reached her cruising altitude, she leveled off and eased back the throttle. Before long they left the St. Lawrence and were heading south once more.

It was several minutes before Bruce spoke. "That was smoother than I could have guessed."

"You didn't really believe that I would give you away, did you?"

"No. Whatever else you are, Emma, you're not stupid." He clicked on his flashlight and twisted around. "The whole operation didn't take more than eight minutes from the time you signaled the ship. Flying under radar, maintaining radio silence, hell, no wonder the coast guard hasn't been able to catch them at it."

"You sound as if it's all a big game to you," she said.

"It's no game. It's my job."

"Right. Upholding the law, putting away the bad guys, that's what you live for, isn't it?"

"We're on the home stretch, Emma. Don't start up now, okay?"

She glanced at the darkness beyond the windshield, watching for the patch of paleness that would indicate the first of the lakes she was using for landmarks. The moon was high in the sky now, providing more than adequate illumination. As long as the favorable winds held, the flight back would be far easier than the flight out. "I didn't see any patrol boats near the freighter."

"They're keeping their distance, but they're there. Units will already be setting up around the warehouse so no one slips away when we're ready to tighten the net." He unfastened his seat belt and maneuvered his way out of the cockpit.

"What are you doing?"

"Checking our cargo."

She glanced over her shoulder. He crouched beside one of the crates, the small flashlight held between his teeth. He took out one of the paper-wrapped packages and weighed it in his hand. A frown creased his face.

"What's wrong?" she called.

He set the flashlight down and put his foot on it to keep it from rolling away. "Doesn't feel the right weight for this size."

"So?"

"This was a smaller load than usual, wasn't it?"

"Smaller than last time."

He shifted to another crate. One by one, he lifted the packages out and inspected them. "None of them feel right."

"What's that supposed to mean?"

Instead of answering her directly, he pulled a knife from a buttoned pocket of his shirt and unfolded a stubby blade.

"Hey. I don't want you tampering with that. I don't want any trouble from McQuaig when I deliver it."

"Don't you want to know what you're delivering?"

She set her jaw and returned her gaze to the instruments, verifying that they were still on course. The homestretch, he had said. And that's what it was. Once she took the cocaine to the warehouse—

"What the hell is going on?" Bruce said suddenly.

Emma looked over her shoulder. "What's wrong?"

"You tell me."

"What are you talking about?"

He picked up the package he had opened and worked his way toward her. "Look at this." He braced one hand against the back of her seat and extended his other hand in front of her. "Is this what Harvey told you to pick up tonight?"

In the stark beam of his flashlight she saw that he had cut away the brown paper wrapping. Instead of smooth plastic underneath, there was more paper. While she watched, he inserted the tip of his knife into the opening and sliced through several more layers of nothing but newsprint. Why would they do this? Was this flight nothing but a test? Didn't they believe that she would follow their orders for her brother's sake?

"I know that you haven't had a chance to tip them off since we left the warehouse. What's going on, Emma?"

She shook her head. "I don't know. I had a deal with them. I don't understand why they would change their minds."

He tossed the worthless package onto his vacant seat and moved back to inspect the others. Tense minutes passed as he checked the contents of each crate. Emma couldn't take her attention away from the controls for more than a few seconds at a time, but whenever she glanced over her shoulder she could see the scowl on Bruce's face deepen. Finally, though, he slit open a package that wiped all expression from his face.

Emma felt her stomach do a roller coaster glide downward. "What is it? What did you find?"

He sat back on his heels and slowly turned toward her. "Where are we now, Emma?"

She glanced out the window and saw a curving gleam between the dark hills. It was shaped like a bird's foot. "About halfway home."

"Can you land here?"

"On water I don't know? Why?"

"What's the closest place to put down?" he persisted.

"Why?"

He tilted his flashlight toward the package he had just opened. "It looks as if you weren't the only one who wanted to terminate your business arrangement."

Emma craned her neck. There wasn't any plastic bag full of white powder in this one, either. Nor was it packed with newsprint like the others. It appeared to be a handful of wires and a clock, of all things. A clock.

"This explains why McQuaig's group didn't want to give you the real thing," Bruce said. "They didn't want to waste it."

The roller coaster did another swoop through her stomach. "What the . . ."

"I'll wedge myself in back here and keep it steady, but I strongly advise you to find a place to bring us down as soon as possible."

The significance of what she was seeing dawned on her all at once. "Oh, my God!"

It was a bomb.

Chapter 9

Bruce used every shred of his wavering control to fight down the instinctive flash of panic. He had to think, to plan, to reason, to stamp out the gut-level terror evoked by what he was holding. He couldn't let himself remember the other time. He had to do his job.

He moved his flashlight, forcing himself to study the explosive device. The dynamite would be enough to blow off the tail of the plane, virtually guaranteeing a fatal crash. He focused on the glowing red numbers on the timing mechanism. They had less than fifteen minutes left. Evidently the bomb was timed to go off while they were over the sparsely populated region of the north woods.

"Throw it out of the plane!" Emma shouted.

"No."

"Why the hell not?"

"What if it hits a camper? Or a lumberjack? What if it starts a forest fire? I'm not going to be responsible for the death of some innocent bystander."

"Then pull out the wires or something."

"I won't risk disarming it while we're in the air. If something went wrong, neither one of us would have much chance of surviving. Stop wasting time, Emma. Land the plane."

"You're crazy. I'm calling for help," she said, reaching for the radio.

"Don't do that, or they'll know you found the bomb."

"So what?"

"McQuaig's people want you dead. If they find out you're not, they'll try again."

"This isn't one of your games, Bruce. I'm not going to risk my life to play along."

"We have fourteen minutes left. The risk is minimal if you can find somewhere to land."

The background noise that they had been shouting over wasn't loud enough to drown out the string of four-letter words she uttered. She shoved the hand mike back into its cradle and nosed the plane downward.

Nausea threatened as Bruce propped his feet against the side of the fuselage and steadied the bomb between his palms.

"I'll try for the lake we just passed," she said. "It's small, but it would take us too long to find a better one. How much time?"

"Twelve minutes."

She swore again, but didn't waste her energy by arguing. She made one quick pass and banked smoothly. Moonlight flooded into the cabin for a breathless, silver instant before the plane completed the turn and began to descend.

Bruce pressed the back of his head against one of the wooden crates and braced himself. The noise of the engine dropped. Sweat beaded on his forehead as he tightened his grip on the bomb. There was no floodlight to illuminate a path for landing, no time to check the surface for obstacles, yet he had complete faith in Emma's ability to get them down safely.

The pontoons struck the water and the plane slewed like a car going through sand. A crate toppled over. Bruce curled forward to prevent anything from striking the explosive. His flashlight bounced and another crate fell, catching him on the shoulder.

"It's going to be close," Emma yelled. "Hang on."

From his position on the floor he could see a dark outline looming in front of the starry horizon. The outline shifted and grew until it became a ridge of trees. The plane bucked as Emma fought to rid them of their forward momentum. A precious minute went by as they slowed. By now the entire sky was filled with nothing but huge pines.

The plane shuddered to a stop with a dull thud of metal against wood. Emma shut down the engine and was out of her seat before the echoes died. She wrenched open the door. "Okay, we're down. Now throw that out of my plane."

Bruce left the bomb where it was and pushed himself up. "Grab whatever you can. Maps, compass, flashlights. Have you got an emergency kit?" He leaned over to take a look outside. They were less than twenty yards from the shelf of pale rock that marked the shore. One of the pontoons had ridden up on a half-submerged log. If they had been going any faster when they struck it, they would have flipped over. "Wrap them in the tarp to keep them dry. We've got seven minutes left."

She lunged toward him and grasped his arm. "What are you doing?"

"In seven minutes this plane is going to blow up, just like your friends expect it to."

Her grip tightened. "You're insane. I'm not going to stand by and let my plane be destroyed."

"This is the only way. For whatever reason, you've been set up. They'll be checking, and they have to believe they succeeded. With my people set to move in within twenty-four hours, I can't jeopardize—"

"To hell with your investigation, Mr. Policeman. I'm saving my plane." She tried to slip past him. When he didn't move, she shoved at his chest. "Get out of my way."

He knew by her tone there was no reasoning with her. He moved swiftly, grabbing her around the waist before she could guess his intentions. Swiveling around, he squeezed out of the plane, hauling her with him. As soon as he stood solidly on the pontoon, he swung her over the water and released his grip.

She shrieked as she splashed into the lake. He paused only long enough to be sure she resurfaced before he ducked back into the plane. A clock in his head was counting off the minutes. Wasting no more time, he took the tarp that he'd concealed himself with and laid it flat behind the cockpit. He snatched up everything that was loose and piled it into the center, added his holster and his gun, then drew the corners up and fastened the whole thing closed with a length of rope.

The plane rocked as Emma clambered onto the pontoon. Bruce stepped to the open door and tossed the bundle to her. "Here, catch."

He heard her hit the water again. This time instead of shrieking, she splashed in rhythmic strokes toward the shore. He picked up his flashlight and shone it one last time around the cabin, looking for anything else that might be useful. Open packages of worthless newsprint littered the floor. Several wooden crates lay on their sides. The numbers on the bomb's timer glowed red as they worked their way downward. Pausing only long enough to grab the nylon sleeping bag from the jumble of Simon's camping equipment, Bruce stepped out of the plane for the final time and eased himself into the water.

The cold was a shock, stealing his breath and sending icy needles through the shoulder that the crate had fallen on during their landing. He raised himself up enough to fling the tightly rolled bag onto the shore, then lowered his head and stroked after it.

Emma sat at the edge of the water, the bundle he'd tossed to her rested high and dry on the rock ledge behind her. Her fingers were a pale blur as she unlaced her boots. She yanked them off, threw them toward the bundle and stepped into the lake. In the moonlight her eyes seemed huge, her face leached of color as she looked toward the abandoned Cessna.

Bruce felt the bottom under his feet and rose in front of her. "Get back, Emma."

She didn't respond.

"It's going to blow in four minutes," he said, reaching for her arm. "We've got to get away from here."

She pulled against his grip and moved further into the lake. "No. I can't let you do this. I can't just stand here and let you destroy my plane."

He could read the desperation in her expression and feel the latent panic tremble through the arm he still held. "Move, Emma. Now."

"No!" With a burst of strength, she twisted out of his grasp and dived into the water.

Bruce plunged after her. He clamped a hand around her ankle and pulled her backward. She came up sputtering and tried to kick out of his hold. The clock in his head clicked another minute toward zero. "Damn it, Emma," he gasped as her foot struck his chin. "It's too late."

"No! Let me go!"

There was no time left. He wrapped his arms around her waist, hauled her out of the water, and flung her over his shoulder.

"Put me down," she yelled, pummeling his back with her fists.

His waterlogged sneakers slipped on the smooth rock at the shore. He went down hard on one knee before he recovered his balance and staggered onto dry land. Keeping one arm like a vise around the back of her thighs, he paused only long enough to take his bearings before he strode rapidly toward a ridge of boulders. Once they were in the shadow of the huge, square slabs of rock, Bruce shifted his grip to allow Emma to slide to her feet. He knew she would make another suicidal attempt to save her plane the moment he released her, so he held her firmly to the front of his body.

The blast blew the white Cessna apart as if it were no more than a paper toy. A second explosion followed the first when the fuel that still remained in the tanks detonated and a sudden fireball burst toward the sky. Debris cartwheeled across the lake and flew in spinning, smoking arcs.

Bruce pushed Emma to the ground and fell on top of her. The boulders provided shelter, but pieces of jagged metal clanked onto the rocks around them. He felt something hot strike his back and the smell of singed cotton mixed with the oily smell of smoke. Ignoring the pain, he remained motionless until the last of the debris had fallen. Cautiously, he levered himself up on his elbows and raised his head.

Emma's eyes were squeezed shut, her face contorted.

Immediately Bruce lifted his weight off her and came to his knees, still straddling her body. "Emma? Are you hurt?"

"Is it gone? Is it over?"

There was no way to soften the blow. "Yes."

With a sob she rolled to her side and slid out from underneath him. Clawing at the boulder for support, she pulled herself to her feet and faced the lake.

Emma didn't want to look, but she had to. She could smell the sting of burning fuel, she had heard the fragments hit the ground around them. She knew with her brain what had happened, but still, she had to see.

It was truly gone. Her plane, the Cessna that was like an extension of herself, the wings that let her soar to freedom, everything was gone. Scattered chunks of wreckage littered the water's surface, some of it smoldering, some of it drifting in lifeless silence like pieces of a shattered ghost. "No," she mouthed, her voice failing her. "No."

"I'm sorry, Emma." Bruce stood beside her and laid his palm lightly on her shoulder. "There was no other way."

Her wet clothes clung, the sodden fabric draining the warmth from her skin, but she didn't feel the cold. She was too numb to feel the cold.

"We'll get out of here. We've got maps and a compass. If we head for the nearest logging road, we can follow it until we find a way to contact Xavier. I don't know what kind of double cross I stepped into between you and your friends, but it won't stop the rest of the team from taking in McQuaig and his group."

McQuaig. Xavier. The names filtered through her head but she couldn't deal with what they meant, what all of this meant. They had destroyed her plane, they had wanted her dead. She couldn't think past that. It had happened too fast, too fast.

"We can turn this setback around, use it to give McQuaig a false sense of security while the net continues to be drawn together."

"And that's what matters, isn't it?" she said, her throat tight with a lump she couldn't swallow.

"That's why I'm here."

"And to hell with anyone caught in the middle. You don't care, do you?" She whirled around, turning her back on the smoking remnants of the plane that had been her only joy. "You're like every other cop I've known. All you see is your job. You don't care who you hurt or use along the way."

He rubbed a hand over his face. His fingers were shaking. "I've heard all this before."

"I could have saved that plane if you hadn't pulled me back to shore."

"There wasn't time."

"Yes, there was. You stopped me."

"You never would have made it. And I already told you, it's best this way."

"Everything's gone. You don't know what you've done."

"I know exactly what I've done. I did my job."

"But I have to make that delivery tomorrow. My brother's counting on me."

"There was nothing to deliver. Can't you see that yet? You were set up. Your deal with McQuaig is off. Your brother will have to take care of himself."

"But I have to help Simon."

"You should be worried about yourself. You're the one they wanted dead."

"Then you should have let me blow up along with the Cessna. That would have guaranteed a successful operation, wouldn't it? Not only wreckage to show McQuaig, but a body?" Tears of reaction burned behind her eyes. She blinked frantically, unwilling to let him see them fall. "Why didn't you let me die, Bruce? I'm no longer any use to you. I can't fly the drugs, I can't lead you to McQuaig. Why did you bother?"

"That's enough, Emma."

Her bare feet slid over sharp fragments of stone as she took a step toward him. "Congratulations, Mr. Policeman. You've just made it a perfect score. The law has taken my family, my home, and all the plans I once had for my life. Now you've taken my plane."

"I'm sorry, Emma. I know—"

"What do you know? You're just a cop. You think with your badge, you feel with your rule book."

A blazing fragment slipped beneath the lake's surface with a hissing splash. The night was suddenly silent, like the breathless pause between a flash of lightning and the inevitable roll of thunder. Bruce stood motionless in front of her, leashed tension humming from his fixed jaw to his curled fists. "Do you think you're the only one who's lost anything?" he asked finally.

Some of the danger in his tone reached through her budding hysteria. She sensed it, but she pushed anyway. "You're still a cop." She poked his chest with a stiffened finger. "You don't care about anything except upholding the law. You're only worried about how this will affect your case."

He caught her by the shoulders. In the colorless silver of the moonlight the angles of his face seemed honed from living steel. "Do you believe no one else has ever been a victim of circumstances that were out of their control, that you're the only one who's had a rough ride from life?"

"You're the one who let my plane blow up, not me."

"Yes, I let it go. It can be replaced. You can't."

She pressed her palms against his shirt front. The wet flannel rose and fell with each straining breath he drew. She could feel his restraint slipping away but she was in no condition to help him.

Bruce slid his hands down her arms and cupped her elbows, pulling her forward, forcing her up on her toes. "Do you feel this, Emma? Feel the heat between us?"

She gasped. His body was hard, vibrating with a primitive, unmistakable need. And just like that, she felt a response, equally primitive, equally unmistakable.

"Part of you may hate me, but there's a part of you that's got nothing to do with the grudge or vendetta or whatever it is that you've got going with the law. You know that. You've known it from the start."

Yes, she'd known it. "But you're—"

"Dammit, Emma! We're *alive!*" He jerked her against him. "Even the hate is better than nothing."

A piece of wreckage that had landed on the shore fell over with a tinny creak. At the sound, something snapped inside her. The events of only minutes ago kaleidoscoped in her mind, suddenly crystallizing into focus. The bomb, the landing, the explosion . . . "You carried me to safety."

He splayed his hand over the small of her back and held her closer. "Yes."

"You sheltered me with your body."

"And you fought me."

Only now was she beginning to realize how close, how very close, she had come to death. "Oh, my God. Bruce, we both could have been killed. If you hadn't checked those packages we wouldn't have had a chance. If you hadn't caught me when I tried to swim back to the plane I would have... I would... oh, *God!*''

"I wasn't going to let it happen. I couldn't. Not again."

She felt the strength of his grip, the sheer virility of his presence, and her breath caught. "You saved my life."

"Damn right, I saved your life."

Desperately she pressed herself against him, flattening her breasts to his chest, feeling his heat and his heartbeat. His arms were like bands of steel around her back. His cheek was like a butterfly's kiss on the top of her head. Her pulse tripped and sped until it matched the rhythm of his. "How can you hold me like this?"

"I have to. Right now, I need to hold you as much as you need to be held."

"After everything we've said to each other, everything we've done..."

"It doesn't matter how much you fight me, Emma. Or how much I fight myself. I still care for you. I have from the very first. I don't think anything's going to change that."

"And you don't want to care, do you?"

"No, I don't. I don't want to admire you, or respect you, or understand you, but I do. Despite everything that's going on, I do." He moved his feet apart, drawing her even closer. "You're ripping me apart inside."

"Because you're a cop."

"Yes. That's what I am. That's all I want to be."

She molded herself to his hardness, savoring each breath she drew, reveling in his familiar scent. Hate, anger, grief, all those emotions were swept up in the primal urge that flooded her body. The bond, the connection that had been there from the start, flared with a power that made her tremble. "You're also a man."

Tension, energy barely leashed, sang through his frame. "Do you know what's happening, Emma? Do you realize what we're doing?"

"We're living, and breathing and feeling."

His hands dropped to her hips, pulling her closer. "There's no door you can bolt out here."

"There's nothing out here. Nothing but you and me. Everything else has been blown away."

"Emma." It was a demand, a warning, a plea.

"We could have died, Bruce. But we didn't. We're alive. Nothing else matters."

He shuddered. His embrace tightened.

Recklessly, she spread her fingers and ran her palms over his shoulders, molding his wet shirt to the powerful breadth beneath. She slid her palms down his arms, exploring the hard muscles that had been able to lift her and protect her so effortlessly. He was so solid, so strong, so...male. Her feelings were too raw to deny the instinctive pull between them. The twisting, wrenching response that surged through her blood was as inescapable and inevitable as time.

A wordless groan rumbled from his chest. And then he was caught by the same storm. He lowered his head and kissed her. Only it wasn't a kiss. It was a melding, a joining. It was the essence of every kiss they'd shared before. The comfort, the tenderness, the anger and the lust, they were all there, finally unleashed, out of control.

Emma parted her lips and welcomed the thrust of his tongue, pressing herself closer, craving more. The kiss that was more than a kiss drew the breath from her lungs and the strength from her knees until her senses spun. The world narrowed to just this place, this moment, this incredible yearning.

Gasping for air, he dragged his mouth from hers. "Emma. Emma." He whispered her name against her skin as he trailed kisses across her jaw. His teeth grazed her neck and she shuddered. When he loosened his hold so that he could fit his hand between them, she leaned back and offered him her breast.

He covered it swiftly, greedily, cupping it in his palm, kneading it with his fingers, sending shafts of sensation to every secret part of her body. She moaned at the force of her response, as helpless to stop the sound from escaping as she was to halt the mindless passion that leapt to match his. His fingers moved to open her shirt. She didn't stop him, she helped him. She fumbled with the clammy cloth, gasping at the jolts of pleasure as each button slid tightly through its hole. She pulled it apart with no thought beyond the moment, baring herself to the moonlight and to the mad, glorious urgency that possessed her.

The sound he made was deep, rough, indiscernible. He fastened his hands at her waist and lifted her, swinging her around until her back was to the largest of the boulders beside them. He sat her on the edge, slipped his arm behind her for support and buried his face between her breasts. At the touch of his lips on her flesh she cried out. Thrusting her fingers into his hair, she held him closer, arching her back, as greedy as him.

"I want you, Emma," he breathed against her skin. "Just this once, I want to forget who we are."

"Just this once," she echoed, shutting out the hopelessness of asking for anything more.

He caught her nipple between his teeth. Pleasure-pain ripped away the last shreds of her control. She moaned and dug her nails into his neck. His tongue swirled and soothed, his lips surrounded, and he sucked her into his mouth. The stars spun overhead and Emma had to close her eyes against the wave of dizziness. Bruce drew back and the cool air puckered the wet nipple to excruciating sensitivity. He took the other one, flicking it with his tongue, drawing sobs and groans that she barely recognized as her own.

She curled forward, her blood pounding, her hands shaking, and reached for the collar of his shirt. She had no patience left. Wet fabric ripped as she pulled it apart and spread her fingers over his chest. She traced the rippling hardness of his stomach, sliding her palm down and down in a sensual path of discovery. When she reached his belt she didn't stop, she couldn't. She drew the leather through the metal buckle and let it fall aside, unsnapped the stud on his waistband and lowered his zipper.

The word he whispered was short and crude and suited the wildness of what was happening between them. He braced his hands on her thighs and straightened to his full height, tilting his pelvis to help her reach him. She ran her fingertips down the straining length, then grasped him in both hands. Her lips parted, her head fell back, and a wave of overwhelming urgency made her sway. He caught her and lifted her from the boulder, bringing her to her feet in front of him.

"I can't stop," he murmured, running his hands feverishly over her hips and between her legs. "Please, Emma." He unfastened her jeans and peeled the damp denim past her knees. "I need this. I need you."

She was beyond rational thought. Her response came from the level of instinct. It was an affirmation of life, of survival, of the strength they shared. It was as impossible to deny now as it had been the first time he had touched her. She kicked off her jeans and underwear and hooked her arms behind his neck. Shamelessly, savagely, she climbed onto him. He grasped her buttocks and lifted her, driving himself upward as he brought her down.

The explosion that rocked them was as powerful, as shattering and as violent as the one that had destroyed the Cessna. Emma screamed and clung to Bruce's shoulders as wave after wave crashed over her. His fingers clenched, sliding her upward for a heart-stopping instant. She twined her legs around his waist and screamed again as he buried himself fully and released his own passion with a long, shuddering groan.

Minutes passed. Or maybe only seconds. Time suspended, then was counted off by their ragged breaths. Emma dragged her mouth over his neck, nuzzling her way past his collar. One of her breasts was squeezed to his bare chest, the other was shielded by someone's shirt, whether it was his or her own, she couldn't tell. Cool air whispered a chill over her naked thighs. She felt drained, exhausted, and she could no longer keep her ankles locked. Gingerly she let her feet slide downward.

"Not yet," Bruce murmured. He slipped his forearm around the small of her back, anchoring her against him. "Not yet."

She felt a sudden tightness in her throat. Reality was returning. They couldn't stay like this. They shouldn't have done this. Oh, God. What *had* they done? Her nipple ached, her nails had broken, she had screamed aloud. *What had they done?* Tension stiffened her body. She twisted away from him, wincing at the tenderness where they had joined. Her feet hit the ground, rock digging sharply into her soles. She staggered.

"Emma?"

She shook her head, covering her face with her hands. She couldn't look at him. She couldn't think about this. They must have been insane.

"Are you all right?"

"I don't know." Her voice was hoarse, unrecognizable. Her ears rang with painful clarity, as if she were waking up after a bout of delirium. The sounds of the night were suddenly loud, the crickets shrilled, the soft sigh of pines in the breeze was a roaring howl, the gentle lap of the water against the shore crashed like ocean surf.

A zipper rasped, a stud snapped. He moved toward her. Although he didn't touch her, she felt his presence. "I don't know what to say, Emma."

"Whatever you do, don't apologize."

He stood silently for long, agonizing minutes. "I should apologize."

"This . . . thing that happened. It was mutual."

He didn't dispute that. It was too obvious to dispute. "I was rough. Did I hurt you?"

She tingled and throbbed. She would probably have finger-shaped bruises in the morning, but right now the physical discomfort was minor. "No."

Still he didn't move away. She inhaled deeply and lowered her hands. She kept her gaze on the ground. She could see the toes of his running shoes—he hadn't even taken off his clothes to make love. But they hadn't made love, not love. No, there was no pretty euphemism to describe what they had just done. It had been as powerful and as primitive as their surroundings. It had been as far removed from anything in her experience as this entire wild situation. She should be ashamed, embarrassed, repulsed....

But she wasn't.

Her tumbling thoughts steadied all at once. No, she wasn't ashamed. What they had done was natural. And necessary. There had been no words of love, only words of need. What they had done was honest, probably the first completely honest act since they had met. She raised her chin and met his gaze.

The naked vulnerability on his face stunned her. In the other-worldly dimness of the moonlight, his chiseled features had never looked more handsome, yet his expression was so lost, so completely confused, that she lifted her hand and cupped his cheek before she realized what she was doing.

Swiftly he caught her wrist, turned his head and pressed a kiss to her palm. His breath tickled her fingers in an unsteady sigh. Without warning, the strength and the fierce passion of this enigmatic man had suddenly been replaced by tenderness.

At the poignant gesture, Emma felt the tentative control she had regained threaten to crumble. They had just shared their bodies, but this was another kind of honesty, one that could be even more devastating. She didn't want this. She didn't need this. It couldn't be excused away. They were skirting the brink of an intimacy far deeper than a mere physical melding. "Don't," she whispered.

Bruce kissed each of her fingers, folded them into her palm and closed his hand warmly over her fist. "If I live to be a hundred," he murmured, "you'll never cease to amaze me, Emma."

Chapter 10

The stars began to fade as streamers of dawn pearled the eastern horizon. A family of wood ducks splashed through the lily pads near the shore, the tiny ripples from their wakes butting against pieces of a charred packing crate. Small rustlings stirred the branches of the looming evergreens that bordered the rock point and birds whistled and trilled to the dissolving shadows. Slowly the clearing took on color and form.

They would need to move soon. Bruce didn't think that he had slept. He hadn't wanted to sleep. He hadn't wanted to miss one second of the time they had stolen. He lay on his side on his half of the canvas tarp, his cheek pillowed on his bent arm, and watched the way the approaching sunrise gave substance to Emma's face.

Her beauty was undimmed by the tangled hair that fell over her forehead and the dark shadows that tinted the delicate skin under her eyes. The sleeping bag that he'd managed to salvage from the plane was tucked warmly to her chin, yet he still saw, and felt and tasted the lush curves that it covered. In his mind he once more saw the image of

Emma standing in front of him, her chin lifted defiantly, her feet braced apart. Clothed in nothing but her gaping shirt, she had been pure, elemental female, still trembling from the sensual storm they had unleashed. She hadn't cried, she hadn't condemned him; she had told him it was mutual and then had touched his face.

Regret slashed through him, cold and stark. They had both lost control. The danger, the adrenaline, the painful memories stirred up by the situation, all those things had contributed to the insanity that had seized them in the darkness. But the regret he felt wasn't from what they had done. It was from the knowledge that neither of them would allow it to happen again.

Not yet, he thought recklessly. *Just this once, we'll forget who we are. You'll smile, you'll sigh, you'll hold me...*

A gull shrieked, its raucous call sounding like a mocking laugh. He closed his eyes and concentrated on the gentle, rhythmic puff of Emma's breathing.

"Bruce?"

The voice had a first thing in the morning huskiness, sending tendrils of tension curling through his body. He blinked. Emma was looking at him, her mountain lake blue eyes probing past the barriers he hadn't had the chance to reerect. He swallowed. He didn't know what he wanted to say, or do. No, that wasn't right. He knew what he wanted to do, he just wouldn't let himself do it.

She shifted, curling her fist into the sleeping bag to hold it to her chest as she propped her other arm beneath her head. Her arm was bare, her shirt spread out to dry on the rock beside her. She glanced around the clearing before catching his gaze once more. "I guess we should leave."

"Yeah. We should."

"There's a compass in the first aid kit."

"From what I could see when I unrolled the tarp, the maps came through in good shape." The ducks near the lily pads took off in a blur of spray and beating wings. He turned his head to follow their progress across the lightening sky. "We should wait until your boots dry out, though, or you might get blisters."

"I thought you'd be in a hurry."

His voice softened. "We can wait a little longer. It would be a shame to disturb any more ducks right now, wouldn't it?"

The smile that nudged the corners of her mouth was as tentative as the mist on the lake. "Yes, it would."

Bruce hadn't realized how much he had missed seeing her smile. She hadn't smiled for days, not since he had shaved off his beard and become himself. She had fought him, had cursed him and had given her body in passionate abandon, but she hadn't smiled. He looked into her eyes, wishing he could stretch out this moment and pretend they were the only two people in existence. Hopeless wishes, mere remnants of last night's insanity.

She tilted her head, muffling a yawn against her shoulder. "Thanks for letting me use the sleeping bag."

"You're welcome."

"I guess you must have been cold."

"I folded an edge of the tarp over myself. It wasn't all that cold during the night." He glanced down at his shirt. It hung open in two places where Emma had ripped the buttons from their holes. "Drafty, but not cold."

She followed his gaze and a flush darkened her cheeks. Her smile faded. She tried unsuccessfully to rake her fingers through her hair, then focused on her broken nails. "Bruce, about what happened last night... after the explosion. Between us."

He should have known there wouldn't be any evasiveness or morning-after denial when it came to Emma. "What about it?" he asked gently.

Her gaze lifted to his and steadied. "I'm not going to pretend it didn't happen."

"No, neither of us can do that."

"And I'm not going to pretend that I'm ashamed. It was understandable, a purely physical reaction to the circumstances."

Was it? Of course, she was right. The physical attraction had been building for days. That's all it was. It couldn't have been more. He wasn't about to open himself up to the pain of loving someone again, he knew better than that. "There were some strong emotions let loose."

"We both went a little crazy, I guess. But you know it won't happen again."

He sighed and rubbed his face. His beard sounded like sandpaper against his palm. "I know, Emma. I do have to ask you something, though."

"I'm all right, if that's what you're worried about. I'm not fragile."

"No, that's not what I meant. Things happened too fast for me to take any precautions."

"Oh. That." She was silent for a while. "It was the wrong time of the month. As you would say, the risk was minimal."

"If you find out, later, you'd tell me?"

The silence stretched out longer this time. "Let's not talk about later, okay?"

They lay side by side, unmoving, while the light strengthened. There was so much more to say, yet neither one of them seemed to want to break the predawn peace. The temporary truce between them had settled in as fleetingly as the dew. It was bound to burn off in the light of day.

"Bruce?"

"Mmm?"

"When you were Prendergast, were you faking your incompetence with a fishing rod?"

The question brought back that memorable day in Emma's canoe and he smiled. "Why?"

"Considering the fact that we're facing more than a day's hike through the bush, I'd like to know what kind of outdoor experience you have. Ever been camping? Do you know how to build a fire, snare a rabbit, keep from walking in circles?"

"I've never been much of a fisherman, but I know how to build a fire. And as long as I have a compass and a good map, I won't get lost."

"That's a relief. Are they teaching survival training along with those disguise courses at the police academy these days?"

"You could say I had on-the-job training. I worked with some park rangers out in Alaska one fall to crack a ring that was killing bears for their gall bladders."

She scowled. "That kind of thing is disgusting. I hope you caught them."

"Uh-huh. Eventually. The stakeouts on that job didn't involve reading books in front of a crackling fire, though."

"I bet."

"What about you? Did they teach fishin' and huntin' at your fancy private school? How did a rich society princess end up owning a pair of broken-in leather hiking boots?"

She rolled onto her back, raising her arms to lace her fingers under her head. "From the time I was a kid, my father used to take me hunting with him. We would spend two weeks a year tramping through the most remote and beautiful areas on the continent, pretending that we were actually trying to bag a trophy, but the point of the trip was the trip itself. We usually came back empty-handed."

"You and your father must have been very close. You miss him a lot, don't you?"

"He was lost to me long before he died in that stupid accident. I should have known he wasn't in any shape to go hunting alone, but I had hoped that it meant he was starting to turn things around, to give up the bottle." She paused. "No matter what your research might have said, it really was an accident. The insurance companies were the only ones who tried to imply my father's death was a suicide."

"They wanted to avoid paying up, right?"

"You guessed it. The media made it into another scandal—the Duprey name has sold a lot of papers over the years. The reporters crossed the line that time, though."

"What happened?"

"They wouldn't leave us alone. They staked out the house, they followed us around. Then some vulture of a photographer started snapping pictures of Simon and me at the graveside. They've got no respect, no compassion, no sense of privacy or decency. The scum deserved what he got when Simon took his camera and—" She stopped abruptly.

"Emma? What did Simon do to that reporter?"

"Nothing."

He frowned, sitting up so that he could face her. "Did Simon hit him?"

She wouldn't meet his eyes. "No, I did."

He braced his hands on either side of the sleeping bag and leaned closer. "Emma, look at me. Don't you think that after last night we could be honest with each other?"

She rolled to her side away from him. "Is my shirt dry? I think I'll get up."

"It's got dew on it but it's drier than it was when you took it off. Stop trying to change the subject. You were charged with assault three years ago, right after your father's funeral. It was that reporter, wasn't it? Simon was the one who struck him, but you took the blame, didn't you?"

"Get off me, Bruce. I want to get dressed. It's too early in the morning for a police interrogation."

Sighing, he pushed away from her. "So we're back to that, are we?"

She inched the bag over and reached out to snag her shirt. Keeping her back toward him, she thrust her arms into the sleeves and started fastening the buttons. "Did we ever get away from it?"

"You know we did. This is just between you and me. That assault case is over and done, you settled it out of court, so I'm not asking officially, I'm asking for me."

"Just because we shared our bodies doesn't mean we share everything else."

He knew she was right. Neither one of them wanted the intimacy to go further, and yet . . . He glanced at the horizon. Dawn was a breath away. Quickly he stretched out his arm until his palm hovered above her shoulder. "Emma, please."

"Why?"

"Why? I want to know the truth, that's all. I'm sick of lies. There always seems to be a good reason for them, but after a while the layers of dishonesty get so thick they can choke you." He completed his motion and let his fingers come to rest on the damp cotton. The contact triggered a wave of warmth through his body. He hadn't touched her since last night. He was surprised by how much he still needed to touch her. "I know what it's like. With the job I have, going deep undercover for months at a stretch, sometimes I live a lie every day. It gets to you, that constant need to suppress what you feel and who you are. It's confusing, and frustrating, and you risk losing yourself."

A delicate tremor traveled through her shoulders. "I've lived a lie for three years."

He knelt behind her and shifted his hand to the back of her head. His need to touch her was more than sexual. He moved his palm, focusing on the way her hair twined over his fingers. Slowly, tenderly, he began to stroke the tangled locks. "You did it to protect your brother, didn't you?"

"This isn't an official question?"

"No, Emma. Like I said, this is for me."

Emma closed her eyes and soaked up his soothing touch. Last night his grip had been hard and uncompromising when he'd pulled her out of the plane and again when he'd forced her to safety. And afterward, his hands had been rough and urgent. This tender, quiet, early morning gentleness was something new, something she'd never known. With anyone. It made her remember all the old dreams of having someone who would be there to wake up with, to share sunsets with, to hold her while she cried. Someone she could trust, maybe even love.

But she knew that someone couldn't be Bruce. They didn't love each other. They couldn't. Want, need, those were the words that applied. Soon the sun would come up and with it would come all the reasons why he shouldn't be touching her and she shouldn't be letting him. Daylight and reality would find them, and they would once more be the two people they had been the day before. But for now, for this stolen instant, she would seize the pleasure he was giving her. She sighed. "Yes. I took the blame for Simon."

He worked his fingers toward her scalp, easing apart a snarl of auburn-streaked hair. "It makes sense, Emma. I know you have a hell of a temper, but you're too smart to get caught punching out a reporter, no matter what the provocation."

"There was plenty of provocation," she said. "It was the reporter's idea to bring the charges against me instead of Simon, though—I'd always done my best to shelter Simon from the publicity our family went through over the years, so he wouldn't have made as spectacular a target. I guess the reporter figured I'd be worth more, maybe sell more copies of his paper. He was happy enough with the money my lawyers settled on him."

"No wonder you tried to intimidate me with that bow when you thought I was a reporter."

"You don't intimidate easily, do you?"

"Nope. Neither do you."

She tipped her head forward as he combed his fingers down to her nape. "I was tired of it, Bruce. I just wanted some peace. That's why I bought the cabin and changed my name. The local people still don't know who I am, and I like it that way."

Carefully he separated the last of the knots that the dunking in the lake and the wild night had left in her hair. When he was done, he settled his hands lightly on either side of her neck. "Your mother died of a drug overdose, didn't she?"

"Tranquilizers and vodka. Why?"

He dropped his hand and moved in front of her, his knees on the edge of the sleeping bag. "Why are you working for McQuaig, Emma? What's the real reason?"

The question wasn't entirely unexpected, yet she had hoped that he might have waited a little longer, might have touched her a little more, maybe smiled and talked about unimportant things like jazz and books and chocolate.

"If you were doing this smuggling in order to thumb your nose at the law, you wouldn't be running drugs. It would be anything but drugs. And if you moved out to the cabin for peace, why would you get yourself mixed up with a group like McQuaig's? You're not stupid. You would know what you were getting involved with." He leaned forward, his eyes vibrant, his gaze intense. "And there's the way you love to fly, but you hated every minute of that flight last night. I saw it on your face."

The sun burst over the horizon with the finality of a thunderclap. The night, and the fleeting truce, was at an end. Emma wriggled out of the sleeping bag and tugged the tail of her shirt over her thighs. Keeping her gaze on Bruce, she backed toward her discarded jeans. "You're not asking just for you anymore, are you?"

"Does it make a difference?"

"You know it does."

His face had already lost the soft sleepiness of the man who had watched the wood ducks. "I guess I can't separate it, can I? I can't even share in some harmless pillow talk without remembering who I am. My job is still my life."

She pulled on the rest of her clothes. An awkward silence descended. She walked across the rock point to retrieve her boots, then sat down and tugged them on. It was difficult to see the laces through the tears she didn't want to acknowledge. "What we did together doesn't change who we are, Bruce."

"What we did together? We made love, Emma. I don't know how you can expect me to forget that."

"It wasn't love."

He hesitated. Raising his hand to his face, he rubbed his eyes hard before he replied. "No, it wasn't love, but—"

"Neither of us has any illusions about it. And I'm not saying I'll forget it, but we can't make it into something more. It was sex, that's all. We weren't thinking straight. Our bodies, our adrenaline and the circumstances were responsible."

"I know that."

"You want to get the bad guys, I want to get my brother. We're stuck together now because we're using each other, that's all."

"We can't get past that, can we?" he said. "We can lie on a rock and watch the sun come up, we can share memories, we can understand each other to hell and back, but we're still the same people, aren't we?"

"The same people, the same problems." She took a deep, unsteady breath and blinked rapidly. "Go ahead and ask your questions."

"Will you answer them?"

The mournful cry of a loon warbled over the lake. The breath of wind that had accompanied the sunrise strengthened, stirring up tart odors from the traces of wreckage and spilled fuel. Reality had returned, whether she wanted it or not. "My deal with McQuaig blew up with my plane. I've got nothing to lose by being honest."

At least a minute passed in silence before Bruce walked across the rock point and squatted down in front of her. "Okay. No more lies. Why does McQuaig want you dead?"

"I don't know."

"You must have some idea."

"I don't know why they want me dead. Maybe it isn't me. Maybe it's you. They might have found out you're a cop, and they saw me leave with you. They might have guessed we'd struck a deal."

"Did they have any reason to think you'd go to the police?"

"No. They knew I wouldn't. They knew I'd do exactly what they told me."

"You've said before that they think you'll do what they say. Why? What's their hold over you? It couldn't be the money, you've got plenty of that. And you don't intimidate easily." He reached out to grasp her chin in his hand and tilt her face up. "It takes a lot to force you to do anything. You weren't even afraid of a bomb. If I hadn't thrown you out of that plane, you would have gone up with it. I've never known a more stubbornly courageous woman, or man for that matter. You'd only risk your life for something or someone you truly cared about."

She was looking into his eyes, so she could see the exact moment when he began to realize the truth. It gave her no satisfaction. It was too late for that.

"They're not threatening you, they're threatening your brother," he said. "You're doing this for Simon. You were desperate to make sure that nothing interfered with this run you were supposed to make, and yet you didn't care what we did to everyone afterward as long as you and your brother got away. But why would they want to get rid of their regular pilot—" He drew in his breath. "That's it, isn't it? You're not their regular pilot."

"I've never run drugs in my life. Last night was the first time. The day you found me crying on the dock I had just found out what Simon was doing and had told him to stop. He tried, but Harvey beat him up, phoned me and ordered me to take Simon's place or they would kill him."

He straightened up and kicked a loose rock into the underbrush at the edge of the clearing. For a minute he simply stared at her without speaking, squeezing his fists until his knuckles went white. "Why didn't you tell me that in the first place?" he asked between clenched teeth. "After we left the warehouse, why didn't you tell me?"

Her reply was brutally simple. "Would you have believed me?"

He had to look away. "No."

"That's your answer."

"There's more to it, isn't there? Lying to a cop is a knee-jerk reaction with you, isn't it?"

"Right. Just like not trusting anyone and not dropping the cop role is a habit with you."

"You were willing to do it again, to take the blame for something your brother did in order to protect him."

"It had worked out before." She pushed to her feet and brushed off the seat of her jeans. "I took a chance. If everything had gone as it was supposed to, it would have worked out again."

"Worked out?" He waved his arm toward the remains of her plane. "Didn't you realize the danger you were putting yourself in? That *I* was putting you in? You were innocent all along. I never would have forced you to make that flight if I'd known—"

"You were using me even before you'd decided that I was guilty, Bruce. You deceived me and manipulated me, so I think it's a bit late for conscience pangs."

"I was only doing my job."

"That's right. And I can't forget what you are. Maybe for a few stolen moments in the dark I could, but not anymore."

A muscle twitched in his cheek. "You were way out of your league with McQuaig, Emma. I know people like him. I've worked with them. They would never have intended for you to take Simon's place. They saw you as a threat to the nice little setup they had going, and they wanted to eliminate you. Once they tell Simon what they did, he'll be too scared to try breaking away ever again. The threat to his life had been a bluff. They wouldn't have gotten rid of their pilot."

"Then he's safe. He's alive. They won't hurt him. At least I accomplished that much."

"Why don't you worry about yourself instead of your brother? He's a grown man. He dug his own hole. When are you going to stop being the one to pull him out?"

She paced across the clearing to the shore. Crossing her arms over her chest, she watched the merciless rays of sunrise slice through the wisps of mist. She had asked herself the same questions only four days ago. She hadn't had the answers then, either. "You won't be bringing charges against my brother when we get back to civilization, will you? That was part of our deal."

"Everything's changed, Emma. If you had been honest with me at the start—"

"Don't give me that bull. You wouldn't have believed me. We still have a deal, don't we?"

"I won't lie to you. Not anymore. I can't guarantee anything as far as Simon is concerned. If he wants to co-operate himself, that's a different matter."

"You'd go after my brother? After what we did together, you'd still—"

"You said it yourself, Emma. What we did together doesn't change who we are."

Slowly she turned to face him. He was standing in a pose almost identical to hers. His long legs were braced apart, his arms were crossed defensively. Even across the space that separated them she could feel the impact of his intense blue eyes. The tenderness that she'd felt when he'd touched her hair was gone. The vulnerability that she'd seen on his face when she'd awakened this morning had disappeared. The splendid, savage lover who had made her claw and scream had vanished with the dawn. He'd drawn into himself, slipped back behind his professional barrier. He was as handsome and compelling as he'd ever been, with the slanting, golden sunlight caressing his face and the awakening breeze stirring his tousled hair. Yet his sculpted masculine beauty was that of a statue. Cold. Distant. Untouchable.

Not yet, she cried silently. *Let's go back, just once more let's forget who we are . . .*

"I hear an engine," he said.

It took a second for the words to penetrate. "What?"

"It's probably someone from McQuaig's group checking their handiwork."

Over the dawn sounds of the awakening birds and stirring trees she heard the low drone of a plane. She turned back to the lake and her gaze dropped to the water. The wreckage of the Cessna hadn't drifted far. A large part had sunk, but some of it bobbed near the shore, more lay scattered across the surface, glittering in the slanting sunlight.

"Better get under cover."

"Maybe it's someone else. We could be rescued, flown out of here—"

"What are the odds that someone else is flying the route they gave you at this time of day?"

"Not good."

"Let's get our gear out of sight."

Reality. It wasn't going to change simply because of her own wishful thinking. Hurriedly she picked up the sleeping bag and stuffed it into its nylon sack.

Bruce tossed the things they had salvaged back into the center of the canvas tarp and quickly rolled it up. The sound of the plane grew louder. "This way," he said, loping toward a break in the underbrush.

She tucked the sack under her arm and ducked past the spruce bough he held aside for her. Fallen needles crunched under her boots. Draping branches wove a dark canopy overhead. "How far do you want to go?"

"This should be good enough. No one will spot us from the air." He set his improvised bundle down beside a mossy log. "I want to see what they do."

The plane was close enough now for her to distinguish the sound. "It's a twin engine, bigger than my Cessna."

He dug through the bundle and came up with his gun and holster. With the smoothness of a motion done thousands of times, he shrugged into the straps and steadied the holster at the small of his back. "Keep your head down."

A squirrel scolded suddenly from the pine beside her and Emma jumped. She grabbed on to a branch, barely noticing the sharp pricks as her fingers snapped off the dead twigs. She kept her gaze on the diamond-shaped patch of sky that showed through the trees. "They're coming from the south. Flying low."

"Right. It fits. They're tracing your course."

Something glinted in the distance. Sunlight flashed from the windshield and all at once a plane took shape. "It's a Beechcraft. No pontoons. They won't be landing."

The plane roared over the trees. They both ducked reflexively. The pitch of the engines lowered as it receded to the north. Emma pivoted to follow its progress. It had barely reached the end of the valley the lake nestled in when wings flashed in a sudden bank.

"They must have spotted something," Bruce said.

The noise approached once more. "It really might be someone else. Anyone would investigate if they thought they saw debris from a crash."

The plane came in even lower this time. It circled the lake in a tight, skidding turn to follow the curve of the shoreline. Emma pressed back against a tree trunk. It was heading straight for them. It passed overhead close enough for her to see the rivets in the fuselage. And the markings on the side. The engines roared again as the plane climbed to clear a hill. It banked more quickly this time.

Bruce crouched down and worked his way back toward the clearing.

"What are you doing?" she called.

"Getting a better look. Stay there."

She dropped the sleeping bag beside the rolled tarp and ran after him. They stopped at the edge of the underbrush where they would have a better view but would still be hidden by the slanting shadows. "That plane belongs to McQuaig."

"Yeah, I saw the CM logo on the side, too."

"I didn't know he had access to his own plane."

"It's registered to one of his legitimate businesses."

"But he could have . . . I mean, why force Simon and me—"

Bruce caught her arm and tugged her down to kneel beside him. "He knows the feds have been watching him, so he wouldn't risk using it for those midnight runs."

The plane swooped over the rock clearing and made a sudden bank at the edge of the trees. For a split second, for a space of time no longer than a heartbeat, the glass cockpit tilted toward them and the occupants were visible. It was only a flash, a quick impression, but the image burned its way into Emma's brain. Her breath whooshed out and she sat back on her heels. There were two men in the plane. She recognized the gleaming bald pate of one of them. And the other—

"I guess they're satisfied," Bruce said. He released her arm as the plane skimmed across the trees on the far side of the lake. The noise of the engines faded gradually. There was a suspended pause of silence, then the air was filled once more with the twittering whistles and rustlings of the morning.

Emma stared numbly at the empty sky.

His thigh brushed her shoulder as he stood up. "We'd better plan our route. There's no reason to hang around here any longer."

"You saw, didn't you?"

"Yes."

"You were right. About everything. They came to check just like you had said. They really did want me dead."

"And as far as they're concerned, you'll stay that way until we can put them behind bars. They're going to carry on with business as usual, and that will give Xavier the chance to shut them down for good."

She thought of the other face she had glimpsed in that cockpit, the one whose boyish charm was buried beneath aviator sunglasses and the crumpled contortions of grief. "Simon thinks I'm dead, too."

"Yes."

"We have to get back."

"We will."

"We have to help him, Bruce. After you contact Xavier again, when you find out how things stand..."

He reached down to cup her elbow and lift her gently to her feet. His voice was soft, his eyes filled with regret, but his jaw was firm. "We've got enough problems ahead of us, Emma. Let's not talk about later, okay?"

Chapter 11

It was late afternoon when Emma felt the blister pop. Somewhere between one step and the next, the skin that stretched over the sharp bone on the side of her ankle finally gave up. It hadn't been weak to begin with, but it had reached its limit. Damp socks, damp boots and six and a half hours of hiking over hills and through spruce thickets were what did it. The discomfort—she wouldn't let herself call it pain—was like someone jabbing a needle into a half-healed burn. She wasn't about to ask Bruce to stop, though. They hadn't yet covered the ten miles they'd agreed to do today.

Whatever he'd done with those park rangers in Alaska had more than prepared him for this pocket of wilderness in Maine. Before they'd left the lake this morning, he had spread out the map he'd salvaged and asked her to point out exactly where they were. Then he had handed her the sleeping bag and had fastened everything else into the canvas tarp, tied it securely, and slung it over his back. He was matter-of-fact about giving her less to carry, not out of any patronizing big strong male attitude, but out of respect for her size and gender. So far she could find no fault with anything he had done, from the route they had decided to follow, to the pace he was setting.

The weather was clear and warm, the bugs practically nonexistent this late in the summer, and the view from the last ridge they had climbed had been spectacular. Thanks to the emergency supplies in the first aid kit, they had enough dried food packs and water purification pills to last them at least two days. Under other circumstances, this hike might even have been an enjoyable challenge.

She slipped on a piece of moss as she followed Bruce around an alder grove and another hot needle jabbed her ankle. Other circumstances? Enjoyable? The tension must be getting to her. This was no stroll through the park, this was a trek for survival. Not only hers and Bruce's, but Simon's. The popped blister was nothing but a minor annoyance. She wouldn't even let herself think about it. They had to do the ten miles they'd planned so that by tomorrow they would reach the trail that had been marked by the broken black line on her map, which would lead to the logging road, which would lead to a telephone and Bruce's colleague Xavier and the chance to help her brother.

Since the twin engine Beechcraft had disappeared over the southern horizon, neither of them had mentioned Simon again.

Neither of them wanted to talk about "later."

A burst of slanting sunshine made her squint as they reached a flat outcrop of glacier-scarred rock. At the crest of a hill a row of leaning white pines stood like windblown sentinels silhouetted against the hazy blue folds of distant ridges. Bruce stopped and shielded his eyes to look over the next valley. "How are you hanging in?" he asked.

"Fine. No problem." She eased the string of the sleeping bag from her shoulder. "How about you?"

"Can't complain." After a careful survey of the area, he took the compass from his pocket and held it in front of his chest. Moving only his feet, he turned until he lined up the direction he wanted. "We'll have to swing around to the north a bit more."

Since she had been the one to lead the way in the morning, Bruce was taking his turn for the afternoon, and he was demonstrating a quiet competence with the task. Although she didn't want to, she couldn't help feeling a grudging admiration for him. "Did you learn about orienteering on that bear gall bladder job?"

"Nope. This is pure Boy Scout."

She let the bag drop by her feet. "You've been leading us for the past four hours from something you learned in the *Boy Scouts?*"

Pushing the compass back into his pocket, he looked at her over his shoulder. The crinkles at the corners of his eyes deepened. "Don't worry. I got a merit badge."

The glimpse of Prendergast's gentle wit startled her. Who was he today? she wondered.

He turned back toward the valley, the plaid flannel of his shirt clinging damply to his broad shoulders. Since noon she'd watched those shoulders shift and flex as he moved. He'd rolled up his sleeves, and the hair on his arms glinted golden in the sunshine. His loose shirttails fluttered around his hips, revealing the outline of Primeau's tight buttocks under his worn jeans. Who was he now?

Bruce. Simply Bruce. The cop who had tricked her, used her and intended to put her brother in prison. The man who had watched the ducks and untangled her hair. The lover who...

The sky blurred as her eyes filled with tears. They'd had a tendency to do that today. She didn't want to admit that this lump in her throat was more than worry about her brother, and about the whole complicated mess with McQuaig. Had she thought that she could simply dismiss what had happened with Bruce? Had she really believed that she could decide it was honest and natural and then get on with her life? She might have moved in the sophisticated, jaded levels of society where sex was as shallow and as meaningless as the phony smiles, but she had never been like that. And she had left it behind. At least, she had believed that she had left it behind. Or was she only trying to soothe her belated sense of morality by considering there might have been more than blind, physical desire involved in what happened with Bruce?

But there couldn't be more. No, not with him. They had both agreed that there couldn't be more. Tipping her head forward, she felt a tear slip down her cheek. Impatiently, she wiped her eyes with her sleeve.

"Are you thirsty?" he asked as he unfastened the rope that held the tarp together and drew out a canteen. He walked to a boulder, sat down, and patted the rock beside him in invitation.

Forcing herself not to limp, she moved over to join him. "Thanks." She unscrewed the top and took a quick swallow, then handed the canteen back to him.

"I think we might as well stop for the day. This looks like a good spot to make camp."

"Now?" She ignored her throbbing ankle and checked her watch. "We still have a few hours of daylight left. We haven't come as far as we'd planned."

"I estimate that we'll be out of the bush by tomorrow night at the latest, so we're doing all right." He put the canteen to his lips, took a long drink and wiped his mouth with the back of his hand. "Actually, we're doing better than anyone could expect. The weather's cooperating, and you managed to land us reasonably close to help."

"The landing was pure luck."

"Hardly. You're one awesome pilot, Emma." He propped his ankle on his knee and looked around the clearing. The outcrop was smaller and not as flat as the one by the lake where they'd spent the previous night. "Seeing as we've got some time before sunset, I think I'll gather some spruce boughs to sleep on."

"Good idea."

"There's no reason why we shouldn't have a fire tonight, since nobody's going to be looking for you."

"I'll scrounge up some firewood."

"I can top off the canteen at the stream we passed near the alder grove. If it's all the same to you, I'd rather reconstitute the dried food we've got with us than go out and snare a rabbit."

"Sure. Whatever." She pushed herself to her feet. "I'll get the water while I'm picking up firewood."

"Sure. Whatever."

Without another word, she took the canteen from his hand and headed back the way they had come. The stream wasn't much more than a trickle, the smooth, rounded rocks in the center lumping high above the surface in the late summer dryness. Emma knelt at the edge of the water and scooped out a hollow in the gritty streambed, then wedged in the canteen so that the flow was directed into the opening. When it was full, she ducked into the underbrush to look for firewood. Within a few minutes she loaded her arms with dry sticks and returned to the clearing.

Judging by the thrashing noises coming from the trees, Bruce hadn't finished cutting their mattress yet. Emma dumped her firewood and sat down on a cushion of moss to unlace her boot. Carefully, she wiggled it off, then looked at the patch of blood on her sock with dismay. Gritting her teeth, she peeled back the sock and assessed the damage. The blister had broken, all right. More than two layers of skin had been worn away and hung in limp tatters around an oozing red center that was the size of a quarter.

The tart aroma of fresh-cut evergreen wafted around her as Bruce walked past and stacked a load of spruce boughs beside the sleeping bag. Whistling a snatch of an old Duke Ellington tune, he knelt down to open the white enamel first aid kit and rummaged through it briefly. "Well, what's your choice, sort of beef stew or noodle surprise?"

"What's the surprise?"

"I don't know." He tilted his head to look at her, a twinkle in his eyes. "The label came off."

Another Prendergast comment. She tossed her boot to the ground and frowned. "Are you going to do the cooking?"

"Sure, if I can find something to use for a stew pot. Have you got any ideas?"

She pointed at the first aid kit. "Unhinge the lid and empty it out. It's enamel, and it's waterproof."

He emptied out the box and went over to where she had dropped the firewood. Using a flat rock, he scraped the moss and dry grass away from a circle and ringed it with stones. Emma leaned sideways to reach the pile of first aid supplies and picked up the bottle of disinfectant. She sorted through the bandages until she found the size she wanted, then pulled her foot onto her lap.

"What's wrong?" Bruce asked. "Are you hurt?"

"No, it's just a blister."

He was at her side before she could blink. His blond curls fell over his forehead as he leaned down for a closer look. "That must have been hell to walk with. Why didn't you say something?"

"We still have a long way to go. It's not that bad."

"There you go again, not worrying about yourself." He sat down in front of her and took her foot between his hands. "Let me do this."

"You're making a fuss over nothing. I'm perfectly capable of taking care of myself."

"I know. That doesn't stop me from wanting to help." He propped her heel on his thigh and took the disinfectant from her hands. "This is going to sting."

It did sting, but Emma didn't flinch. She handed Bruce the bandage and watched as he peeled off the wrapper and positioned it. "Thanks."

He smoothed his thumbs along the adhesive strip. When he was finished, he didn't release her foot. "Give me the other one."

"Why?"

"I'm going to check it for blisters and then give you a massage," he said matter-of-factly. He lifted her foot and took off her boot and sock, then moved back so that she could stretch out her legs. Cradling her heels on his lap, he did a quick inspection, nodded, and began squeezing her toes. "How's that?"

It was bliss. It was exactly what she needed. She braced her arms behind her and sighed. "Why are you doing this, Bruce?"

"Because I'm a nice guy."

She shook her head. "No, your alter ego with the beard and the weight problem was a nice guy. You're a cop."

"Okay. I'm doing this to be sure you'll be in shape to hike out of here tomorrow so that I can contact Xavier and get back on the case as soon as possible. Is that what you wanted to hear?" He flexed her foot up and down a few times and rubbed her instep.

"Won't Xavier be starting a search for you? I mean, don't you need to check in regularly or something?"

"Not when I'm playing out a deep cover like Primeau. He'll know something went wrong with the plan when he doesn't hear from me today, but he won't risk the operation by launching an all-out search. Not yet, anyway. I've been in tougher spots before, and he knows I always manage to land on my feet."

"At the moment, you don't look very much like Primeau to me."

The hint of a smile flitted across his face. For a minute he hesitated, then he leaned forward, tightened his jaw, lowered his eyelids and let his voice deepen. "Don't I, sweet thing?"

Her fingers dug into a patch of crunchy moss behind her as her mouth dropped open. The transformation had been instantaneous. "Bruce?"

"Mmm?" Slowly, seductively, he slid his hand to her good ankle, pushed up the hem of her jeans, and wrapped his fingers firmly around the bottom of her calf. His touch was no longer soothing, it was sensual.

Awareness tingled through every inch of her weary body. She looked at his arm, at the hard, cording muscle below his sleeve, the tension in his broad shoulders and the arrogant tilt of his head. Everything about him radiated raw, animal energy. Beneath the lazily lowered lids his eyes gleamed. Her pulse accelerated as she responded helplessly to his blatant masculinity. "Good God," she whispered. "How do you do that?"

He moved his thumb. That was all, just a subtle, almost imperceptible motion against her skin, but it sent heat racing up her leg. "Do what? This?"

She tried to inch backward, but his grip was deceptively firm. "Let go of me."

"I only did your feet. What about the rest of you?" Wind sighed through the pines around them, denim whispered against his palms as he slowly stroked his way to her knee. "You could take off these jeans."

Instantly, the heat flared higher. Too vividly she remembered how it had felt the last time, how her bare thighs had rubbed over the folds of his jeans, how his strong hands had held her against him. Raw need throbbed insistently, stealing her breath, her caution, her sense...

No. Not again. This wasn't last night. She was in control of herself, there was no excuse. This game they were playing was too dangerous. It couldn't continue. She had to... "Stop. We can't."

His hand curved around the back of her knee. "I watched you walking in front of me all morning, saw the way your hips swayed, memorized the shift and flex of your—"

"Bruce, stop it!"

His expression lost Primeau's cocky smirk, his face eased back into the one she was familiar with. Yet the sexual awareness was still there. He moved his hands to her thighs and rose to his knees, straddling her legs. "Are your feet better now?"

"What?"

His gaze focused on her mouth. "I was touching you only so that you'd be able to walk tomorrow."

"Of course. I know that."

The breeze pulled at the front of his shirt, exposing a palm-size patch of bronzed skin. She had done that, had ripped those buttons off, had been too far gone to care. She had felt the texture of the short, crisp curls on his chest and had learned the rippling strength that lay beneath. He was breathing hard. Tension, shared memory, shared restraint vibrated between them as neither one of them moved. No excuse, she told herself, her fingers clutching painfully at the rock and the moss. It was broad daylight, they were both completely rational; this time there would be no excuse.

Bruce clenched his jaw and lifted his hands from her thighs. With a low curse he pushed himself to his feet and turned away. His movements stiff, he walked to the pile of firewood and bent down to select the thinnest sticks. The dry wood snapped harshly as he broke it into short lengths. "Did you ever go hunting with Turner?"

Emma exhaled shakily. "What?"

"Turner. The man you were engaged to once."

"I know who he is. I'm surprised at your question, that's all."

"You said you enjoyed those vacations with your father. Did your fiancé like the outdoors as well?"

"Not really. Unless you counted the two acres of manicured lawns and formal flower beds around his parents' house."

"He took you to a lot of those society events, didn't he?"

"Of course."

"Did you like all of that? Are you sorry you gave it up when you moved away?"

"No. Why are you asking me this?"

He propped the sticks against each other in the center of the circle he'd cleared. "I'm curious. Ever since you told me why he broke the engagement, I've been wondering why you would have wanted to marry him."

"It was all part of the life I'd thought I would have had."

"And what would that have been? Tennis lessons, bridge clubs, charity work?"

"Probably."

"Did he like to fly? Did he share your interest in books? Did he like chocolate?"

She pulled her feet toward her and wrapped her arms around her legs. No, Turner hadn't liked her plane, or her reading habit. She couldn't remember whether or not he liked chocolate. The subject probably hadn't come up. He had told her that he loved her, he had been her first lover, yet there had been some things they had never shared. She watched Bruce as he struck a match and coaxed a curl of smoke from the twigs. Her thighs still tingled from the touch of his hands, her pulse still sped from the look in his eyes. The current of awareness that flowed between them was something else that she'd never shared with Turner. And her fiancé had never made her scream.

"No," she said softly. "He didn't like to fly."

Bruce blew on the tiny flame. It crackled and grew, licking along the wood greedily. He fed the fire until it was burning strongly, then tipped back his head to look at the row of pines at the side of the hill. "I like it out here. If we had a tent and maybe a few more supplies, it would be a nice place to camp, don't you think?"

Instead of looking at their surroundings, she continued to watch Bruce. When he had been Prendergast, she had found him fascinating. He still was. There were so many aspects to his personality, such a keen intelligence behind his unique blue eyes, it was too bad that... No, she wouldn't let herself think that way. Last night was over. It was over. "Under other circumstances it might be."

Sparks flew as he jabbed a stick into the fire. "Can't forget those circumstances, can we?" he muttered.

The tightness in her throat had nothing to do with the puffs of smoke that blew her way. "No."

He prepared their food in silence.

* * *

The dying fire sent long shadows flickering outward across the bare rock and low bushes. Emma inched closer and tossed another thick branch onto the embers. It seemed colder tonight. It probably wasn't, but without the adrenaline of the night before, she had no defense against the creeping chill that accompanied the darkness. She hugged her arms around herself for warmth and looked at the place where they would sleep. Shortly before sunset they had trimmed the spruce boughs and had layered them into a springy pad on the other side of the fire. The tarp was spread on top, an extra layer of protection from the cold. Bruce sat cross-legged in the center of it, his elbows on his knees, his chin propped in his hands. He'd been quietly studying the flames for the past hour.

"Do you want to use the sleeping bag tonight?" she asked.

"No, you should have it."

"I had it last night. It would be only fair if you had a turn."

"Keep it, Emma. I'll be okay."

There was another solution, of course. They could share it. Considering his size, it would be a tight fit, but not if they wrapped their arms around each other and pressed themselves together. She hid her eyes against her arm, but the image of their bodies entwined wouldn't go away.

He cleared his throat. "I'd like to get an early start tomorrow. When I was cleaning up our stew pot I thought I heard a truck in the distance."

She looked up. "Where?"

"Toward the north. It was several miles away, but it could have been on that logging road we're heading for." He pulled the sleeping bag from its nylon sack and spread it out on the side of the tarp closest to the fire. "Come on, we'd better get some sleep."

In the glow of the flames, she saw a patch of charred fabric on the back of his shirt. She'd noticed it earlier, during the afternoon, but she hadn't mentioned it—she'd been too busy watching him move. "What happened to your back? Your shirt's burned."

He twisted his neck to look over his shoulder. "That's from last night."

A quiver tickled through her stomach. "You mean I did that?"

He chuckled. "No. I mean the explosion did that. A piece of debris hit me."

"Oh." She pushed to her feet and walked around the fire. "Better let me take a look at it."

"Why?"

"You don't want it to get infected."

"It's okay."

"You don't know that." She picked up the disinfectant that he'd used on her ankle. "Take your shirt off and I'll see how bad it is."

Reflections from the fire danced in his eyes as he looked up at her. For almost a minute he didn't move. Then he slowly undid what remained of his buttons. The plaid flannel slid from his shoulders, revealing firm, rangy muscles. Taut skin gleamed in the flickering orange light, shadows played over the crisp hair that covered his chest. He dropped the shirt beside him and waited.

Emma knew she was staring and tried to stop, but it was no use. The sun was down. The isolation of the firelit clearing, the slow embrace of the deepening darkness only strengthened her already heightened awareness. He didn't need to put on his Primeau persona to make her pulse trip. His masculine aura wasn't part of an act. Drawing a slow, steadying breath, she sank down to her knees beside him. "Turn away from the fire. I'll be able to see your back better."

Still cross-legged, he swiveled around and braced his hands on his thighs. The position tensed his spine, sending a subtle ripple across his shoulders. "We were pretty lucky. Those rocks blocked out most of the big stuff."

She saw the fresh burn immediately. The skin was red and shiny in a mark about the length of her finger. It hadn't broken, though. "It doesn't look too bad."

"I told you it was okay."

Her gaze moved up gradually. "You've got a nasty bruise on your left shoulder."

"A crate fell on it when we landed. It doesn't bother me."

She continued her scrutiny, even though he clearly didn't need her help. She simply didn't want to move away from him so soon. "What happened to your neck? Was that from the debris?"

He reached behind him and touched one of the long, thin scratches that arced over his skin. "You mean here?"

"There's dried blood on it." She opened the bottle of disinfectant and dabbed it over the scratches. "Maybe something from that bundle you made out of the tarp was rubbing against it today."

"I got those last night, too."

"It all happened so fast, I think I hadn't realized how bad that explosion was." She rested her fingertips on the curve of his shoulder blade. "I should thank you for sheltering me the way you did. You got these from trying to protect me."

"Not exactly."

"Bruce, I know I said some awful things to you, but I do appreciate the way you used your body to..." She felt a tremor go through the skin beneath her fingers. "What's so funny?"

"Those scratches weren't from the explosion, Emma."

"Then what..." Her question trailed off as sudden heat came to her face. It was so obvious now. She looked at the regular spacing, the curve, the width, then focused on her broken nails. "I did that, didn't I?"

He turned his head and caught her gaze. A smile crinkled the skin beside his eyes. "I didn't notice it at the time."

"I'm sorry, Bruce."

"There are plenty of things between us that probably could use an apology, but believe me, Emma, that's not one of them."

She had drawn blood last night. She had marked him. Another thing she should be ashamed about. But wasn't. What was happening to her? A log fell over behind her with a soft hiss, sending up a plume of flame. In the sudden flare of light she noticed a patch of pale skin low on his side. She put down the bottle of disinfectant and leaned closer. It was scar tissue, the lumpy, stretched kind of scar from a deep wound. It had healed over, but the pain he must have suffered was obvious. "What happened here?"

"Where?"

Carefully she ran the tip of her finger along the perimeter of the scar. "Down here near your waist."

His smile disappeared. He reached for his shirt. "A souvenir. From another explosion."

"When did it happen?"

He moved away from her. "Years ago. I don't want to talk about it."

She caught his arm. "Why not? You learned everything there is to know about me before I told you. Why can't we even things up a bit?"

He shook off her grip and thrust his arms into his sleeves. "Are you sure you want to know, Emma?"

Did she want to know? He had learned about her because of his job, not because he was interested. She had no excuse. She should forget all this, crawl into her sleeping bag alone and close her eyes to these dangerous feelings that stirred inside her. "Yes," she said softly, placing her hand back on his arm. "I'd like to know about you, Bruce."

The muscle beneath her fingers hardened with tension. "The scar is where a piece of my car got embedded in my ribs. I never knew which part of the car it was. I never asked. The bomb had been wired to the ignition. I was walking back to my house to get something. I don't remember what it was. It couldn't have been important. I was halfway across the lawn when the blast went off.''

She swallowed hard. "You could have been killed."

"That was the general idea. I was due in court to testify that morning. I was just a beat cop in the suburbs back then, but I had stumbled onto an outfit that was pirating videotapes. Videotapes. They killed an innocent human being over something as trivial as illegal copies of some meaningless movies."

Killed? The tension in his arm spread. She could see his shoulders stiffen. What he had said clicked in her mind. The bomb had been wired to the ignition, but he had been walking across his lawn. "Who was in the car, Bruce?"

"My wife."

The pain in those two words slammed through her without warning. She leaned her forehead against his back. His wife. "I'm sorry," she whispered.

He inhaled shakily but he didn't pull away. "It was five years ago, one of those April days when the leaves are just starting to come out and the smell of warm earth is in the air and the birds are going crazy finding mates and building nests. Lizzie wanted to drop me off at the courthouse on her way to her doctor's appointment. She was in a hurry. She was always in a hurry. She was the original Type A personality."

"You must have loved her deeply," she said. "I can hear it in your voice."

"God, yes, I loved her. She was everything to me. She was one of those people that you'd instinctively gravitate toward if you walked into a roomful of strangers. We thought we'd have the rest of our lives. We'd made so many plans. And when she found out about the baby—" He broke off, his breathing ragged.

The pain just kept getting worse. Emma closed her eyes and moved her head from side to side in a slow negative. "Oh, no."

"She was three months pregnant when they killed her."

Without hesitation Emma slid her arms around his waist and pressed her cheek to his back. The night closed around them, the cocooning quiet broken only by scattered crickets and the muted rustle of the dying fire. "How did you ever survive?"

"When I got out of the hospital, I changed jobs. That was my first undercover assignment. It took only three weeks."

She didn't need to ask what it was. "Did you get them?"

"Yes. The one who planted the bomb never made it to trial. I wasn't proud of that case. It was vengeance, not justice. The next case was easier. That's when I found out that I could lose myself in my work. With the badge and the rule book, I could forget about the pain."

Echoes of her angry words of the night before came back to her. She tightened her hold on him. "I'm sorry, Bruce. I'm so sorry. I didn't know. All I could think about was myself. I wish I could take back those things I said."

"It doesn't matter."

"But I hurt you. All those times I taunted you about your devotion to your job, when I think about that now I feel sick. I was so cruel. I should have thought—"

"We've both done our share of hurting. I haven't forgotten what I did to you, how I betrayed our friendship, and how I wanted to use you. I've had to take a good look at myself lately, and I realize that all I see is my job, my rigid picture of right and wrong. I haven't cared who I need to hurt or use along the way."

"But what you've told me explains so much."

He covered her hands with his, lacing their fingers together. "It's a hell of a situation. It has been from the start. You see, I understand why you hate cops, because I know all about grudges. I recognize the rage you feel toward the people you hold responsible for destroying your family. I felt the same way, only I was able to do something about it. I got them. Every time I finish a case, I get another one of them."

She hung on. She didn't want to move. He knew about grudges because he knew about loss. He had lost his family and all his plans for his life. He had been a victim of circumstances beyond his control. They were alike. They were both survivors. The bond between them, the instinctive connection she had never been able to explain went far, far deeper than she had ever imagined.

This had happened before, this sudden shift in perception. It was like the time she had seen Bruce without the beard and the fake belly and had realized that her view of him had been all wrong. Only this time it was worse. He wasn't the unfeeling robot she had wanted to believe. No, he felt, and he hurt and he'd lost. It made sense now. She could understand why he buried himself in his work, why he didn't want to be close, or to care. She rubbed her cheek against his back, her eyes filling with tears. Yes, she understood. The bond between them was deep. And the problems between them even deeper.

Being a cop was more than merely a job to him. It was how he dealt with the pain he had endured. Hating cops was how she dealt with hers. Oh, God. It was hopeless.

"Last night," she said. "The bomb in my plane, the explosion, everything must have brought it all back for you."

"I shouldn't have told you."

No, he shouldn't have, she thought, her mind reeling. "That's why you lost control, that's why we...did what we did."

"What we did was because of *us*, Emma. You and me. We weren't thinking of the past, or the future. We needed each other because we needed to reaffirm life."

"And surviving."

He paused. "Yes. Surviving. We both carry around the scars of our past, and we've both found our own ways of dealing with it." He pried one of her hands away from his waist and raised it to his lips. His breath puffed warm and rapid over her knuckles. "It's late. We'd better get some rest."

Emma had never felt more connected to another human being in her life. She didn't want to release her hold on him. She wanted to pull his head to her breasts and let their bodies spin them to the sweet oblivion they had shared before. But they couldn't make love. Because if she gave in to the urging of her heart at this moment, that's what the act would be called. And she couldn't love him. Not him. Please, not him. A tear slipped from beneath her tightly closed eyelids and soaked into the soft fabric of his shirt.

A shudder rippled across his back and he dropped her hand. "Go to sleep, Emma."

Her arms felt empty as she let them fall to her sides. The cold of the night rushed over her the moment she no longer touched him. Shivering, she eased into her sleeping bag and turned away, curling up on her side. The spruce boughs rustled as Bruce stretched out behind her. The air crackled with emotions held back, with dangerous words left unspoken, with the invitation neither of them was willing to utter. Together, but apart, they lay motionless while the embers of the fire faded to blackness.

Chapter 12

The noise of the engine rose from a roar to a throaty scream as the truck rounded the curve. Logs creaked against the crib of steel ribs that enclosed them, gravel flew from the deeply treaded tires and clouds of dust billowed behind the wheels like a smoky white parachute. Bruce waved his arms over his head, then jumped off the road and braced himself for the rush of air as the truck rumbled past.

Emma coughed and squinted against the dust. "He doesn't look as if he's going to stop."

"Give him a minute. Fully loaded like that it's going to take him a while to slow down." Red lights flashed on as the brakes hissed. Bruce grabbed their gear and loped along the edge of the road. "Come on."

The truck didn't manage to stop until it was halfway to the next bend. They caught up to it just as the door on the passenger side squeaked open.

"Where the hell did you two come from?" A powerful aroma of oil, sawdust and spearmint rolled outward as the driver leaned toward them. Straight black hair fell over his forehead. From beneath bushy eyebrows his dark brown eyes focused carefully on each of them in turn.

Bruce put on an awkward, harmless, unthreatening smile that Emma recognized immediately. "Man, am I glad to see you. Our van died a few miles up that trail. I'd appreciate it if you could give us a lift to a phone."

The truck driver shifted a wad of gum the size of a golf ball to his cheek, causing one corner of his drooping moustache to twitch. "Sure. Climb on up." The engine growled as he leaned back into his seat and shoved the gear lever. The truck shuddered and began to move forward. "Let's go. I'm working on bonus."

Emma quickly grasped the handle beside the door and swung herself onto the narrow step. The wheels hit a pothole, throwing her into the cab. Bruce leapt to the step behind her, tossed their belongings to the floor and steadied her with his hands on her waist. "There's only the one seat," he said, raising his voice over the increasing noise of the engine. "I'll slide in and you sit on my lap."

It was all she could do to remain upright as the truck started to pick up speed. The trees beside the road marched past. Bracing her arm against the dashboard, she waited until Bruce slammed the door shut and maneuvered himself into the seat. The wheels hit another pothole and she fell backward against his chest.

"Hang on," he said, wrapping his arm around her waist. He angled his knees to one side and positioned her securely on his lap. "Are you okay?"

She had to loop her arm around his shoulders for balance before she twisted her head to look at him. "Sure. Are you?"

His face was so close to hers she couldn't miss the trace of strain around his eyes. With each bump in the road, some part of her rubbed or brushed or bounced against some part of him. "I'll be fine," he answered tightly.

She looked away. She couldn't ignore the forced contact of their bodies, but she had to try. They both had to try.

"What were you folks doing out here?" the driver asked, his voice a near shout.

"We're on vacation." Bruce pressed her to his chest in order to angle his right hand toward the other man. "My name's Prendergast. This is the missus."

He lifted his hand from the shift knob for an instant to clasp Bruce's. "I'm Smitty."

"Thanks for picking us up."

"No problem." His mustache twitched rhythmically as he concentrated on chewing his gum. With the air rushing through the open windows, the crunching of the gravel beneath the huge tires and the roar of the engine, there was no more chance for conversation. Smitty kept his attention on the road, for which Emma was grateful. By now they were traveling fast enough for the trees to blur. Shadows lengthened and fingered across the windshield while one bumpy, dusty mile blended into the next.

They were dropped off much the same way as they were picked up. The wheels barely stopped moving long enough for Bruce to grab their gear and jump out. He held up his arms to catch Emma and swung her to the ground beside him as the truck jerked into motion once more. She shook her head in an attempt to clear the ringing in her ears, then looked around to study their surroundings. A white church spire poked above the rooftops in the distance. On the other side of the road there was a gas station with old round-topped pumps, a restaurant with a weathered soft drink sign over the door and a handful of stores. On this side she saw a bank and a post office. She had missed the sign at the edge of the small town, but this could have been Castlerock for all she cared.

"We made it," she said. "We actually made it."

"I never had any doubts."

A pickup truck rattled past. A mournful beagle sat in the back, turning its head to stare at them. Emma brushed the dust from her jeans and straightened her shirt.

"You look fine, Emma."

She glanced up at him quickly. "I'm surprised that dog didn't bark."

He didn't smile. The blond stubble on his cheeks shifted as his jaw clenched. "It would take more than two days in the bush to dull your looks."

She could say the same about him. Even more. The sun had darkened the light tan on his face, making the startling blue of his eyes more intense. The wrinkled, ripped shirt only added to his aura of rugged masculinity. She hitched the string from the sleeping bag over her shoulder and looked away. "Thank you."

"It was a statement of fact, not a compliment."

"Thank you, anyway."

"Would you like some dinner?"

"Sounds good to me."

"There's a restaurant across the road. After we eat something, we can check into the motel I noticed when we came through town."

"How are we going to pay for it?"

"I've still got my wallet."

"They might not serve us, considering what we look like."

"I've still got my badge, too."

Of course, he'd have his badge. Can't forget that badge. She pressed her lips together and fell into step beside him as they crossed the road. The exhilaration of making their way out of the bush unscathed was short-lived. Reaching this town meant more than a good meal and a hot bath, and they both knew it.

The motel was a long, low, salmon-colored building set into the remains of the woods that encroached on the outskirts of the town. A large station wagon with a baggage carrier attached to the roof was parked in front of one room, a dusty truck cab minus its trailer was in front of another. Business was slow, so even with no vehicle and questionable luggage, Bruce hadn't had any trouble obtaining a room.

Wisps of steam and the scent of the motel soap wafted around him as he paused in the bathroom doorway to rub his hair with a towel. The place had the impersonal, anonymous neatness of any number of motels in any number of small towns that he'd passed through. A television was bolted to the wall in the corner, the color scheme was a bland beige and rust, and the double bed was made up as tight as a cracker box. How many nights had he spent in his own bed this year? He couldn't remember. He never objected when the job had taken him away from home for months at a stretch. The apartment wasn't really a home, though. He had no home, not anymore.

The mattress creaked as Emma sat on the edge of the bed to comb her wet hair. Bruce tossed the towel over the shower rod and pulled on his shirt, uncomfortable with the silence. She had barely spoken during their dinner at the restaurant, but then, neither had he. Oh, they'd been hungry enough to ignore the curious stare of the waitress and polish off steaks that could have choked a lumberjack, but that wasn't why the conversation had died. The tension between them was getting worse. He didn't know why he was putting off this phone call. They'd been in town for almost two hours now. Their time together was nearing an end. He had to forget how she'd shuddered in his arms, and how she'd cried against his back....

The sex two nights ago had been understandable, but what had happened last night had been a real mistake. Why the hell had he told her about Lizzie? He didn't tell anyone. He'd closed off that memory as efficiently as he'd closed off his heart. Dredging it all up again should be reminding him of why he'd made the decisions he had, and why he wanted to be nothing other than what he was. Only it hadn't worked that way. Now that he'd unearthed that memory for Emma, he'd been remembering other things, not just the pain. He'd been remembering what it had felt like to have a woman by his side, to see that warm glow of love in someone's eyes, to know that he didn't have to face life alone.

Yet whatever memories had been stirred up, it shouldn't make any difference. It was only physical, the way Emma drew him. They'd both agreed that's all it could be. They were almost finished with each other. Once he called Xavier, he would know where they stood. By tomorrow she'd be back in Bethel Corners and he'd be wherever he was needed. Dragging this thing out would only make it worse.

Taking a deep breath, he walked to the other side of the bed and picked up the telephone.

Emma must have been waiting for this. She tossed down the comb and braced her hands on her knees. "What are you going to tell him?"

"The truth."

"Everything?"

"Everything that concerns the case."

"What are you going to say about Simon?"

He put the phone back down, keeping his hand on the receiver. "Would you rather tell them?"

"No. I couldn't. I'd feel as if I were betraying my brother."

He'd known how she'd feel. After all, he understood her. "Your loyalty to your brother is misplaced."

"No, it's not misplaced. He's the only family I have left, and I'll do everything I can to help him. I know I've probably made mistakes in the way I've tried to protect him, but my loyalty won't change. We can't help who we love."

"He's broken the law."

"He gambled and was in debt. He was doing the smuggling to pay off what he owed. He deserves leniency."

"Do you condone what he was doing?"

She angled her knee onto the bed and turned to face him. "Of course not. I might not like the law, but I know right from wrong."

"Your brother's fate isn't up to me. Or you. If he wants to straighten himself out, then that's up to him. Let it go, Emma. You've done all you could."

Her chin lifted. For a moment it seemed as if she wanted to argue further, but then she swallowed hard and averted her face. He lifted the receiver to his ear and punched in the number.

The familiar gravelly voice came on the line after six rings. Time seemed to collapse on itself. Bruce felt an instant of disorientation until he automatically slipped back into the role he was more accustomed to. As concisely as he could, he told Xavier what had happened from the moment the Cessna had lifted off for the rendezvous in the St. Lawrence. Emma's spine stiffened as he reported what he had learned about Simon, but he told everything, just as he'd said he would.

"Sounds like one hell of a mess," Xavier growled when Bruce had finished.

"That's an accurate assessment. What's been happening at your end for the past two days?"

"Another mess. McQuaig pulled up stakes."

"What?"

"Cleaned out the warehouse, got rid of the freighter, generally sank back under his rock. Something spooked him. Could have been that woman. You're sure she's on the level?"

Bruce didn't even hesitate. "Yes. I'm sure."

"And you're sure she couldn't have tipped them off?"

"Positive."

"Okay. If that's the case, McQuaig might just be playing cautious. As long as he thinks the Duprey woman is dead, he might be tempted to resume business. I'll send someone to pick you up tomorrow morning and bring both of you back to Bethel Corners. We'll firm up our plans then. Meanwhile, keep out of sight."

"Why Bethel Corners?"

"Jurisdictional politics, couldn't be helped. I'm due to meet Sheriff Haskin tomorrow."

He frowned. "I don't like Haskin."

"Who would? From what I've heard, he's a living, breathing stereotype of the small-town bully. He gives the whole profession a bad name, but we have to work with him."

"Why?"

"He ran the plates on your 'Vette, dug around a bit and found out something was going on in his territory. We had to bring him in on the investigation." Papers shuffled briefly before Xavier spoke again. "Do you think there's a chance of Simon Duprey turning state's evidence?"

"It's possible. Why?"

"It might be a useful angle. Let me fill you in on what else we've found out."

Bruce's frown had deepened when he hung up the phone a few minutes later. Emma was watching him closely, her face carefully blank. "Well?" she asked.

"Well what?"

"What have you learned about Simon?"

"He's apparently healthy, still willingly working for McQuaig."

"What's going to happen to my brother now?"

"Like I said before, that depends on him. Not you, not me."

Her fingers twined together restlessly. She was silent for several minutes. "When are your people going to move in?"

"I don't know anything for sure, but it will be soon. You need to keep out of sight a while longer, though."

"I can't play dead indefinitely." She rose from the bed and paced across the room. "I've got a business to run. And if word of my death gets out, my investors might panic."

"We'll talk it over with Xavier tomorrow. It's only been two days. Could your business run without you for a few more?"

"Only two days," she repeated, slowing her steps. "It seems longer."

He knew what she meant. So much had been compressed into the time they had spent together, it seemed hard to believe that so little time had passed. "It's for your own safety, as well as the good of my case."

"I'm not under arrest, though, am I?"

"I could cite you for obstruction of justice, but I'm hoping you'll cooperate on your own."

She paused in front of the door and fingered the chain. It rattled against its slot hollowly. "Do you still think I'd warn McQuaig if you let me go?"

"No. I don't think you would."

"Then why did you get only one room?"

Bruce inhaled sharply. She'd done it again. Her quiet question slid neatly beneath the rigid, professional armor he was struggling to maintain. It was unexpected, and dangerous. He didn't want to answer, because he didn't want to examine his motives too closely. Why? He glanced at the bed. *One* bed. They had slept side by side for two nights. They had lived together for longer than that. He hadn't even considered getting separate rooms. Why? He didn't want to get any closer to her than he already was, he knew they shouldn't repeat what had happened after the explosion, he knew she still hated him and everything he stood for.

"Bruce?"

He met her gaze, and the answer came to him. "I didn't want to be alone, Emma."

She twisted away, pressing her forehead against the door. "Don't do this."

No, he shouldn't do this. There was no point, no future. Still, he moved around the bed to stand behind her. "Do you want a separate room?"

"I should."

"That's not what I asked."

"Then what exactly are you asking?"

He lifted his hand and spread his fingers a breath away from her shoulder. What was he asking? What did he want? "Damned if I know."

The sound she made could have been a laugh, or a sob. "Damned if I know, either."

"It's late. There's nothing we can do about Simon or McQuaig until tomorrow."

"No, there isn't. Do you think we could watch the sunset?"

The sudden switch in topic startled him. "What?"

She slipped past him and moved to the window. Her hand was unsteady as she reached out to tug the curtain aside. An orange beam slanted into the room, gilding her delicate features and sparkling in her eyes. "The sunsets from my cabin are spectacular. Sometimes the colors are hushed and subtle, as if the day is surrendering gracefully. Sometimes the rays stream from behind the clouds like paths to heaven. On warm nights I go down to the edge of the lake and watch it from my dock. In the winter it comes early. The blue of the sky is cold then, but the snow on the lake seems to capture the light and glow long into the night. I love sunsets."

He followed her. The view from the window showed the parking lot and the other side of the road, nothing but an ordinary scene in a small town. Yet the sky was alive with streaks of color. He wouldn't have noticed it on his own. "You're a constant wonder to me, Emma."

"Don't you ever take the time to watch a sunset?"

"Not lately. With my job..." He paused, thinking over the excuse he was about to make. It no longer seemed valid. His job had been ruling his actions for years. Except for the past week. "The sunrise we watched together was beautiful. I'll never forget it."

Her hand tightened to a fist, bunching the fabric of the curtain into fat folds. "I'm twenty-eight years old, and I've watched too many sunsets by myself. I don't want to be alone tonight, Bruce."

He lowered his head until his cheek touched her hair. She smelled of the same shampoo he had used, as well as sunshine and warm, honest woman. Honest wasn't a word that he would have thought to associate with Emma, but there had never been any doubt about the physical side of their relationship. "You won't be."

"You make it sound so simple. But it's not. How can I want to be with you when you and your people could take away my brother's freedom? How could I live with my-self—''

"Shh." He slipped his arms around her waist and crossed them beneath her breasts. "Let's call another truce. Just for tonight, it's only you and me. Whatever you want to do. Or not do."

They stood together until the sun sank behind the trees and the light from the sign at the entrance to the motel washed out the last traces of dusk. Emma felt his breath stir her hair and his warmth chase away the shadows. She released the curtain and watched the folds fall back into place. *Whatever you want to do.* He still had no idea, did he? He didn't know about the yearning she felt, or the hopelessness. He didn't know that she wanted more than a temporary truce, or just one night.

"Emma?" His deep voice was like a caress, sweeping aside her caution. He stepped closer, pressing himself full length against her. Tightening his arms, he rocked gently from side to side, swaying their bodies to a rhythm that needed no music.

She closed her eyes and let her head fall back against his shoulder. "I'm tired of fighting, Bruce."

"Then stop fighting." He brushed a kiss along the edge of her jaw, trailing his lips toward her ear. "I can't keep away from you. I've tried, God knows, I've tried. I've lost count of the number of times we've both gone over the reasons that we shouldn't do this again, but the pull I feel toward you keeps getting stronger."

"I feel it, too. I've always felt it."

"You're a woman of deep passions. I've seen your anger. And your desire. I can't forget either one."

Anger and desire. That's all he'd seen, all he wanted to see. She understood why, but that didn't make this any easier. No, understanding him only made it worse.

He shifted his grip and his arm nudged the underside of her left breast. He tensed, flexing his muscle, and her breast lifted. "I can't forget what you looked like in the moonlight," he said. "Your skin glowed like silver satin.

There were droplets of lake water at the base of your throat. I licked them off. They tasted like sunshine, warm and full of life, like you.''

Arousal awakened inside her, curling and stretching, a mindless creature driven by nothing but animal instinct. She felt herself tingle and swell. She turned in his embrace and lifted her hands to his face, cradling his bristly cheeks in her palms.

He tilted his head, capturing her thumb between his teeth. He nibbled gently, then ran the tip of his tongue to the inside of her wrist. ''You still taste good.''

She pressed her face to his neck. ''You smell good. That's something that didn't change, no matter who you were pretending to be. Your scent stayed the same.''

''It was frustrating to be Prendergast and not to be able to touch you, or to let you touch me.'' He took her hands in his and brought them to his chest. ''Do you remember how you stroked that arrow when we met? I watched your fingers glide along that shaft and I pictured them on me.''

''When you shook my hand that day, I felt as if I'd touched lightning,'' she replied.

''I thought of you when I shaved off my beard. I was afraid you'd never want to touch me again once you learned who I was.''

''When you strutted into that warehouse as Primeau, I thought I was going insane.'' She parted his shirt and raked her nails through the crisp, damp curls. ''I couldn't figure out why that lowlife character would make my palms sweat.''

''You look like royalty, whether you're wearing hiking boots or a designer dress. *You* make *my* palms sweat. You make me ache.''

''Even when we were fighting, I couldn't help wanting you. The way I react to you...'' She rubbed her nose against his collar. ''It's so primitive. Sometimes I don't believe it myself.''

''Take it off.''

''What?''

"My shirt." He dropped his arms to his sides and waited while she tugged the sleeves down. The soft flannel slid off his shoulders, bunching at his waist until she freed his hands. "I want you to see me as I really am."

Her pulse raced with a sudden burst of power. She clutched the cloth in her fingers for an instant before she let it drop to the floor. When she raised her gaze her vision was filled with a bare expanse of gleaming skin stretched taut over lean muscle. He was as magnificent as he'd appeared last night in the firelight, but now it was better. She was free to touch him.

"You're beautiful," she said, splaying her hand on the subtle ridges above his navel.

He stepped back. "Wait."

"What's wrong?"

His hand went to the pocket of his jeans. Holding her gaze, he withdrew a flat leather folder and tossed it to the floor on top of his shirt. "Tonight it's just me." He unfastened the buckle of his belt. Leather slid through denim loops with a soft hiss. He opened the zipper of his jeans and pulled them off, then kicked them aside and stood before her completely naked. "Just me."

A quiver shook her frame. Her lips parted. He had stripped away his clothes to strip away his personas, but he was all of them. He was sensitive and sexy, restrained and raw, vulnerable and virile and enough man to make her weep.

He smiled and held out his hand.

Emma knew that the image of him at that moment would be seared into her memory forever. Her breath hitched unevenly as she stepped over his clothes and his badge. He didn't wait any longer. Scooping her up in his arms, he whirled around and strode to the bed. She hung on to his neck as he leaned over to pull back the covers. Then the springs creaked and his weight settled over her, pushing her into the mattress.

"I wanted to go slow this time," he said, his voice rough. He rose to his knees, straddling her legs, and unfastened the buttons of her shirt with shaking fingers. Leaning over, he pressed an openmouthed kiss on her breast. "I don't know if I can."

Sensations whirled through her at his touch. She arched her back, blood surging and tightening. "I don't know if I want you to go slow."

His hands dropped to the zipper of her jeans. He pulled off the rest of her clothes and threw them over his shoulder. They landed with a soft thump on top of his. "You're incredible." He slid lower, his lips grazing her belly. "You even taste like sunshine down here."

There was no room for shyness, or shame. Emma reveled in what he was doing to her, gloried in it. She stretched her arms over her head and flattened her palms against the headboard, her entire body thrumming to his kiss. At her response he made a low sound of satisfaction and grasped her hips, lifting her closer, taking her higher. She flung her hand over her face, biting down on her knuckles to stifle her moans. Bruce moved on top of her, nudging her hand aside so he could cover her lips with his, taking her moans into his mouth.

Emma could lie still no longer. She pushed at his shoulder until he rolled over, then used her lips and her tongue and her teeth to explore his body as thoroughly, as possessively, as he'd explored hers. He'd wanted her to see him as he really was, and she did. She had seen past his appearance long ago. When she curled her fingers around his bicep she saw the strength within, his determination and tenacity. Her lips grazed the pulse that hammered at the base of his throat and she saw his will to survive. Her thigh rubbed the hot, hard, throbbingly masculine length of him and she saw the passion that needed no words to describe. Bracing her hands on his chest, she raised her head. She looked at the sun-streaked blond hair that curled boyishly over his ears, at the stubborn chin, the sensual mouth, the laugh lines at the corners of his incredibly brilliant blue eyes and she saw more than his handsome face.

She saw the man she loved.

"Emma?"

Her lungs heaved. She had forgotten to breathe. "Oh, Bruce," she whispered.

His beautiful, sensual mouth stretched into a smile. He slid lower on the bed, grasped her shoulders, and pulled her downward until her nipple brushed his lips.

With a sob, Emma rolled onto her back. No. She couldn't love him. Oh, no.

"Was that the one I bit?" He covered her breast with his palm. "I'm sorry. I didn't realize—"

"No, I'm fine." She didn't want to think. She didn't want to love him. Not love. Not him.

"What do you want?" he murmured, his thumb toying with her nipple. "Tell me. We'll do whatever you want."

I want to make love, she thought recklessly. Real, honest, love. You and me, Bruce and Emma, one soul to another.

The desire she felt deepened, and blossomed. She grasped his wrist and pulled his hand to her mouth. She kissed his thumb, his palm, his long, strong fingers. A sob rose to her throat, along with the knowledge she couldn't deny. She started over again, touching him, tasting him, because now it was different. This was why she saw him as he really was.

The truth couldn't hide when she looked with her heart.

They rolled over, limbs twining together. She wanted all of him, everything, his passion, his pain. Her fingertips glided over sweat-slicked skin, rubbing across the crisp hair, memorizing his contours and textures by touch. She explored hollows and angles, hard and soft, until he quivered beneath her caress. And when her hand brushed the tender, puckered skin low on the side of his back, she came to her knees on the bed beside him, leaned over, and pressed her lips to the scar.

He trembled. With a wordless growl he flipped her onto her back and knelt between her thighs.

She didn't speak aloud, but the words were there, in her arms as she pulled him close, in her eyes as she looked

helplessly into his. She could feel the wave of emotion
surge over her out of control, her need suddenly unbear-
able.

Bruce gathered her against him, tilting his face so that
their mouths fitted together as perfectly as their bodies.
His tongue plunged past her lips, taking up the rhythm of
their hips as she met every thrust. She clung to him, her
senses spinning.

And they flew.

They soared.

Even before she opened her eyes, Emma knew that
Bruce wasn't beside her. She stretched out her hand, letting her fingers absorb the traces of his warmth that lin-
gered on the sheet. How could she feel so replete and yet
so empty? How could she have experienced such fierce joy
and yet feel this overwhelming sadness? Why did there always have to be so many other emotions tangled up with
love?

A shadow moved near the window and she turned her
head. Bruce was standing in front of the curtains, his head
bent, his shoulders held rigid. Against the predawn gray-
ness his naked form was highlighted as if etched by a mas-
ter's hand.

For a moment she indulged herself, looking her fill.
Beautiful wasn't a word usually used to describe a man,
but she could think of nothing else that came close to ex-
pressing the physical perfection of his leanly muscled body.
Simply looking at him started the familiar throbbing deep
inside, the primal need that he'd satisfied again and again
during the stolen hours of the night.

He shifted, and she saw that he held something in his
hand, something flat and dark and rectangular. She knew
what it was. It was the black folder that he'd taken from
his pocket and thrown to the floor before he'd felt free to
carry her to the bed. It was his badge, and now he'd picked
it up. He hadn't picked up his clothes, but he'd picked up
his badge. Maybe he'd never really put it down. Maybe he

couldn't. His job was his defense against the pain of loving again. His sense of duty was as necessary to him as her own loyalty to her brother. It would always be there between them. Yet even if her brother wasn't involved, even if Bruce hadn't lied to her and used her, it still wouldn't make any difference. He still wouldn't love her. He wouldn't let himself love her.

His image blurred. She had kissed the scar that marred his back, but the scar on his heart was probably too deep to heal. How many times had he told her that he didn't want to care about anyone, didn't want to get close, didn't want to have a life outside the black-and-white world of the law? He'd wanted her body, her passion, not her love; he'd asked for one night, not a lifetime. In a matter of hours, they would resume the roles fate had given them. In a matter of minutes their truce would be at an end.

Not yet, she cried silently, blinking back the tears. *Just once more, one last time, let's forget who we are. We'll smile, we'll make love...*

Bruce lifted his head and slowly turned around. In the dim half light his eyes gleamed. His hands were empty as he held his arms out to her.

Swallowing a sob, Emma slipped from the bed and walked into his embrace.

No words were spoken. His kiss was tender, almost gentle, his touch reverent as he smoothed his hands over her curves, awakening the flesh that glowed for him. This time they did go slow. The raw edge of their need had been eased, but the desire was somehow stronger.

He led her back to the bed and knelt in the center of the mattress with her, thigh to thigh, her breasts tight against his chest. Cradling her face in his palms, he tilted his head and kissed her again, his breath melding with hers.

She soaked up his taste, his scent, his texture. When she swayed, he wrapped his arm around her waist and lay back, draping her over him. They slid together naturally, perfectly, their bodies moving with unhurried care, prolonging the moment even as they whirled toward the end.

Not yet, not yet. But his arms tightened, crushing her against him as he surged inside her.

Emma hovered on the brink, her skin tingling, every nerve humming for completion, as she hopelessly tried to hold back the dawn. Then Bruce lifted his head and licked a tear from her cheek, and she shattered.

Afterward, Emma curled onto her side, the tremors that shook her no longer from passion. Bruce kissed the nape of her neck. He didn't ask any questions, he didn't make any empty declarations or false promises. He pulled the sheet over them, looped his arm around her waist and snuggled her firmly into the curve of his body. The light from the window strengthened and he held her, simply held her. While she cried.

Chapter 13

There was a distinctive aroma common to every police station Emma had visited. It was a unique mixture of ink, coffee, sweeping compound and sweat. The small brick building that served as the Bethel Corners sheriff's office was no exception. The moment Emma had stepped through the back entrance, she'd felt suffocated by that smell. It had struck her like the echo of an unwelcome memory, stirring up glimpses of lawyers and judges and prison visiting rooms.

Here in Haskin's private office, with the venetian blinds levered shut and the door securely closed, the atmosphere was rife with it. Emma breathed shallowly and curled her fingers around the hard wooden seat of her chair.

A high scale map of the Bangor area was pinned to the cork bulletin board beside Haskin's desk. Bruce, O'Hara and Xavier Jones were gathered in front of it, talking quietly among themselves. Bruce had donned his policeman identity even before he'd put on his clothes this morning. Emma tried not to look at him, and he'd been doing his best to avoid her gaze. They'd barely spoken to each other, but then, what was there left to say that hadn't already been said?

Her fingers tightened as she focused on O'Hara, the man who had driven them here. At first glance he looked like a rumpled construction worker on his day off, but once she'd seen past the easy grin and the relaxed posture, she recognized the detached intellect behind his light green eyes and the hint of zeal in his movements that marked him as surely as a uniform.

There was no mistaking the profession of the third man in the group, though. In his dark blue suit, with his graying hair clipped into a military-crisp haircut, Xavier Jones radiated the steady energy of someone who had spent most of his life in a position of authority. No smile touched his face, no weakness eased the stiff line of his back. He was the epitome of the dedicated career cop. And in another twenty years, Bruce would probably look exactly like him.

Emma set her jaw and moved her gaze to the fourth man in the room. Sheriff Haskin sat with his feet crossed on his desk, his eyes narrowed. When he had come to the cabin to hassle her three days ago, he hadn't been a player in this undercover scheme. From the time this meeting had started, it was obvious that he was now highly annoyed over joining the game late. His head swung toward the corner where she was sitting and his scowl deepened. "Should she be here?" he asked loudly.

Bruce turned around and fixed the sheriff with a cold stare. "Miss Cassidy is cooperating with this investigation and needs to remain here until it is concluded."

Haskin snorted. "Cassidy? Her name's Duprey, and she's as crooked as her old man and her brother. She's been lying to me for years."

Emma lifted her chin and met his scowl with one of her own. "My past is my own business. And why are you complaining? I've always given you precisely as much respect as you deserve."

"I'm going to see that sleazy brother of yours behind bars, lady, so don't try any of your smart-mouthed remarks with me."

She pointed suddenly to the front of his shirt. "What's that on your uniform, Sheriff?"

He blinked and automatically glanced down. His chin folded in on itself like a crumpled sock.

"My, my. Looks like strawberry jelly to me," she continued. "Why don't you go back to the Stardust Café and have another doughnut? That's the type of police work you're most familiar with, isn't it?"

His feet hit the floor with a thump as he straightened up. "Listen to me, you lying b—"

"Sheriff, please!" Xavier interrupted firmly. His arm shot out, blocking Bruce when he made a move toward Haskin. "Prentice, settle down. Let's try to keep our attention on the case, all right? Miss Duprey?"

She waited until the sheriff had subsided behind his desk before she crossed her legs and folded her hands demurely in her lap. She realized that the effect was probably ruined by her grimy jeans and wrinkled shirt. "Yes, Mr. Jones?"

"Tell us again exactly what you saw and heard when you were at McQuaig's warehouse."

With exaggerated care she recited every detail she could remember. When she was done, she asked a question of her own. "Who's going to replace my Cessna?"

Xavier lifted an eyebrow. "Don't you have insurance?"

"By some oversight I neglected to get a policy that covered dynamite. Since the plane was lost as a direct result of a police investigation, you owe me compensation."

"I'll send you a form to fill out."

She nodded once. "Fine. Now, about my brother," she began.

Xavier glanced at Bruce. "Didn't you explain it to her?"

"Explain what?" she asked.

"Yes, I told her that our original deal was off," Bruce said, not meeting her eyes.

She abandoned her pose of calm and leaned forward. "What else is going on?"

"Perhaps in this instance, Sheriff Haskin might have a point," Xavier said, exchanging a silent look with the other men. "There's no need for Miss Duprey to know more than necessary."

O'Hara nodded. "There's enough of a risk already—"

"Risk? I thought everything was under control, that all you had to do was catch McQuaig with the drugs before you tighten the net around him. It was supposed to be neat and simple." She looked at Bruce. "You told me once my plane blew up McQuaig would have a false sense of confidence and it would be business as usual."

Bruce raked his hands through his hair distractedly, the first chink he'd allowed in his composure since they'd arrived here. "The plans have changed, Emma."

She rose to her feet and stepped around Haskin's desk in order to get closer to the bulletin board. There was a red pin stuck into the map. "What's this?"

Xavier moved in front of her smoothly, blocking her view. "It doesn't concern you, Miss Duprey."

"The hell it doesn't. What happened?"

"You'll hear all about it at your brother's trial," Haskin said. "If the little creep makes it that far."

The sheriff's mocking tone made a hard knot form in her chest. She looked past Xavier to Bruce. "What does he mean?"

He hesitated for a tense minute. Then he sighed and rubbed his jaw. "McQuaig changed his supply route after he sabotaged your plane. At first we thought that he'd gone to ground, but he's too greedy for that. Last night the coast guard managed to observe an exchange between a fishing boat and a small launch in Frenchman Bay. The launch—"

"Prentice," Xavier said tersely. "She doesn't need to know."

"Yes, she does," he said firmly. "Emma has every right to know, considering what she's gone through."

"Are you going to take responsibility for the consequences? She's only a civilian, a hostile witness at best."

"Yes, I'll take full responsibility." Bruce brushed past Xavier and grasped Emma's elbow, steering her toward the door. "Is there another room where I can speak privately with Miss Cassidy, Sheriff?"

Haskin leaned back in his chair, lacing his hands over the jelly stain on his stomach. "We don't have any guests downstairs today. Help yourself to one of the cells."

Pausing only long enough to mutter something to O'Hara, Bruce ushered Emma past the deputy's desk toward the hall that ran along the rear of the building. They went through a metal door, then down a set of brightly lit stairs to a basement corridor, their footsteps loud on the linoleum. They came to a large room painted a ludicrously cheerful yellow. An old wooden table with a swivel chair and a telephone was on one side, but as soon as Emma saw the two barred cubicles, she dug in her heels. "Now wait a minute."

Undeterred, Bruce tightened his grip on her arm and pulled her into the cell on the left. He unrolled the thin mattress with one hand and sat on the bunk, tugging her down beside him. "I have to make this quick, so if you want any answers, don't waste time arguing, okay? I'm going out on a limb for you here. Xavier's right, you don't need to know what we're planning, but I realize how much you care about Simon and I want you to be prepared for what might happen."

She jerked away from his grasp and strode across the floor, turning around when she reached the bars that formed the side wall. "All right. Tell me."

"Don't you want to sit down?"

She looked at his tousled hair, the weary curve of his broad shoulders, the lines of strain around his mouth, and she wanted nothing more than to sit beside him and take him in her arms. Or maybe crawl into his lap. But they had left that behind along with the rumpled sheets of the motel bed. "I'll be able to concentrate better if I'm not touching you."

"That's putting it bluntly."

"There's never been anything subtle about what's between us, has there?"

He leaned back, letting his head bump against the cement block wall behind him. "Emma, I didn't want it to end this way."

"What does it matter? We both knew it had to end," she said quickly, struggling to maintain control over the emotions that were seething inside. She dug her nails into her palms and breathed deeply, but all she gained from that was another whiff of police station smell. She pressed her back against the cold bars. "Please, don't drag this out. Just tell me about my brother."

The sympathy she saw in his eyes almost broke her, but then he rubbed a hand over his face and began to speak. "There's no question any more about the degree of Simon's involvement. He's in deep. He was on that boat last night, and he helped transfer the cargo to his Jeep. He's got a red Wagoneer, doesn't he?" At her nod he continued. "McQuaig's operating out of a place he's got close to one of the ski areas near Bangor. The feds already have it under surveillance. We're coordinating a raid tonight before McQuaig has a chance to distribute the cocaine to his dealers or destroy any evidence. It won't have the finesse of an undercover sting, but at this point we're prepared to use force. As long as we have the element of surprise, the risk will be—"

"A raid?" she said, her voice hoarse. "You mean dozens of cops driving in with guns blazing?"

"We hope it won't come to that, but we don't want to wait any longer. It's not only drug smuggling anymore, it's attempted murder. Yours."

"But we weren't hurt when the Cessna blew up. Couldn't you do it some other way? Some safer way? There's too much risk of someone getting shot."

"As long as Simon doesn't resist, he won't get hurt."

With a shock she realized that her first thoughts hadn't been of her brother's safety but of Bruce's. "He doesn't even know how to use a gun. He doesn't want to be with those people. Couldn't we warn him to stay out of the way?"

"No, Emma."

"But—"

"No!" He rolled forward and got to his feet. "There's no room for discussion on this. The plans are already set. We move at 10:00 tonight."

It was going too fast. From the time she had first laid eyes on this man, she had been swept along on a flood surge of events beyond her control. Her fingers curled around the hard steel of the bars behind her as if the cold solidity would anchor her. "I feel so helpless. How can I stand by and do nothing?"

"That's exactly what you have to do. You'll stay here, out of sight, until the operation is finished." He moved to stand in front of her and grasped her shoulders. "I've endangered you once. I was so caught up in the job I was doing, I almost got you killed. I won't let that happen again."

"You didn't know about the bomb, or the double cross. You thought I was guilty, anyway."

"It shouldn't have made any difference whether you were guilty or not." His grip tightened. In the stark light from the caged bulb overhead, his face was all harsh planes and angles. "Emma, I understand your loyalty to your brother."

Loyalty? How could she resolve her loyalty to Simon with the love she felt for Bruce? "We don't have any choice about the people we love," she said, her voice breaking. "It can't be turned on or off."

"And I realize that you'll do everything in your power to help him."

"He's all I have left." Her eyes filled. "It hurts too much to lose someone you love, but you know that, don't you?"

"Yes, I know. The pain is a dull ache behind your heart. You learn to live with it, but it never goes away." He brought her against his chest, enfolding her in a sudden embrace that crushed the breath from her lungs. "All along, you've asked me not to apologize, but I have to say it, Emma. I'm sorry. God, I'm sorry."

There was nothing dull about the pain she was feeling now. It was a wrenching, tearing misery. "I'm sorry, too."

"What we shared was precious. I'll never forget it. I'll never forget you." He lifted his hand and tangled his fingers in her hair, pressing his cheek to her head.

Sliding her arms around his waist, she clutched him as if she had the power to make him stay. "You're saying goodbye."

"Yes. I'm sorry."

The door at the top of the stairs opened and closed with a heavy clang. Footsteps gritted closer.

Bruce released her slowly, pulling back to look into her face. "Please, try to forgive me, Emma."

Her fingers cramped when she tried to let go of him. "There's nothing to forgive," she whispered.

He reached behind him and caught her wrists, then joined their hands together and brought her fingers to his lips. "Oh, yes. There's plenty to forgive. But I have to do my job."

"I know you do. I know *why* you do."

O'Hara shuffled to a stop outside the cell and cleared his throat. "Xavier's already left, Bruce. Are you ready to go?"

He nodded once, his gaze never wavering from hers. "Like I said, Emma, I realize that you'll do everything you can to help Simon. I don't blame you for it, I understand it."

The sympathy was too much to bear. She pulled her hands from his and crossed her arms tightly, as if she could hold in her emotions by physical force. She glanced briefly at O'Hara, who was plainly waiting for them to finish. "Thank you for telling me what's going to happen."

"You deserved that much." Bruce backed away from her, pausing in the open cell door. "Forgive me, Emma." Clenching his hands at his sides, he turned to the other man. "Okay, go ahead."

O'Hara took a ring of keys from his pocket, stepped around Bruce and slammed the door of the cell shut. Before the echoes had faded, he inserted a key into the hole on the flat metal plate and clicked the lock.

Emma's breath whooshed out as if someone had punched her in the stomach. "What..."

"Sorry, Miss Duprey, uh, Cassidy," O'Hara said. He backed away and put the keys on the table on the other side of the basement. "I had my orders."

She leapt at the door, but of course it was too late. She grabbed the bars and jerked with all her strength. Nothing moved. "Let me out!"

O'Hara shrugged and looked at Bruce. "We'd better go."

"You can't do this to me!" She twisted sideways and rammed her shoulder against the steel. "Open the door!"

Bruce raked his hand through his hair and rubbed the back of his neck. "This is for your own good. I said I was sorry."

"I didn't know what you meant. I thought you were apologizing about..." She swallowed hard. "How can you do this? You tricked me."

"That wasn't my intention. I want to keep you safe. You were willing to take crazy risks to fly those drugs for your brother's sake. I couldn't take the chance that you'd do something reckless now."

She kicked the bars. Her leather boot provided scant cushioning against the force she applied. "I cooperated with you. And you said I wasn't under arrest." She kicked again, sending sharp pain spearing up her leg. "I should have known better than to trust a cop."

"You're in protective custody. It's only temporary. Haskin will release you the minute our operation is over."

"You don't trust me, do you? That's what this is all about. Even after everything we've gone through, and what we did last night, you still don't—"

"Too many lives are at stake, Emma. If even a hint of this raid gets out, things could turn ugly real fast. My feelings don't count. I have to go by the book on this."

"Do you think I'm going to betray you? Is that it? Do you think I'm so shallow that I'd share my body with someone and then go behind their back to—"

"This is my job, dammit. You said you understood."

O'Hara started off for the stairs. "I'll wait in the alley for you, Bruce. Sounds as if you've got some personal business to settle."

Bruce glared at him. "Forget you heard that."

"I didn't need to hear it to figure it out. There's been a high-voltage field crackling in the air since I picked you two up this morning. Take a minute to get your head straight. I don't want your mind wandering when you're supposed to be watching my back."

Swearing under his breath, Bruce waited until the door at the top of the stairs clanged shut behind O'Hara. "It's for your own good," he repeated, frustration edging his words.

"Right. Fine. Hide behind your badge, Bruce." She slapped the bars and stepped back from the locked door. "You're so damn worried about caring for someone again, you had to find some way to push me away, didn't you? No trust, no emotional attachment, no pain."

"I do care for you, Emma. What we had together—"

"Is over. Over." She sniffed hard and waved her arm at the bars between them. "Take a good look. Opposite sides, Bruce. How much clearer could you make it? You're not doing this for my safety, you're doing it for yours. Well, you didn't need to. I knew the score. You locked your heart away five years ago when your wife died."

He flinched as if she had struck him. "I have to go."

"So go."

Without a word, he walked to the stairs.

"Get another one of them, that's what you're doing, right? Put every bad guy in the world away, one by one."

He placed his foot on the bottom step.

"It won't bring her back, Bruce."

He whirled around and strode to the front of the cell. "Devoting your life to coddling your brother won't bring back your parents. And it's easy to blame the law for everything that went wrong, but your life wasn't so great to begin with, was it?"

"If my father hadn't been arrested—"

"I've had it up to here with that story." He sliced his hand roughly against his forehead. "Things happen. Plans change. Circumstances aren't always in our control. If you're strong enough, you survive. That's what you did. That's what I did. But now you hide behind your hate so you won't have to take another chance with life."

"I have good reasons to hate the law."

"Do you? Or are you using it?"

"What's that supposed to mean?"

"You're afraid. You act tough, but underneath you're so scared of opening yourself up to more pain you channel all your feelings into this misguided devotion to your brother and your useless grudge."

"You don't know—"

"But I *do* know. We've both built our lives around lies of one kind or another. For our own reasons, we've lied to each other and to everyone else. But when you can't face the truth about yourself, that's the true lie, the really dangerous one."

How much more of this could they hurl at each other, how much more could she take? She moved back from the bars as each one of his words struck home.

"Before you judge me, Emma, take a good look at yourself."

She retreated until her shoulders nudged the cement wall. Fingers shaking, she raised her hands and covered her face.

His stride was swift and angry as he moved away. He sprinted up the stairs and slammed the door behind him.

In the long silence that followed, she could hear nothing but the pounding of her pulse in her ears. When she finally gained the strength to look in front of her, she was alone.

"Bruce." The sound of his name bounced off the bare walls in a hopeless refrain. He was gone. She had told him to go. She hadn't even told him goodbye. "Bruce, don't leave like this." She went to the door and pressed her face to the bars, her anger dissolving in her tears. "I don't hate you," she whispered. "I love you."

The declaration sounded hollow, because no one was there to hear it. He didn't know. The way things were turning out, he probably never would.

The afternoon dragged into evening. A young deputy brought Emma a plate of food from the Stardust Café, but she couldn't bring herself to take a single bite. She sat on the edge of the bunk, the plate on her lap, the fork forgotten in her fingers.

"Is something wrong, ma'am?"

She pushed her hair behind her ears and glanced up. The deputy was sitting on the edge of the desk across the room. He was vaguely familiar, like everyone who lived in Bethel Corners. Red-haired, with skin freckled like whole wheat bread dough, his earnest face was creased with concern. She had heard Haskin tell him that she was being held until her brother could pay her speeding tickets. Although the deputy looked sympathetic, so far he had ignored her demands for release. Emma looked down at her plate and jabbed at a lump of mashed potatoes. "I don't feel like eating. What time is it?"

"Around 8:00. Is there anything you need?"

Her freedom, she thought immediately, but she didn't bother saying it. "No."

"Okay. I'll be back to get your plate in half an hour or so. I've got some paperwork to do upstairs, but I'll leave the door at the top of the stairs open, so just yell if you need anything."

She nodded, poking at a piece of chicken. "Thank you."

"No problem," he said easily as he moved away.

Emma set her plate aside and leaned back against the wall. She wasn't good at waiting, she never had been. Bruce had mentioned they would raid McQuaig's place after 10:00 tonight, so it would happen soon. It was hard to accept that there was nothing more she could do for her brother, but maybe it was high time to let him pull himself out of the hole he had dug. And maybe it also was time to stop blaming all her problems on the law.

Wearily, she rubbed her eyes. Bruce had been right. She was afraid of taking another chance with life, terrified by all these tangled emotions that had been let loose. She'd been hiding behind her hate the same way Bruce had been hiding behind his badge. She had been lying to herself because she hadn't wanted to risk loving someone, and she was as much to blame as he was for the emptiness of the future she faced.

Last night she should have told him how she felt. She should have admitted it to herself long before that. And she should have gone to the police in the first place and forced Simon to turn himself in, but instead she had let her old grudge, the old reflexive antagonism, rule her actions.

And now her brother was still in danger. Worse than that, so was Bruce. She should have ignored the threats McQuaig's man Harvey had made on the phone, but how was she to know it was a bluff? Just thinking about that deep, tomblike voice made her shiver. The memory of it was so vivid, for a moment she imagined that she actually was hearing it.

The hair on her arms lifted and she held her breath. It wasn't her imagination. She *was* hearing it.

Quietly she eased off the bunk and tiptoed to the front of her cell. A cool draft blew from the direction of the staircase, carrying with it fragments of a hushed conversation. Emma remembered passing the rear entrance to the police station when Bruce had brought her down here. That must be where the draft was coming from. Someone must be standing at that door, talking to whoever was in the alley outside. But that voice . . .

She turned her head to press her ear to a space between the bars. The words were difficult to make out because the exchange was harsh and rapid. She tried to tell herself that it couldn't possibly be Harvey. It must be her nerves. What business would someone like that have at a police station? She was about to move away when a single phrase came through with sudden clarity.

"They're planning a raid tonight."

She pressed back against the bars so fast she scraped the side of her forehead. Squinting against the sharp pain, she held her breath and listened.

"We'll have to move up the timetable. You should have gotten word to us sooner."

There was no mistake. That was the voice she remembered clearly from the phone and the warehouse. He really was here. But who was the other man?

"Not my fault. I was tied up with this damn task force all day, and the number you gave me has been disconnected."

"Yeah. We had to change location."

"Have you got my envelope?"

"Don't bother counting it, it's all there." The draft strengthened, swirling across the floor. "You'd better come with me and we'll set up a welcoming committee for them. It'll be a regular turkey shoot."

"Hey, killing wasn't part of our deal."

"It is now. If we go down, you go down, Haskin."

At the sound of the name, Emma jerked. Her knuckles clunked dully against the metal.

For a moment there was silence. Then she heard Harvey's voice again. "Where are your deputies?"

"Don't worry, we're alone. Thibault is out on a call and I gave enough paperwork to Duff to keep him busy all night."

"Anyone down there?"

Another silence. Then Emma heard the scrape of a shoe at the top of the stairs. She pivoted quickly and dived for the cot. Heedless of the plate of food, she curled up on the mattress and faced the wall. Heavy footsteps approached across the floor and stopped just outside the cell. She forced herself to remain motionless and breathe evenly. Her flesh crawled as she felt his gaze move over her.

After what seemed like an hour but what only could have been a minute, the footsteps crossed back to the stairs. Emma was about to move but caught herself just in time. She continued to feign deep sleep, the rhythm of her breathing never changing. Another hour-long minute passed before Haskin finally climbed the stairs. There was the sound of a door opening and closing, then nothing.

Emma curled her fingers into her palms and stayed where she was, counting off another two minutes, but he really was gone this time. Warily, she lifted her head and looked behind her. The basement was empty. She rolled over and came to her feet in an instant, muttering a short oath.

Haskin. A crooked cop. No wonder Simon had panicked at the idea of going to the police. Was that why Haskin had always been asking about Simon? Was he keeping an eye on him for McQuaig's group? He had been out to the cabin the day before the Cessna had blown up. What else was he doing for McQuaig?

She ground her teeth together so hard her jaw ached. The question wasn't what Haskin had been doing, it was what he was about to do.

"Oh, my God," she said, as the full implication of what she had heard finally hit her.

Haskin had warned them. That meant Simon would be able to get away after all.

But for how long? Wouldn't it be better if he was forced to face up to his actions now, before he only got in deeper? Maybe the prospect of being arrested was less dangerous than continuing the involvement with the drug smuggling.

But the raid was no longer a surprise. What kind of welcoming committee was Harvey going to set up for the police?

What would be the price of her brother's freedom?

Lives are at stake. If only a hint of this gets out, things could turn ugly...

Suddenly all the tangled emotions, all the conflicting loyalties didn't mean a thing. There were no sides to choose, because her heart had already chosen.

She leapt to the door. "Hey," she yelled. "Hey!"

There was no response.

She kicked the bars until the steel rang. When no one came to investigate the noise, she took her discarded plate from the mattress, dumped the food on the floor, and started clanging the plate against the bars. In the enclosed space the din was deafening, but Emma persisted until she saw the red-haired deputy descend the stairs.

"What's all that for?" he demanded the moment she lowered the plate. "What's the matter with you?"

"Please, you have to help. Call off the raid."

"What raid? I don't know what you're talking about."

"The raid on McQuaig's estate. Sheriff Haskin warned them. You have to get word to Bruce Prentice. He's working with Xavier Jones."

"Ma'am, I've never heard of either of those characters."

"They were here this morning with another man. They're working a special undercover assignment to stop a ring of people who are smuggling cocaine into the country...." She paused, seeing his disbelief in his raised eyebrows and narrowed eyes. "I know it sounds crazy, but it's true. Please, you have to warn them they're being set up."

"Cocaine smuggling? In Bethel Corners?" He laughed. "That's crazy, all right. Those guys were no cops, they were from the county roads department. The sheriff told me that himself."

"He didn't know who they were until yesterday. He's been working for the drug smugglers. He's setting up an ambush."

"Ma'am, if this is supposed to be a joke, it's not very funny. I don't know what you think you'll get out of it, but—"

"I'm not lying!" She might have laughed, if the situation hadn't been so desperate. One of the few times she was being honest with someone in uniform, and he wouldn't believe her. Clenching her fists against a wave of helplessness, she whirled around. Her gaze fell on her uneaten dinner. The chicken gravy had spread across the floor in a splatter of lumpy blotches. Mashed potatoes were smeared on the toe of her boot and partway up her calf from where she had been lying on the plate. She had been standing in front of the mess, so the deputy wouldn't have seen it yet.

"Now, I think it would be best if you settle down and stop making up stories about Sheriff Haskin. He doesn't seem to be too pleased with you as it is."

Swiftly she wrapped her arms around her waist and doubled over. Groaning, she staggered closer to the spilled food.

"What's wrong now?"

"I don't feel well. I think...I'm going...to be...sick."

"Uh, ma'am?"

"Help me, please, I don't know if I can..." She positioned herself strategically and collapsed within easy reach of her dinner plate, then drew her knees to her chest and moaned loudly.

But not loudly enough to drown out the sound of the key in the lock.

Chapter 14

Bruce sipped a mouthful of lukewarm, tasteless coffee and tried to quell the uneasiness that tightened his gut. The interior of the panel truck was crammed with only a small portion of the team that Xavier had been putting together over the past week. Apart from O'Hara and himself, there were DEA people, two representatives from the Bangor Police, a coast guard official and some perfumed and high-heeled advisor from the justice department. What had begun as a fishing trip based on a hunch had snowballed into a major narcotics bust. Bruce didn't like it. With so many people involved, there were too many chances for something to go wrong. At least Emma would be safe. Furious, but safe.

"Forget about her, Bruce," O'Hara said quietly.

There was no mind reading involved here, Bruce thought. O'Hara knew him well enough to realize that his attention wasn't focused on the case. "Right."

"You had to do it. We couldn't have her running around loose."

"I know that."

"She's made it clear that she doesn't think much of the ₁w. Xavier filled me in on her background, and she's a ₁d risk."

"I wanted her out of the way for her sake, not ours."

"Whatever. Quit beating yourself up about it. It was ₁othing but nature taking its course. She's a good-looking ₁oman. Considering the circumstances—"

"Damn the circumstances!"

Several heads turned in his direction. Xavier looked up ₁om the aerial photograph he was studying. "Problem?"

"No. No problem." Bruce drained his coffee in one ₁ulp. Focusing on the paper cup in his hand, he tore off ₁ieces of the rim and dropped them inside.

Xavier murmured a low comment to the woman from ₁e justice department and made his way to the rear door ₁f the truck. "Let's get some air, Prentice."

Bruce crushed the cup in his fist and tossed it to O'Hara Whatever you say."

Xavier held the door open against the wind until Bruce ₁ad stepped outside, then eased it shut and walked a short ₁istance away. They were behind a deserted gas station that ₁as about a mile from McQuaig's place. Several other ve- ₁icles gleamed dully from the shadows nearby. Xavier ₁alted beside one of them and turned up his collar. "We ₁ove in less than two hours. Anything you want to say ₁efore then?"

The clouds that had rolled in at sunset had brought the ₁ng of rain. The air was charged with expectancy and the ₁reat of change. Frowning, Bruce shoved his hands into ₁e pockets of his borrowed coat. "I don't like this."

"Any particular reason?"

"It's gotten too big."

"McQuaig *is* big. We need the help. Anything else?"

"No, just a bad feeling."

He was silent for a few moments. "You don't have to ₁ke part. You've already contributed more than your ₁are. Why don't you stay in the truck and man the radio ₁is time?"

"No. I want in. I want to find Simon Duprey."

"You're too close to this one, Bruce. Considering you involvement with the sister—"

"Leave Emma out of it. I want Simon Duprey becaus he's our best chance of nailing McQuaig. He worked fo them under duress, and despite his problems with the law it's my guess that he'd choose a deal over prison."

"We've already discussed that possibility."

"And if we've figured it out, so could McQuaig. Du prey might not last long enough to do us any good. I can' let that happen."

"Because of the case or because of the woman?"

Bruce couldn't answer. He hunched his shoulders an turned his back to the wind. "There's something else want to talk to you about."

"Go ahead."

"This is my last case. I'll give you my badge when it' over."

Crickets chirped shrilly from the long grass at the edg of the road. The wind gusted in whispers through the stan of birch that bordered the gas station. Xavier swore softl and stepped closer. "You're burned out. Take some tim off. You've got it coming. There isn't any reason for yo to do something this drastic. You're a good cop. Wh throw that away?"

"Because that's all I am."

"You've worked undercover for too long. I've seen before. Take a vacation, get some perspective on the situ ation."

He shook his head. "This isn't something that a trop: cal beach can change."

Twin beams of light swung around the curve of th road. A car slowed and pulled off on the shoulder. Xavie glanced toward it and stepped away. "We'll talk about thi later. Once you have a chance to rest, you'll feel differ ently." He started off toward the car. "In the meantime you keep that badge, because if you try to give it to me, won't take it."

With an odd sense of detachment Bruce watched four more men emerge from the car. Xavier wasn't taking any chances. Already there were units unobtrusively surrounding McQuaig's estate. The planned raid was taking shape, but instead of feeling the thrill of anticipation or the low-level excitement of the chase, he was filled with an overwhelming sense of emptiness.

His heart simply wasn't in this anymore. He had known early this morning, when he had stood by the window and stared at the glinting piece of metal in his hand, that he would never be able to go back to the way things were. He'd always known that Emma Cassidy was a dangerous woman, but he'd never imagined how dangerous. With the vulnerability in her mountain lake blue eyes and the generous, healing passion of her body, she had managed to destroy the defensive wall that had shielded him for five years. No, there was no going back. He closed his eyes briefly, and into his mind flashed the image of Emma's face as the cell door had clicked shut.

He hadn't wanted to say goodbye like that. He hadn't wanted to say goodbye. Ever.

Muttering an apology under her breath, Emma locked the cell and tossed the keys on the table, then ran up the stairs and closed the metal door on the deputy's outraged demands. Cautiously, she peered around the corner. There was no one at the front desk. Normally there were two officers on duty at this time of the evening, but from what she had overheard Haskin say, one of them, Thibault, was on a call. The other one, who must be Duff, was nursing a sore head in the basement. Haskin had already left with Harvey, so temporarily she had the place to herself.

Moving swiftly, she went straight to Haskin's office, slipped inside and closed the door behind her. With a quick glance to assure herself that the blinds were still shut, she crossed to the desk and picked up the phone. It was only when she was listening to the dial tone that it struck her—she didn't know what number to call.

"Damn," she whispered. She bent over the desk and sorted through the papers, her anxiety mounting. She found the map that had been pinned to the bulletin board, but there was no trace of the files that Xavier had placed here this morning. The dial tone switched from a hum to a squeal and she jabbed at the zero.

"Give me the Bangor Police," she told the operator. But when the connection was made and she heard the first ring, she hung up the phone. McQuaig had the Bethel Corners sheriff on his payroll. Did it stop there? Or were there others? Could she trust them to deliver her message? What if her attempts to warn Bruce's people backfired?

Frustrated, she shoved the map into her pocket and paced across the room. This was too much. All her life she had claimed that she couldn't trust cops. Now she wished she could. Bruce had asked her to give the law a chance, and she was trying. A week ago, when she had told him that Simon was in trouble, he had attempted to convince her to... She skidded to a stop. He had wanted her to go to the police. He had picked up a pen and scrawled a number on the back of an empty envelope and had said that it belonged to Xavier Jones.

"That's it!" she exclaimed. Even if Xavier himself couldn't be reached, someone at that number would be able to get the warning to him. She glanced at the clock, her stomach knotting. If she ignored the speed limits, she could be at her cabin in fifteen minutes.

If she had a car.

Chewing her lower lip, she looked around the room until her gaze lit on the set of small hooks beside the locked gun rack. One set of keys dangled from the center hook. With the tip of her finger she lifted a slat from the blind and looked outside. Haskin's patrol car was still parked in its usual spot in front of the station. Of course. He wouldn't have wanted to draw attention to himself when he left with Harvey. Without giving herself time to think about what she was doing, she snatched the keys and ran outside.

Her estimate had been off. She made it to the foot of her driveway in less than twelve minutes. Heedless of the damage the boulders were doing to the undercarriage of the patrol car, Emma gunned the engine and shot to the crest of the hill. She was out and running the moment she yanked on the brake. Before the echoes of the engine faded, she leapt over the rock that formed her doorstep and burst into her cabin.

The telephone was gone. With a frustrated sob, she grabbed the zippered bag that Bruce had left under the desk and emptied it on the floor. Clothes, a pair of cowboy boots, two telephones and a modem fell in a heap at her feet. She untangled the cord of one of the phones and plugged it in behind the couch, then yanked open the top drawer of her desk. In less than ten seconds she held the envelope with Xavier's number. Lungs heaving, Emma knelt on the floor and dialed the phone.

"Come on, come on," she whispered, holding on to the receiver so tightly her knuckles cracked. She heard two rings, then a series of clicks before it started ringing again.

A tired voice came on the line. "Yeah? Epstein here."

Another cop. She hesitated for a split second, then decided if he was in Xavier's office, she had to trust him. "I need to get in touch with Xavier Jones or Bruce Prentice."

"They aren't here right now." The tone sharpened. "Could I help you?"

"This is an emergency. I need to get a message to them. McQuaig knows about the raid."

There was a brief silence. "Who is this?"

"That's not important. Please, just tell them that McQuaig knows. The raid on his estate near Bangor is no longer a secret. You have to warn Bruce and Xavier they've been set up."

"Where did you get this information?"

"I overheard Sheriff Haskin talking to one of McQuaig's men. He's working for them."

"The Bethel Corners sheriff? Are you sure?"

She ground her teeth. "Listen, Epstein, I'm trying to help. Can you get a message to them or not?"

"I'll see what I can do."

"Don't play games with me. Lives are at risk. If you can't contact them and get this stopped, then I'm going to take my chances with every law enforcement agency in the state and hope that I don't hit another one of McQuaig's flunkies. Then I'll go to the media, and if I do that, nobody wins. Either you give me some guarantee that—"

"If you publicize this, you'll be responsible for endangering more people yourself. If you're on the level, you'll let us handle it. Why don't you give me your name and your number and—"

She slammed down the phone and covered her mouth with her hands, her fingers shaking too badly to grasp the receiver. Anxiety burned along her nerves. She had to warn Bruce, she had to help him. She couldn't imagine a life without him.

"Oh, God!" She rocked forward on her knees. Everything was happening too fast. By now Harvey would have alerted McQuaig about the raid and would already be on his way to Bangor. It would take over an hour for him and Haskin to drive there, but that would still give them plenty of time to prepare for the police. Epstein would relay her warning, wouldn't he?

She looked around the cabin, suddenly conscious of the silence. She had lived alone here for three years, but all it took was a week with Bruce and now the place seemed empty, as if a vital part were missing. Without him, a vital part of *her* was missing. How could she go back to this solitude after he'd shared it?

She glanced at the reading glasses that rested on the coffee table and she remembered how he'd looked over the rims at her, his hair burnished in the soft light, his eyes sparkling with vitality. Something glinted on the floor and she leaned over, pushing aside the edge of his bag. Biting her lip, she picked up a gold earring and let it dangle from her fingers. What had seemed hopelessly complicated was now painfully simple. She loved him, and that wouldn't change, no matter where he was or who he decided to be...

Something underneath a crumpled shirt caught her eye. She lifted it aside and saw the corner of a black-and-white photograph. Grasping the white border of the photo, she tugged it free and found herself staring at her own face. He must have taken this the day they had met. She remembered wearing that shirt and canvas hat, but the expression on her face startled her. Did she really look that lonely, that lost? The edges of the photograph were dull with fingerprints and one of the lower corners was bent, as if it had been handled frequently. Something shifted painfully inside her. Bruce had taken this, his hands had held it, his fingers had left those marks. He must have been studying her picture from the day they had met.

She set the photo down on the floor and looked through the pile of things that had been in his bag, but there were no other photographs. Why had he saved this one? He had kept it with him even when he had thought the worst of her. He had said that he cared. Was it more than caring?

Would she ever get the chance to ask him?

She smacked her palms against the floor and rose to her feet. She loved him, and she had lost too many people that she loved. She'd be damned if she was going to sit here and wait for it to happen again.

An ambulance rushed past, its siren whining to the blackness. The red lights glittered through the raindrops on the back windshield as Emma glanced in the rearview mirror. Her hands tightened on the wheel. Nearly an hour had passed since she had left her cabin. She had followed the map carefully, so this had to be the right road. She almost wished it wasn't, not if that ambulance meant she was too late. The car hit a pothole and she jerked her attention back to the rain-slicked blacktop in front of her. The moment she rounded the next bend, any lingering doubts about her route vanished. A police car was parked at the

side of the road, the flashing light bar on its roof making
eerie shadows across a stand of birch trees.

Emma felt her pulse thudding hard and thick at the base
of her throat as she drove past. She expected to be con-
fronted any second, to be taken back into custody before
she had the chance to be certain her warning had gotten
through. But no one stopped her. Just as no one had tried
to stop her from doing twenty miles over the speed limit on
the I-95. Of course, they wouldn't think of stopping one
of their own.

She exhaled shakily and fumbled for the switch that
would reactivate her flashers. She hit the siren by mistake,
grimacing at the loud whoop that escaped before she could
shut if off. Another mile rolled past before she saw a glow
through the trees. When she steered around the final bend,
her empty stomach knotted.

The three-story house on the hillside was ablaze with
light, from the casement windows under the eaves to the
glass doors beside the rock terrace. Groups of people
moved freely between the gaping front entrance and the
dozens of vehicles that lined the sloping driveway and
ringed the lawn. Blinking blue, red and orange blurred and
glimmered through the slanting rain. She rolled down her
window and listened, but she could hear nothing except the
sound of her engine. No shouts. No shots. Whatever had
happened was over.

Her message to Bruce and Xavier must have gotten
through after all. But the raid hadn't been called off. It had
been moved up.

Another ambulance pulled away from the house and
headed down the driveway. Emma watched it approach.
Who was in there? Bruce? Simon? Both of them? She
clutched the wheel, leaning her forehead on the back of her
hands until the ambulance had passed, then slowly,
woodenly, she nosed the stolen police car onto the lawn
and turned off the engine. No, they were all right. They
had to be all right. If they weren't she would have been able
to tell, wouldn't she?

Keeping to the shadows, aided by the night and the confusion, Emma managed to make her way to the house unchallenged. She stood behind one of the pillars at the front entrance, waiting motionless, while two rifle-carrying cops walked by. They held their weapons loosely and grumbled about the weather, obviously relaxed now that the raid was over. If she approached them, would they tell her what she wanted to know? No, she couldn't risk being sent away, not yet. The moment they passed her, she melted into the shrubbery and worked her way around the house.

When she got to the edge of the terrace, she paused. Through the open glass doors she saw that the room was an office or study of some kind. It was dominated by a huge, carved mahogany desk on one side and an ornate archway on the other. Her heart skipped, then thudded into a strong steady rhythm as she focused on the tall, blond man who stood in the center of the floor. His back was toward her, but she would recognize him anywhere, just as she'd always been able to recognize him. She didn't even pause to wonder why she had been able to find him so easily—whatever had drawn her to this room was probably the same inexplicable and primitive bond that had drawn her to him from the start.

Time seemed to slow. The rain was no longer as cold, the flashing lights that ringed the house faded from her vision. The wave of relief that flooded through her was so strong she swayed, taking a step closer.

But then he moved, and she caught sight of the smaller man who stood beyond him.

No. She had wanted them safe, she had wanted them healthy, but not like this. She had thought that she had prepared herself, but the reality was something else. It was a scene from a nightmare, not the one she had been fearing the most, but a nightmare just the same. It was a tableau that embodied all the conflicting loyalties and emotions that she'd thought had been resolved. Part of her wanted to retreat to the shadows and disappear, run back to the isolated safety of her cabin and pretend she could forget the image that was now etched on her brain....

It was no use. Even across the distance that separated them, she could hear the metallic click as Bruce snapped the handcuff around Simon's wrist.

The fine hairs at the back of Bruce's neck tingled. Although he couldn't identify any sound that had alerted him, suddenly he knew he was no longer alone with his prisoner. Warily, he snapped the second cuff closed and turned around.

A lone woman stood on the terrace on the other side of the open doors, a shadowy figure in black. She must be an apparition from the storm. She couldn't really be here. She was safely locked into a cell seventy-two miles away. Speechless, he watched a droplet of water trace a path down her face and fall into her collar. Her gaze caught his, the deep, pure blue swirling with pain. Her lips formed a silent denial.

His prisoner shifted restlessly. "Well, don't you read me my rights or something now? Or are we going to stand around here all..." He paused as he followed Bruce's gaze. The arrogant expression drained from his face. "Emma!"

As if caught in a trance, she moved closer. "Hello, Simon."

He took a step toward his sister. "You're alive! Thank God. McQuaig told me you were dead."

"He lied."

"Oh, Emma, it was terrible. I thought they were going to kill me, and then when they told me that you had crashed, I didn't know what to do." He reached toward her, stopping when the chain of his handcuffs cut off the motion. "Help me, Emma."

"I've been helping you."

He held up his manacled wrists and took another step. "Don't let the police lock me up. Please. I couldn't survive if they did that."

Bruce fastened his fingers around Simon's upper arm, preventing him from going farther. He had to finish this.

You're under arrest. You have the right to remain silent. Anything you say—"

"Stuff it, cop. I'm not going anywhere with you."

Setting his jaw, Bruce completed the familiar recitation. With each word he said, Emma moved nearer. As she stepped into the square of light that spilled from the room, he could see that not all the moisture on her cheeks was from the rain. He was able to see something else, too. The hunting bow, the one that had rested on the wooden rack in the cabin wall, was slung from her back. Black-fletched arrows bristled from the quiver that was strapped to her thigh.

The fact that she was truly here was difficult enough to accept. The knowledge that she had come armed was like a sudden fist to the gut. How? *Why?* Bruce thought of the gun that was concealed beneath his jacket. But he didn't reach for it.

"You've always come through for me, Emma. Don't let me down now," Simon urged. "Help me get away."

Her chin trembled as she shifted the bow to her hand. She was silent for a moment, balancing the weapon on her palm. When she finally spoke, her voice was low and unsteady. "Why did it have to be you, Bruce?"

He felt his control slipping. "Put it down, Emma. It's all over."

"Do you know him?" Simon asked incredulously.

She nodded. Her hair was wet and wild, slicked down against her head as it had been in another time, another place. Another disaster. "Yes," she answered, her gaze never leaving Bruce. "I know him."

"Your sister and I have been..." Bruce hesitated on the word. "We've been working together."

"I don't believe it. Emma, you'd never help a cop."

"I did it for you, Simon. I had to get you away from McQuaig. I couldn't let them hurt you."

"Emma, how did you get here?" Bruce asked. "Why did you come?"

Her breath hitched on a laugh that held no humor. "
broke out of jail, I stole Haskin's car. I called Xavier'
number, but then I had to come to make sure you got th
message. I did it for you, Bruce." Another tear joined th
raindrops on her face. "I couldn't let them hurt you, e
ther."

"You were the one who tipped Epstein?"

She nodded again.

"Your warning probably saved a dozen lives. Xavier ha
us move in the moment Epstein radioed. We all ow
you—"

"You warned the cops?" Simon cried. "But you didn'
warn me? Do you know what you've done?"

Her fingers trembled as she wiped the moisture from he
eyes. "Yes. I know exactly what I've done."

"It's not too late," Simon said quickly. "I still have
chance." He lunged toward her but Bruce hauled hir
back. "Emma, for God's sake, it's just the three of u
here. Do something before someone else comes around
You got in, you can get me out. They've arrested Mc
Quaig. I saw him being put in the wagon with the others
They won't bother us anymore. Please."

"You'll get a light sentence if you cooperate with us
Duprey," Bruce said. "I already explained that to you."

"Emma! We're all that's left of the family. Don't tur
your back on me now. Prison killed our father, and seein
him there killed our mother."

"I know that. I can't change it."

"Then don't let me down, sis. I love you."

She pressed her lips together, inhaling deeply throug
her nose. "I love you, too, Simon."

Sudden anger flashed through Bruce as he watched th
effect Simon's pleas were having on Emma. He turned
shaking Simon roughly by the arm. "Stop it," he gritted
"Can't you see you're tearing her apart?"

"Shut up, cop. You don't know anything."

"I know that your sister's loyalty is more than you de
serve. Her love is unconditional, but you're using it as

weapon.'' He shook him again. ''Do you have any idea of what she's done for you, of the chances she took and the danger she faced? If you had only a fraction of her courage you'd never have gotten yourself into this mess to begin with. Grow up, Duprey. It's past time you faced the consequences of what you've done and let your sister go.''

''Bruce.''

The sudden ice in Emma's tone made him snap his head around.

There was no longer any indecision on her face. Her eyes were narrowed, her jaw clenched with determination. She widened her stance, angling one foot over the threshold of the room and aligning her body. Smoothly she drew an arrow from the quiver. ''Move over, Bruce,'' she said, her voice barely above a whisper.

No. He wouldn't believe it. After everything they had gone through together, everything she had come to mean to him, she wouldn't do this. She'd never hurt him, of that he had no doubt. But it couldn't end like this, could it?

''Emma.''

The arrow wasn't one of the blunt-tipped target practice kind. Light gleamed from a trio of spiraling metal blades. With deadly, purposeful grace, she nocked it and raised the bow.

His gun weighed heavily against the small of his back. Echoes of the last time he had faced that bow shimmered through his mind. Every nerve tingled with the urge to move, to act. If he rolled to the side he'd be able to draw his weapon and fire a shot that would take control of the situation. But he knew he wouldn't. He couldn't. All the training and the years of experience had cracked and fallen away, all the defenses he'd clung to were gone.

He had no defense against her. He never had.

Her wet shirt molded to her lithe, athlete's body as she hooked two fingers on the string and drew the bow.

It was too late to plead, too late to beg. The angry words he had flung at her when he'd left her this afternoon weren't the ones he'd wanted to say. Would it have made a difference if he'd told her he loved her? Or would it have made her cheeks even wetter with the moisture that wasn't from the rain? Her love for her brother was unconditional. But so was Bruce's love for her. He dropped his hands to his sides and moved away from Simon. She had made her choice.

He never saw her release the arrow. It happened too fast to see. He felt the kiss of rushing air on his face and heard a hard, splintering thud behind him.

"That's far enough, Sheriff," Emma ordered. She slid another arrow from her quiver and readied the bow as she stepped into the room. "Put the gun down, or the next one's going to hit square on your jelly stain."

Reality shifted and realigned itself as Bruce turned around. Haskin stood just beyond the archway that led to the rest of the house. The revolver that he held in his hand slowly lowered. An arrow vibrated in the wooden doorframe at the level of his ear.

Chapter 15

Footsteps, rapid and heavy, approached from the hallway. Seconds later O'Hara appeared beside Haskin and took the gun from his fingers. None too gently, he spun the man around and shoved him face first against the wall. "We caught your bald friend in the lab, Sheriff, but you're both about an hour too late. Good thing we started the party without you, huh?"

Like a man waking from a nightmare, Bruce shook his head groggily. He focused on his hands. They were trembling. She had done it to him again, had turned him inside out. Amazing, astounding, enigmatic woman. He had an insane urge to laugh. Instead, he walked over to the archway and ran a fingertip along the arrow.

O'Hara did a brisk search for concealed weapons, then wrenched Haskin's arms back and snapped a set of handcuffs around his wrists as he read him his rights. "You okay, Prentice?" he asked over the sheriff's loud protests. "Those idiots from Bangor were supposed to patrol the perimeter but..." His words trailed off when he saw the arrow. His mouth pursed into a low whistle. "Where the *hell* did that come from?"

The steel head had bored a hole the diameter of a golf ball through several inches of wood and plaster. Bruce grasped the shaft and tugged, then braced his foot against the doorframe and yanked again, but he could dislodge nothing but a shower of splinters and plaster dust.

Emma lowered her bow and carefully eased the tension from the string. "I saw Haskin sneaking down the corridor. He was watching you, so he didn't see me. When he raised his gun, I had a clear shot."

"You were aiming at the sheriff," Bruce said hoarsely.

"No, I was aiming at the doorframe. I already told you, I always hit what I'm aiming at."

Roughly he raked his hands through his hair. Reality was still shifting, reforming into something he'd only dared to dream of. There stood Emma, with the rain a sparkling curtain behind her and her weapon poised to defend him and ... *she had made her choice.* "You were trying to help me, weren't you? That's why you brought the bow."

"I didn't know what I'd find when I got here." She slipped the second arrow back into her quiver. "I had to bring my bow. I don't own a gun."

Haskin jerked out of O'Hara's hold and spun to face the room. "Arrest her! She tried to kill me. That's assault on a police officer."

"You're no police officer." The gravelly voice came from the hallway. Xavier Jones stepped forward and surveyed the scene with a gaze that missed nothing. He gave a start of surprise when he saw Emma. "Miss Duprey!"

"She's with us," Bruce stated. "I'll take care of her. The explanations can wait."

Scowling, Xavier glanced at the open terrace doors. "How did she get in?"

"Probably the same way as Haskin. I told you this operation had gotten too big."

Muttering under his breath, Xavier turned his attention back to the sheriff. "It's convenient you decided to turn up. Saves us having to come after you. We've just gained access to your bank records, and those regular deposits sure aren't from a sheriff's salary. How long have you been working for McQuaig?''

"I don't know what you're talking about, Jones. You can't prove anything."

Bruce looked at Simon. "Well, Duprey? What'll it be? Are you going to do the time while your friend here goes free?''

Emma hitched the strap of the bow over her shoulder. "It's your choice, Simon." She went to him and grasped his arms. For a moment she was silent, gazing at his handcuffs, but then she sighed and slid her arms around him in a quick, hard hug. "It's your life. What you do now depends on *you*. Not me, not our parents, not the past. You say you want your freedom, so try freeing yourself from your hate."

"It's not that easy."

"Easy? It's hard as hell, Simon, believe me. But this is something you have to do on your own."

His eyes filled. "I want you to be proud of me. I've always tried so hard, but nothing works out. I didn't want to get mixed up with McQuaig, but Haskin wouldn't leave me alone. He got me into that poker game, then when I kept losing he hassled me until I agreed to get involved—"

"Shut up, Duprey!"

Simon blinked hard and curled his imprisoned hands into fists as he turned to face the sheriff. "The monthly envelopes you got weren't enough. You wanted a share of the stuff I was transporting. It's because of your greed and stupidity that the cops traced us to Bethel Corners."

"I said *shut up!*"

O'Hara smiled grimly and grasped the sheriff's elbow. "You know the routine. Let's go."

"I should have shot you when I had the chance, Duprey, you double-crossing piece of sh—"

"I said, let's go." O'Hara emphasized his order with a firm tug that propelled the man down the hall.

Xavier looked at Simon and motioned after them. "Come with me, Duprey. I've got someone from the Justice Department who will want to hear what you've got to say."

Pressing her lips tightly together, Emma touched her fingertips to her brother's cheek. "I'm sorry," she whispered. "But it's for your own good. I do love you, Simon."

He squared his chin with a hint of his old belligerence and moved away. Without a word or a look in her direction, he walked over to Xavier.

"Just a minute," Bruce said before Xavier could leave the room. "There's one last piece of business I want to take care of."

The older policeman scowled. "I already told you, Prentice. I'm not going to accept it, so don't bother."

Bruce reached behind his back and brought out his gun. He turned it over, studying it for a moment as if he didn't recognize it, then he slapped the weapon into Xavier's palm. "Take it."

"Prentice, don't."

Ignoring the protest, Bruce shoved his hand into his pocket and pulled out the flat leather folder that held his badge. This time there was no hesitation as he dropped it on top of his gun. "Find someone else to play your games, Xavier."

"I'll consider this a leave of absence, not a resignation. Give you time to think about it when your head's clearer."

"It won't make any difference."

Xavier lifted his shoulders in a shrug and stepped into the hall. "We'll see. Being a cop is in your blood, Prentice, just like it's in mine. You'll be back. Come on, Duprey. Time to get started." Grasping Simon's elbow with his free hand, he ushered him toward the back of the house.

Emma listened until their footsteps faded down the hall. From the depths of the house she heard voices, the ringing of a telephone, doors opening and closing. From behind her came the sound of rain striking the stone terrace, car doors slamming, the crackling static of a radio. Her wet shirt felt clammy, her knees shook. Time had sped up again, and the adrenaline that had brought her this far was finally wearing off. Her brother would be all right now. She had to believe that, just as she had to believe that he would eventually forgive her. As she had already forgiven Bruce.

Bruce. Across the width of the room she looked at him, noting the lines of strain beside his mouth and the rigid set of his shoulders. She wanted to run to him, throw herself into his arms, kiss those lines from his face.... And yet she stood where she was, her nerves quivering with uncertainty.

They were alone. Simon was gone, so were McQuaig and his gang. The case that had brought Bruce to Bethel Corners and into her life was resolved. It was over. Finished.

The tension that still hummed in the air was from something else entirely.

Was it really over?

"Why did you do it?" she asked softly.

"He'll be all right. As long as he cooperates, he'll get fair treatment."

"No, I mean, why did you hand in your badge?"

He rubbed his face with his hands, then looked at her over the tops of his fingers. "Maybe I outgrew it."

"But I thought..."

"That I needed it? That I wanted to live the rest of my life without a real home or anyone who cares whether I live or die? That I want to wake up in the morning and wonder who I'm supposed to be?" He shook his head. "Not anymore. I want a life, not a role, not a masquerade."

"There are different kinds of cops, Bruce. You don't have to stay with Xavier's undercover operations."

"You're trying to talk me out of it, aren't you?"

"I guess I am."

The lines eased from his face as he smiled wryly. "Have I ever told you that you always manage to surprise me, Emma?"

"Do I?"

"I thought you'd be happy to see one less policeman in the world."

So did she. "Maybe I outgrew my hate."

He began to walk toward her. His stride was long and easy, his body moving with the animal grace that had never failed to evoke a response in her. As it did now. Even with half the police in the state wandering around the lawn outside the room, and her feelings still churning from the emotional scene with her brother, she couldn't help the tingling, or the tightening, or the jolt of . . . rightness.

"I should thank you," he said, reaching out to ease the bow from her shoulder. "What you did tonight probably saved my life."

"There's a good possibility Haskin was aiming at Simon."

"Somehow I doubt whether he always hits what he's aiming at." Bruce moved his hands to her waist and unbuckled her quiver, then undid the strap that held it to her thigh and lowered it to the floor beside her bow. "You're one dangerous woman, Emmaline Cassidy Duprey. I knew it from the moment I first laid eyes on you."

"What do you mean?"

"Aside from the obvious, such as breaking out of jail, stealing cars, and deciding to crash a police raid with a hunting bow?"

"Yes, aside from that."

A hush fell around them as he slipped out of his jacket and wrapped it around her shoulders. His warmth soaked into her chilled form like sudden sunshine. Stepping closer, he cradled her face in his palms. His thumbs gently traced the contours of her cheekbones, leaving her damp skin tingling with heat. "You make me want to take another chance."

She raised her gaze to his face, and her heart leapt. His vivid blue eyes were sparkling with an emotion she'd never thought to find there. Hope—crazy, delicious, irrepressible hope—swelled inside her. For the first time, his gaze was so completely open, so stripped of barriers, she imagined she could see clear to his soul. "What kind of chance?"

"You, Emma, with your courage, and your generosity and your sense of loyalty, you're the one who's made me want another chance at life. And a real home. And having someone who cares whether I live or die."

The hope turned to promise. To fierce yearning. Holding his gaze, she turned her head to press a kiss to his palm. "Oh, I care, Bruce."

"You make me want to risk loving someone. And opening myself up to the risk of losing everything again."

Her eyes misted. She slid her hands to his chest and felt the beat of his heart, and remembered the scar on his back. "Our past helped to make us what we are. Knowing that happiness can be taken away doesn't mean we shouldn't grasp it. It means we should treasure it."

"I don't want to let this chance slip away, Emma. I don't want to say goodbye again."

"Would it scare you if I told you I loved you?"

Tipping back his head, he heaved a sudden, unsteady breath. "Oh, Emma." When he looked at her once more, his expression was intense, strained, a poignant mixture of longing and hope. "It would terrify me if you said you didn't."

Her fingers tightened on his shirt as she lifted her face. "I love you, Bruce. Whatever you do, whatever you look like, wherever you go, I'm still going to love you. I thought I had known what love was, but what I feel for you is so deep, and so rich, and so necessary...I couldn't stop it, even if I tried."

A tremor went through him. With a muffled groan, he brought his mouth to hers in a kiss that unleashed old dreams and desires and made them possible, a kiss that revealed new visions and made them real.

Joy blossomed inside her and she stood on tiptoe, clasping her arms around his neck, molding herself against him as the jacket he had draped around her shoulders slid to the floor. He lifted her, and she clung to him, reveling in the power of the bond that had been there from the start. How had she known? Throughout it all, how had her heart recognized him as the man she was meant to love?

The words were there, in his lips, his hands, his body. She hadn't realized she was hearing them until she felt his breath on her ear. "I love you, Emma." He kissed her cheek, her nose, her eyelids, letting her slide down his body until she stood on the floor. A smile of aching sweetness curved his mouth. "I love every reckless, stubborn, hot-tempered passionate inch of you. And I love the compassion you had for a shy man, and the defiance you had for a bold man. And all the other aspects of you that will take a lifetime to learn."

"Lifetime?"

He caught her hands and laced her fingers with his. "Starting tonight. When I take you home, I want to stay, Emma. Share those sunsets, and sunrises and everything in between."

She hesitated. "Would you be happy at the cabin?"

"As long as you're there."

"We're going to need more bookshelves."

He grinned. "Once I clean out my apartment, we might need an extra room."

"I love the way you look at me over your reading glasses."

"And I love the color of your hair in the firelight. We'll have lots of fires." He dipped his head and captured her mouth once more, his lips and tongue promising a different kind of heat. He moved their joined hands between them, rubbing his knuckles over her breasts.

Emma swayed, her world spinning as a tremor of need surged through her, so powerful it made her gasp.

He pulled back and looked at her, his eyes gleaming. Man to woman, hunter to hunted, love that was beyond the power of words. His hand moved again. And he smiled.

"Bruce?" She barely recognized the trembling, husky voice as hers. But she recognized the jungle cat sensuality in his smile. Her pulse pounded, her breath caught. "Bruce!"

He swept up her bow, her quiver, and his jacket in one smooth movement, then looped a firm arm around her waist and steered her toward the terrace doors. "I love you, Emma, but I have a sudden, overwhelming urge to continue this discussion somewhere more . . . private."

So did she. Oh, so did she. "It's a long way to the cabin."

"Then it's lucky you stole a car with a siren, sweet thing."

Epilogue

The mist was thick this morning, hiding the golds and reds that had begun to appear among the somber pines on the far shore of the lake. Frost glittered from the yellowed patches of grass on the hillside, a powdery breath of the season to come. Pulling her robe more tightly around her, Emma moved closer to the window.

"Is it still there?"

She smiled. "Oh, yes. It's there."

Glinting in the slanting sunlight, the white Cessna rocked gently at the end of the dock. The paperwork had taken almost two months to go through. The plane was a newer model than the one she had lost, and she hadn't had the chance to learn its capabilities or its personality quirks yet, but it was everything she could have wanted. Wanted, not needed. From the first moment she had slid into the pilot's seat and taken the controls, she had realized that more than the plane had changed. Once it had been her way to escape. But now...

Bruce stepped behind her and crossed his arms over

hers, enveloping her in warmth. "Are you taking it up today?"

Her smile softened as she relaxed into his embrace. There was nothing in her life that she wanted to escape. "Maybe later, after you get home."

He lowered his head, propping his chin on her shoulder. "I could always stay here with you and play hooky."

"On your first day at your new job? What kind of example would that set?"

"I don't care. My wife is very wealthy, you know." His hand felt around until it slipped into the opening of her robe. "What do you say? Want to go flying?"

"Mmm. I've got a conference call scheduled for 9:00... Ah." Tingles chased across her skin. "That feels so good."

He nosed aside her collar to nuzzle her neck. "I don't mean the kind of flying you do in your new Cessna."

"I know." She turned in his arms, linking her hands behind his head as she planted a lazy, lingering kiss on his mouth. "You're insatiable."

"Nope. Just crazy about you."

She smoothed a curl off his forehead, then ran her fingers through his hair. The sun-bleached streaks were growing out, leaving rich, burnished gold. His tan had faded, but the blue of his eyes was somehow more brilliant. Perhaps it was the love that shone so clearly each time he looked at her. "I'm crazy about you, too."

"Despite what I'm wearing?"

There was a trace of uneasiness beneath the surface of his teasing. Emma straightened his tie and studied him carefully, knowing her answer was important to him. "Actually, you look sexy as hell in that outfit. How long is your lunch break?"

He burst into laughter and gave her a hug that made her consider disconnecting the phone. "You really don't mind my new job?"

"No, Bruce. I don't. When I said for better or worse, I meant it."

"Is this the 'worse' part?"

She lifted up to rub her nose against his. "No, it is most definitely not the 'worse' part. Every day, when I wake up beside you and know I'll be back in your arms that night, it just keeps getting better."

"It does, doesn't it?"

"Yes, it does." With one last kiss, she slipped out of his embrace. "But for now, my insatiable husband, we both have work to do."

Sighing noisily, he picked up his coat from the back of a chair and let her walk him to the door. "Well, what else have you got planned for the day, besides that ridiculously early conference call?"

"I thought I'd call Hugh."

"The Hugh from the gas station Hugh?"

"The very one. I'm going to ask him to recommend a contractor to put on that extra room we were talking about."

"I certainly don't have any complaints about the pilot he recommended last summer. But why start the room now? Can't stand tripping over my books anymore?"

She tightened the belt of her robe, fidgeting with the ends for a moment. "How would you feel about having another person live at our cabin next spring?"

He paused, his coat hanging from one arm. "You don't mean Simon, do you? I'm not sure he'd be comfortable around me, but if it's what you want—"

"No, not Simon. He told me that Xavier's arranging a job in Chicago for him when he gets out. It's with an ex-con who owns his own business and evidently is as tough as he is fair."

"I hope he can straighten himself out."

"So do I. But he already knows that it's up to him."

He finished putting on his coat and reached for her hands. "Would you rather have your brother here?"

"Not really. I think it would be best for him if he had a chance to establish his independence."

"I'm sure he will . . ." His gaze sharpened. "Who's the room for, if it's not Simon?"

She stepped closer, reached for his hand and placed it over her stomach. She had meant to tell him last night, but they'd watched the sunset, then sat in front of the fire, and the words had gotten lost in the loving. And there was so much loving.

"Emma?"

"I love you, Bruce. Have I told you that yet today?"

"If you count body language, you shouted it clearly about an hour ago."

"Well, I do love you. And I love our child."

Understanding spread over his face. His fingers splayed. "Our child?"

She nodded, her smile watery.

With a whoop that echoed from the cabin's rafters, he scooped her into his arms and whirled around. "Oh, Emma! When?"

"Next May."

"May!" He rained smacking kisses on her nose, her forehead, the corners of her eyes, wherever he could reach. "A new life, another beginning. It really does keep getting better, doesn't it?"

"Yes, it does."

He whirled around again until she buried her face against his neck. "May. That's only seven months away. We have to make plans. Maybe we should get a place in town..." He paused, his eyebrows lifting. "May?"

"Yes."

"But..."

She tipped her head back and smiled. "The due date the doctor gave me works out to exactly nine months after my last Cessna blew up."

"But you told me it was the wrong time of the month. I remember."

Her eyes gleamed. "I lied."

"You lied?"

"It was a reflex action, considering the circumstances." Her smile grew. "Do you mind?"

He backed up until he could collapse onto the couch with her on his lap. "Mind?" He yanked off his coat and tossed it to the floor. "My wife presents me with the ultimate gift of love and she asks me if I mind? Emma!" He ran his hands over her body. His long, strong fingers trembled. "I treasure you, and the happiness you've brought into my life. I'm going to cherish our child—" His voice broke. His palm settled over the place where their new life grew and he kissed her with all the passion that their love had taught him to grasp.

And on his first day at the job, the new sheriff of Bethel Corners was late for work.

*   *   *   *   *

COMING NEXT MONTH

#661 CAITLIN'S GUARDIAN ANGEL—Marie Ferrarella
Heartbreakers/50th Book
Heartbreaker Graham Redhawk had never been under the illusion that
his job—his *life*—was easy. And protecting ex-love Caitlin Cassidy
from a vengeful murderer was proof positive. But in keeping Caitlin
alive, Graham found the perfect solution to keeping custody of his son.

#662 A TWIST IN TIME—Lee Karr
Spellbound
Colin Delaney was endeavoring to solve his grandfather's scandalous
murder. So when unsuspecting Della Arnell discovered a piece to the
puzzle, he sought to get closer...to the woman and the truth. But a twist
in time transposed past and present, shedding a dark light on their
budding love—and the killing about to occur....

#663 TIGER IN THE RAIN—Laura Parker
Rogues' Gallery
Murder target Guy Matherson had many regrets, but none as potent as
his longing for the beautiful stranger who'd changed his life—then
disappeared. Now Michelle Bellegarde was within reach, but still
worlds away. For in claiming Michelle as his own, Guy would surely
be signing her death warrant.

#664 TROUBLE IN TEXAS—Leann Harris
Alexandra Courtland had seen the face of death and wanted only to
forget. But her temporary stopover in Saddle, Texas, revealed a town—
and a lawman—in desperate need of her help. And slowly, sweetly,
Alex found that in salving Derek Grey's wounds, she was healing
her own.

#665 MONTANA ROGUE—Jessica Douglass
Kidnapped! Courtney Hamilton's prayers for rescue were answered by a
most unlikely—and unwanted—hero. Jack Sullivan seemed every inch
the mountain man he resembled, but she soon recognized his face—his
touch—as those of the lover who'd once cruelly betrayed her.

#666 GIDEON'S BRIDE—Amelia Autin
Rugged rancher Gideon Lowell had three young children who needed
a mom, and mail-order bride Rennie Fortier definitely fit the maternal
bill. And as Rennie charmed his kids, she also warmed the coldness
Gideon kept locked inside. Until he learned of her past...

SPELLBOUND
ROMANCE

**A CENTURY-OLD MURDER...
A TIMELESS LOVE**

leads to

A TWIST IN TIME

by Lee Karr

Colin Delaney was desperate to discover
who had killed his grandfather a century ago.
So when unsuspecting Della Arnell discovered
a piece to the puzzle, he sought to get closer—to
the woman and the truth. But a twist in time
transposed past and present, shedding a dark
light on a new love—and an old killing
about to occur.

**Don't miss A TWIST IN TIME (IM#662)
by Lee Karr
available in September, only from—**

Join RITA-award-winning author Emilie Richards as her miniseries "The Men of Midnight" concludes in August 1995 with MacDOUGALL'S DARLING, IM #655.

Andrew MacDougall believed in his two best friends, a misty loch creature...and little else. Love and marriage were certainly not meant for him. But Fiona Sinclair's homecoming stirred up memories of their long-ago bond, one he knew still existed by its hold on his heart.

Don't miss MacDOUGALL'S DARLING, Emilie Richards's magical finale to "The Men of Midnight" miniseries. Only in—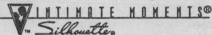

PRIZE SURPRISE SWEEPSTAKES!

This month's prize:

BEAUTIFUL WEDGWOOD CHINA!

This month, as a special surprise, we're giving away a bone china dinner service for eight by Wedgwood**, one of England's most prestigious manufacturers!

Think how beautiful your table will look, set with lovely Wedgwood china in the casual Countryware pattern! Each five-piece place setting includes dinner plate, salad plate, soup bowl and cup and saucer.

The facing page contains two Entry Coupons (as does every book you received this shipment). Complete and return *all* the entry coupons; **the more times you enter, the better your chances of winning!**

Then keep your fingers crossed, because you'll find out by September 15, 1995 if you're the winner!

Remember: The more times you enter, the better your chances of winning!*

*NO PURCHASE OR OBLIGATION TO CONTINUE BEING A SUBSCRIBER NECESSARY TO ENTER. SEE THE REVERSE SIDE OF ANY ENTRY COUPON FOR ALTERNATE MEANS OF ENTRY.

**THE PROPRIETORS OF THE TRADEMARK ARE NOT ASSOCIATED WITH THIS PROMOTION.

PWW KAL

PRIZE SURPRISE
SWEEPSTAKES

OFFICIAL ENTRY COUPON

This entry must be received by: AUGUST 30, 1995
This month's winner will be notified by: SEPTEMBER 15, 1995

YES, I want to win the Wedgwood china service for eight! Please enter me in the drawing and let me know if I've won!

Name_____

Address _____ Apt. _____

City   State/Prov.   Zip/Postal Code

Account #_____

Return entry with invoice in reply envelope.

© 1995 HARLEQUIN ENTERPRISES LTD.   CWW KAL

PRIZE SURPRISE
SWEEPSTAKES

OFFICIAL ENTRY COUPON

This entry must be received by: AUGUST 30, 1995
This month's winner will be notified by: SEPTEMBER 15, 1995

YES, I want to win the Wedgwood china service for eight! Please enter me in the drawing and let me know if I've won!

Name_____

Address _____ Apt. _____

City   State/Prov.   Zip/Postal Code

Account #_____

Return entry with invoice in reply envelope.

© 1995 HARLEQUIN ENTERPRISES LTD.   CWW KAL

OFFICIAL RULES
PRIZE SURPRISE SWEEPSTAKES 3448
NO PURCHASE OR OBLIGATION NECESSARY

Three Harlequin Reader Service 1995 shipments will contain respectively, coupons for entry into three different prize drawings, one for a Panasonic 31" wide-screen TV, another for a 5-piece Wedgwood china service for eight and the third for a Sharp ViewCam camcorder. To enter any drawing using an Entry Coupon, simply complete and mail according to directions.

There is no obligation to continue using the Reader Service to enter and be eligible for any prize drawing. You may also enter any drawing by hand printing the words "Prize Surprise," your name and address on a 3"x5" card and the name of the prize you wish that entry to be considered for (i.e., Panasonic wide-screen TV, Wedgwood china or Sharp ViewCam). Send your 3"x5" entries via first-class mail (limit: one per envelope) to: Prize Surprise Sweepstakes 3448, c/o the prize you wish that entry to be considered for, P.O. Box 1315, Buffalo, NY 14269-1315, USA or P.O. Box 610, Fort Erie, Ontario L2A 5X3, Canada.

To be eligible for the Panasonic wide-screen TV, entries must be received by 6/30/95; for the Wedgwood china, 8/30/95; and for the Sharp ViewCam, 10/30/95.

Winners will be determined in random drawings conducted under the supervision of D.L. Blair, Inc., an independent judging organization whose decisions are final, from among all eligible entries received for that drawing. Approximate prize values are as follows: Panasonic wide-screen TV ($1,800); Wedgwood china ($840) and Sharp ViewCam ($2,000). Sweepstakes open to residents of the U.S. (except Puerto Rico) and Canada, 18 years of age or older. Employees and immediate family members of Harlequin Enterprises, Ltd., D.L. Blair, Inc., their affiliates, subsidiaries and all other agencies, entities and persons connected with the use, marketing or conduct of this sweepstakes are not eligible. Odds of winning a prize are dependent upon the number of eligible entries received for that drawing. Prize drawing and winner notification for each drawing will occur no later than 15 days after deadline for entry eligibility for that drawing. Limit: one prize to an individual, family or organization. All applicable laws and regulations apply. Sweepstakes offer void wherever prohibited by law. Any litigation within the province of Quebec respecting the conduct and awarding of the prizes in this sweepstakes must be submitted to the Regies des loteries et Courses du Quebec. In order to win a prize, residents of Canada will be required to correctly answer a time-limited arithmetical skill-testing question. Value of prizes are in U.S. currency.

Winners will be obligated to sign and return an Affidavit of Eligibility within 30 days of notification. In the event of noncompliance within this time period, prize may not be awarded. If any prize or prize notification is returned as undeliverable, that prize will not be awarded. By acceptance of a prize, winner consents to use of his/her name, photograph or other likeness for purposes of advertising, trade and promotion on behalf of Harlequin Enterprises, Ltd., without further compensation, unless prohibited by law.

For the names of prizewinners (available after 12/31/95), send a self-addressed, stamped envelope to: Prize Surprise Sweepstakes 3448 Winners, P.O. Box 4200, Blair, NE 68009.

RPZ KAL